THE

WESTWARD

HOURS

Extraordinary Books
Gable House, 18–24 Turnham Green Terrace
London W4 1QP
www.extraordinarybooks.co.uk

Published in Great Britain in 2026 by Extraordinary Books

ISBN 978-1-917569-23-1
eISBN 978-1-917569-24-8

EU GPSR authorised representative: Logos Europe
9 rue Nicolas Poussin, 17000
La Rochelle, France
contact@logoseurope.eu

Printed and bound in Great Britain by Clays Ltd, Elcograf S.p.A.

THE WESTWARD HOURS

Dennison Smith

Written with gratitude to the Navajo family who took me in as a motherless hitchhiker, treated me as kin and shared their songs. And with gratitude to the shards and rocks of The Basin that stood me on my feet after a monster knocked me down. And deep thanks to Mitch Albert, who has steadfastly believed in me and championed this story through copious interminable drafts.

This is for my daughter, Oceana.

I

ULYSSES

On the last night of our marriage, the silence between Joel and me didn't feel like peace. But *peace* is so often a word devoid of feeling.

On the thirty-third floor of the Grand Hotel in the frontier metropolis of Ulysses, my husband sat on the edge of his queen bed, appraising the other queen bed and wondering whether he'd made a mistake by not booking a single shared king. Joel liked space to himself and hated me throwing off the blankets, which I had done throughout our marriage but even more since the first flush of menopause. But with the option of two identical beds, he couldn't be certain whether my queen was not the better one while he'd chosen the dud.

The silence was nothing but a lull in the night's hostilities. The bedside clock read 21:47:00, 63.9°, 12/09. The hour was late, the room freezing; another year had almost spent itself, and Joel had declared a ceasefire, but only because he had to work: Yácorp closed Human Interface at 23:30. Loosening his belt and untying the laces of his black dress shoes, Joel made himself comfortable for remote-interfacing with his colleagues at Central Hub.

Glancing at me, he said, "I don't get you, Dorothy."

He didn't need to say more, because I got *him*. I understood that he didn't 'get' why I'd accompanied him to −101, ostensibly to admire Ulysses, if all I wanted was war.

"It's a flying visit," he'd said when I'd asked to come along.

"I arrive late and have meetings the next day. There won't be any sightseeing. And you'll miss your Christmas fête."

"I can amuse myself," I'd said. "And I hate the university party. It's boring. I don't have anyone to talk to. Also, I haven't been to Kansas –" I was forever slipping up. It was so hard to break the habit of state names. "To -101," I'd corrected myself, "since my mom died. Forever ago. And I want to see Ulysses. I want to see your handiwork."

"Handiwork?" he'd said.

"Whatever you want to call it."

He disapproved of the word, which he felt was better suited to my mother's needlepoint than to masterminding a city out of rubble. But he had not caught the reversal: how, the previous year, I'd loved the faculty Christmas bonanza and had insisted he attend it with me, even though he was suffering from a cold. "You'll meet the genius in Biogenetics," I'd told him that Christmas, "and he'll cure your sneeze" – a remedy that had consisted of Joel getting very drunk and gazing blindly into a retinal camera and other equipment in the genius's lab.

But it was true enough that I had no one to talk to at faculty parties, because you don't share intimacies with your colleagues if you've married into Yácorp, or into any of The First and Last One Hundred: Mobil, Unilever, Meta, Bayer Crop, Coca-Cola, etc., but especially Yácorp. Everyone knew the jingle: *Yácorp, Number One Govcorp.* Teaching in the Recent History department, and forbidden to use my maiden name, I insisted students call me by my first name, because "Saunders" was as toxic to some as "MacAllister" was to most. Joel was Yácorp's darling, their Idea Man, and not everyone loved Yácorp.

As a specialist in the Sacrifice War (as documented from the vantage point of peace, or what passes for it) and the leading expert on the MacAllisters, I was accustomed to internal dissonance and the silence that supports it. Keeping quiet about my husband was easy, especially as there were 2.7 billion other subjects to discuss – that being the number of people who'd died in The Change.

In the RUSA (Re-United States of America) alone, forty-six million had died in the Migration Era and another twenty million in the Early Reconstitution, the period after the Sacrifice War was deemed to be 'over' and everything west of -101.35 was fenced off. As for the nonhuman death toll, from elephants to ants, it was never tallied, and history being anthropocentric, it was not my role to remedy this oversight. Suffice it to say that corporations proved hardier than wolves or sharks or any other big predator, and any creature who survived got lucky.

Life is the first stroke of luck; and in mathematics, three is the first lucky prime, while in Greater China, the number three is considered lucky because it sounds like their word for *alive*. Sometimes I think *one two three go* means *get going before your luck runs out.*

As I said, it was the last night of our marriage. And though Joel would find the end abrupt, if he ever looked back with open eyes, he'd see the clock had been ticking from the beginning. The first time we ever kissed, he tasted like antibacterial soap, but I'd already determined to overlook what couldn't be changed about him, for of all the human delegates representing Yácorp at the Chicago Interdomal Intercorporate Futures Symposium, Joel was the only one who could possibly pass for handsome. According to matchmaking algorithms, he was several inches too short for me, but he wasn't unpleasant-looking, and though his ideas were classified, he wasn't a natural secret keeper, being too eager to display the fact he had them.

"I do just two little things," he'd bragged the day I met him at the symposium. "I dream big and make dreams into reality."

He'd been cocky, saying that much to a stranger. But now

I wasn't a stranger, was I? And despite our quarrels, Joel still considered keeping a secret to mean keeping it from everyone but me. Telling his wife didn't feel like telling *someone*.

We were fighting about Ulysses, Stage II. Stage I was the city itself, and there it was out the window and in plain view for everyone to love or hate. Whether or not I believed in God, I had to give the Devil his due: it really was impressive. Productive. Imaginative. High-risk, of course, a city without a dome in the wretched heat, and in the middle of Peacetime Terrorism. But hubris was part of its greatness. It was eco-friendly, in a sense, using volcanic tuff, cinder blocks, inflated plastic cells, aluminum, vermiculite roof-screed-growth-and-incubation-mediums and anti-climb obsidian, all locally sourced beyond the Sacrifice Fence, through which only the tiniest necrophages, like fire ants and sandflies – or my husband – could enter or exit the West. All in all, Ulysses represented unhampered economic growth for shareholders, as provided by forced labor in the National Sacrifice Area (usually just called "Sacrifice") and the cost-cutting advantage of subtracting human and environmental welfare from the budget.

But Stage II remained proprietary. If I hadn't been Joel's wife, I would never have been in the loop. Tomorrow, Yácorp's Idea Man was suing for final dispensation from the Christian Brigade Association to make the city of Ulysses the doorway to the mythical past. Even Disney World Rising had never tried anything like it: reenactment tourism in Sacrifice – last stop, Ambush at the MacAllister Ranch. It was Joel's most ambitious idea to date.

The silence wasn't peace. I stood there, tight-lipped and seething, my slip draped over the vinyl back of the hotel's vanity chair. Thin and butt naked, I'd grown leaner and meaner, or maybe just slender and older: it was one of many subjects about which we'd never agree, but one that Joel took personally. Why spend hours each day with a trainer when he preferred me plump, what I called *fat*? Or had *he* called me fat? We'd been married so long, our boundaries had gotten blurred.

While the years had made me fit and hard, or merely single-pointed, nonetheless, far more than most people, I remained unchanged by Time. At the age of forty-seven, I still had hair long enough to sit on and cream-in-coffee skin and 20/20 bitter-chocolate eyes. And though there was, in my dark hair, a migrating drift of white, like a fable of snow, it was there one month, gone the next, only to return a few months later to another quadrant of my head. I was a woman on the verge of a euphemism – "a certain age" – with all the typical internal symptoms but few of the external ones.

"How is that possible?" Joel once asked, in a peaceful moment.

Witchcraft, I'd mouthed, because walls have ears and, flagging the word, someone in Central Intelligence might have believed the joke.

As a historian, I had to be particularly careful: it was generally accepted that a witch could dig up a corpse, blow on it to shrink it, and sing to make it grow and bring it back to life. Which is suspiciously similar to what a historian does.

Accustomed to surveillance, and used to being visible and unseen, I thought nothing of standing naked in the hotel window, out of which was a half-mile drop into the city that was my husband's brainchild. Firstborn. Stage I. His futuristic baby. We'd failed to have the flesh-and-blood kind, and I imagined it was too late, unaware that accidental pregnancies in early menopause are surprisingly common.

I gazed out on Ulysses. Seeing the potential in the wasteland thresholds and the unutilized service population living in the shanties along the Fence, Joel had dreamed of a world-class city built daringly without a dome and forged from a weed-and-oil backwater on the border of the dead zone, where proximity to industry meant money. After years of planning, he had realized his dream: there were luxury hotels, casinos and even a desert waterpark. Next up, trainloads of tourists would stream through the Fence for the thrill ride of their lives, delighting in popular bloodbaths. Joel was ahead of his time, if time is linear.

I was trying not to fight with him, and he was trying too, for we each had other things to do. But both of us were failing. I can't say when our marriage soured, though Central Intelligence audio could probably reveal the change. We'd once used the word *we* all the time but seldom used it now. And we hadn't had sex in months, which according to the metric of some couples isn't very long, but we'd been so good at sex.

An orgasm had been the one thing I'd never had to fake. Our marriage had been sealed and sealed again by nights in which we'd screwed and slept and woken up and screwed and slept and woken up again, groggy and sweaty on top of the sheets, and stumbled to the bathroom to brush our teeth and then back to bed to dream an identical dream, because the deepest sex can work such magic, and I knew Joel as the Bible defined it. Joel dreamed without censure, regardless of whether his fantasies became other people's nightmares. But the shameful secret was, as much as he'd never admit it, his dreams had been my idea.

"We should go to Sacrifice for our honeymoon," I'd said, after making love, slammed up against his office's wall-to-wall aquarium.

Laughing at me, he displayed his stark white teeth, made brighter by the myriad grow lamps in the tiny underwater ruins.

"I'm not kidding, Joel," I said and fed the carp, catfish, halibut and squid.

"No one can go to Sacrifice."

"*You* can. And you can convince Yácorp to let me come along. I'm dying of curiosity."

"Curiosity killed the cat."

"Are there really still wolves in Sacrifice?"

"Where in the world did you hear that?"

Not wanting to answer, I pouted back at the carp wallowing in its tank and said, "My colleague in Biogenetics told me something interesting: scientists used to think that wolves were related to dolphins. It's hard to imagine the resemblance."

"Sacrifice isn't a safari, honey."

"Show me what it's like, darling?"

Sitting down on his fake-wood desk, I pushed aside our engagement photo: him in a Heatwick suit and me in a black number and stilettos. Then, picking up his Yácorp palm-reader – not the pocket-sized travel one but a silver titanium full-screen that matched the steel-and-tempered-glass interiors of his office – I gave it to him with one hand and placed my other hand in his crotch.

"When I was a teenager," I whispered in his ear, "I used to steal my parents' car at night and drive from Wichita to the Fence and be back by morning."

I could feel him hardening up again, inspired by the thought of his fiancée as a teenage runaway. So I told him all about it. I told him about the shantytown of Ulysses, where I'd smoked up in the lesser heat of the night and watched the moon rising over a white-capped sea of tents.

"My mom never knew," I said, "or pretended not to. Or knew but couldn't admit it to herself. I even brought it up. I asked her if she'd been to Ulysses. She said it was a cute, quiet town, though she hadn't visited since before the war. I told her I thought it had changed. 'Well, if something can change,' she said, 'it can change again. God can do what He likes.'"

"Sounds like your mother," Joel said. He didn't like Brigaders, though he believed them a necessary evil.

Yet Joel was in love with a Brigader's daughter, and he was scrolling into negative longitude to prove it. He logged into Yácorp's vault and entered the elaborate code necessary to access data west of -101.35, the easternmost boundary of Sacrifice.

"Do you know how much you help me?" I asked, as he zoomed into ghost towns. I kissed him lightly on the ear, then offered my full attention as he explained how Govcorps, always economical, had deemed demolition to be superfluous.

"Unless located on an asset," he said. "Even your precious MacAllister ranch – what's left of it – is still standing."

The ranch was mine like Joel was mine. Not even married yet, and he had already echoed back to me the lexicon of my profession. *My* Connie; *my* Twins, Tom and Tam; *my* girl-who-got-away, whose name had not been verified; *mine* as opposed to some other historian's rendition or the pulp-fiction monsters depicted by New Hollywood. Mine, because, as I told my students, a person exists not as an independent entity but in the changeable moment between herself and another: herself and her students, herself and her husband, herself and her parents, herself and her grandparents, herself and her homeland, even herself and herself.

I became visibly excited, as any historian would be. "Can I see it?" I asked. But that request overreached.

Blacking out the screen, Joel lied, "I can't access that sector. Anyhow, we don't want to go there for our honeymoon, not unless God changes everything again."

He laughed at his little joke, either to cover the lie or because he didn't believe in God.

But that night, in his bachelor-pad bed, Joel conceived a big idea. Having made love again, I lay naked on my back, admiring a vintage poster on his wall: Evel Knievel was rocket-propelled into the air above Snake Canyon while, on the floor below, a week's worth of Joel's dirty laundry had mounded up like speed bumps. I heard Joel suck in his breath. In that moment, his brainchild was conceived, though it was so grotesquely large it would take our entire marriage to push out.

Things change.

Now, above Joel's queen bed in our room at the Grand Hotel, there hung a still life of a glass of Gatorade Fast Twitch, and in the ensuite steam bath, sullied towels would be magicked into fresh ones in the morning, while outside the window, down in the streets, people were being killed for the sixty percent of a body that is water.

After so many years of marriage, little gestures reveal long stories. Like Joel feeling the right to eat my chocolate as well as his. Sprawled on the hotel bed, he crossed his ankles and pulled his expandable palm-reader from his shirt breast pocket. Then, while it activated to maximum size, he absently reached over the gap for the last complimentary goodie, the one on my pillow. That he didn't want to fight, especially about candy, didn't stop him from popping the chocolate into his mouth.

Seeing me watching, he asked with his mouth full, "Did you want this piece? I haven't chewed. It's nougat, though, and I know you don't like nougat."

"No," I said.

"I think it's nougat. I might taste rum. Rum and nougat's not very nice. You sure you don't want it? I haven't chewed."

"I don't need a sugar high," I said, "on top of everything else." I was finished with surrogates for love.

"Suit yourself," said Joel.

"Evel Knievel never actually jumped the Snake."

I was not really changing the subject, for the subject had never been candy. And although Evel Knievel appeared to Joel to come careening out of nowhere, the motorcyclist's pretend victory was a good example of distorted history, which is, in fact, what we were fighting about.

"The crosswinds dropped him in the river," I said. "Also, people swear he attempted the Grand Canyon, but he didn't. And when he did try to leap a string of London double-decker buses, he broke his pelvis. Then, when someone wrote a book about his violent temperament, he beat the author with a baseball bat for lying and was sentenced to three years in prison."

"I know," Joel said. "You told me that already."

Implying I had Alzheimer's was a tactic to shut me up. And though, being adopted, I was no more likely than anyone else to develop the genetic disease that had killed my mother, for a moment the strategy worked, because the truth is I don't trust my memory.

I remember some things all too well, but I don't have a steel-trap scholar's mind befitting my profession. As an academic, I was good at analysis, excellent at synthesis, but woefully poor at retention. I couldn't wheel out a quotation, date, anecdote, or citation, or recite, as Joel so often demanded, "exactly what I said that you found so offensive." All arguments got twisted into the question: how could I be trusted to remember anything, professionally or personally? As a result, Joel won all the battles, even if I planned from the beginning to win the war.

"It's gone," he said, as if candy were in fact the problem. "Don't blame me when you want some chocolate later."

As he glanced toward the bathroom door, because the nougat was sticking to his teeth and he was considering jetting it, I turned away toward the window and lay my hand on the glass.

Things change, I thought again.

A banal generality, worthy of the worst of my students. *What* things change, *exactly*? Minds, marriages, allegiances, bodies, genders, faith, climate, governments, memories, mothers, motivations, worlds or love? Names change, obviously. That was self-evident.

Neutralization, as well as the Longitude and Latitude Coordinate Shift, had unnamed the land in order to reduce the Earth to resource and Earthlings to externalities. The RUSA understood what, even as a colonizer, the USA had not: the articulation of names is a subversive act. On twentieth-century Rand McNally road maps, words had played like flutes whittled from human bones, forever calling people home. There was Idaho, meaning *enemy* (Plains Apache); Illinois, *he speaks normally* (Algonquian); Michigan, *large water* (Odawa); Nebraska, *flattened water* (Chiwere); Ohio, *beautiful river* (Seneca). There were scores of towns like Ponchatoula, from the Choctaw language, meaning *flowing hair*, which I like to imagine was shorthand for singing, *Oh this place, how we love her, with those mosses hanging from the trees!*

Govcorps razed it all: no more Idaho or Illinois, also no New England. Ulysses, yes, but no Kansas, from the Kaws or Kansa people, derived from the word for *south wind*. LA, yes, but no California, named for a fictional island in a Spanish novel and the now-mythical location where the MacAllister twins had been born. Also, definitely no Four Corners, that checkerboard nexus where the Sacrifice War began.

"What's in a name?" I often asked my students, who did not recognize the quote, because Shakespeare had been censored as psychologically subversive. They invariably shrugged to say "not much," though the correct answer was "a hell of a lot."

Yácorp was Yescorp before the war. *Yá* means *sky* in Navajo, and in Spanish *ya* (minus the accent) means *now, already, later* and *no longer*, while in Japanese *yā* means *wild*, literally *open country*, and is hybridized to create *bastard, prostitute* or *desert*. Yácorp's stocks soared with a simple change of prefix, which lent it the exotic air of dangerous languages – the first two banned in the RUSA, the latter banned in Greater China.

Things change. History is "things change."

But "things repeat" is also true. The landmass west of -101.35

being designated as Sacrifice, for the purpose of wresting resources from private ownership and tribal holdings, was not a new idea. Back in the 1970s, the United States Department of Energy proposed that the Four Corners locality, long considered a dispensable region inhabited by dispensable people, become a National Sacrifice Area, allowing for total corporate freedom and unbridled exploitation of resources. Had the proposal succeeded, the evacuation of populations would have gone uncontested, safety and cleanup from strip-mining would have been deemed unnecessary, and lawsuits would have utterly stalled out. Luckily, because the powerful corporate lobby wasn't yet all-powerful and corporate interests weren't yet synonymous with survival, the proposal never reached the floor of Congress. But corpses can kick around a while before they are resuscitated.

I was surveying the view from the hotel window, where a coordination of dusky blues, with tiny inoffensive roses, patterned the navy drapes and matched the late-night sky. No longer just a blip on TerraGoogle and now visible from space, Ulysses was "bright and beaming," like clean laundry in a bleach commercial. I could even see the stars, because shielded lamps kept the glare aimed downward so that migratory birds – what was left of them – could navigate above the roofline. (Govcorps weren't above contradictions: building codes protected the birds.)

I stood with my back to Joel. I stood naked in the window, visible from other windows if anyone cared to look, which my husband didn't, too busy licking chocolate off his fingers.

But how did I know that? I didn't have eyes in the back of my head – a saying that had always scared my mother. Married to a man for so many years, somehow you just know things.

A star shot across the sky, and I made a wish.

"I don't dislike nougat," I said, and I think I said it sullenly, but after so many years observing Joel, I sometimes neglected to look at myself.

"Yes, you do," Joel said, because although he needed to interface, he felt a greater need to correct me.

"I dislike caramel," I said, "and you always confuse the two. You purposefully confuse things."

"Have it your way," he said, as if indulging me in a lie.

So I wheeled around and shouted, "I'm a fucking historian! I should know!" Obviously, I wasn't talking about nougat.

I was resuming the fight exactly where Joel and I had left it, with Joel and Yácorp choosing to believe, and in Stage II intending to depict, the grossest and most exaggerated accounts of the MacAllisters – accounts which, in a court of law, if such an institution had still existed, would never have held up. You could not know the past beyond a shadow of a doubt in a day on which the sun cast shadows everywhere and the only survivors were children, whose memories are the progenitors of myth. But monsters are more lucrative than humans and black-and-white more fucking marketable than fucking gray.

"What's with all the *fucks*?" Joel asked, not even bothering to raise his voice. He was lying like a sultan on his back, and I had resorted to repetitive swearing. "I thought you had a PhD vocabulary." He spoke calmly and condescendingly, for winning was a habit. "If tourists want to see a brother and sister torture people or fuck each other's brains out on a cactus, stop taking it so personally."

"Of course I take it personally. It's my life."

"Stop being overdramatic."

"It's my field."

"And how many times have you been wrong?"

"Gotcha," he thought – because I'd been wrong a lot. The MacAllister ranch still standing: I'd refused to believe it until he finally admitted having access to the region and pulled it up and showed me. Outlaws surviving in Sacrifice: he'd produced the infrared footage of unsanctioned human movement near the Lechuguilla Cave mouth, Carlsbad Caverns and Canyon de Chelly, just to prove he was right.

"And now you're really going to claim that your Twins weren't having sex? Stop being such a prude," he said.

"The last thing I am is a prude."

"And stop shivering," he commanded. "Put on some clothes."

My standing naked and shivering was irritating him. Did I expect him to turn down the air-conditioning when I could wrap myself in a hotel bathrobe, with deep pockets for icy hands? But I didn't want to put on my clothes: I wanted Joel to take his off.

Though he'd removed his shoes, due to the insistently cold central air, he'd retained his shirt and tie, his socks and modal-blend pinstripes and was sitting on his billfold, which was called a billfold though it did not contain bills – only philanthropists carried cash. Nor did it hold photographs of loved ones, because who exactly would that be? Certainly not me anymore.

Though plastic was technically unnecessary, his billfold bulged with credit, business, dining and security cards, because retro technologies were the rage. Even Yácorp was nostalgia-friendly, providing what they called "safety in the palm of your hand:" a shiny security chit, which, together with the latest iris recognition, granted my husband, Joel Saunders, entrance into Sacrifice or absolutely anywhere he wanted to go. Which wasn't into me, not in the last several months.

I sat down on the edge of his bed. "You can't be comfortable in your trousers," I said softly.

He moaned and moved his feet, though I was sitting nowhere near them. "Why can't you put something on?" he said, as if my nakedness were a trap.

I glanced over at the window, where the illuminated temperature and carbon count on the Climate Tower blinked on and off: 108°, 412.89 ppm.

"Because it's hot out there," I said.

"You're in here," he answered.

He flicked his eyes toward the emerald numbers on the radio alarm clock, and for a moment Joel resembled the halibut in his office aquarium. The eyes of a flatfish begin life on either side of its head, but as it prepares for bottom-feeding and partial burial in the ocean floor, one eye migrates toward the other until they sit side by side.

"Is that the time?" Joel asked.

"I don't know what else it would be."

"I haven't gotten any work done."

But he knew he didn't really need to. He was already fully prepared for tomorrow's meeting and his strategy already perfect. He just didn't want to look lazy in front of his Yácorp colleagues, particularly after balking at their suggestion that, upon his late arrival in Ulysses, he take a midnight limo tour of Sacrifice. "I don't need a visual on a wasteland," he'd said, "I need a good night's sleep."

"Really, you can't be comfortable in your trousers," I said, crossing my arms at my chest so my breasts rose like buoys in a mirage of water.

I wanted him to notice, but he didn't. He saw so very little. And though I was speaking English, I might as well have been speaking Mandarin or Navajo because, suddenly returning to interfacing, Joel didn't bother to answer.

22:25:56 now.

I stood at the hotel window. Orion was so near I could have hanged myself with his belt. I nudged closer to the drapes as if they'd keep me warm. Their tiny blue roses were, on closer inspection, not solid blue but bicolored: silver-tipped leaves and midnight-tinted blooms.

Down below, The Real Thing, Coca-Cola's Optical Wave, strobed across Patriot Plaza, and on the curved front of the monolithic Agricultural Institute, SynFeast projected blue corn bending in a pleasant breeze, and the words from an old musical – HIGH AS AN ELEPHANT'S EYE – released as pollen with every gust. Farmscrapers grew in multicolor, and foliage-insulated condos and casinos in monochromatic green. Rainbow lights masked the lightning spires and on stormy nights played an optical lullaby, because the rhythm of flickering lights was a proven anxiolytic, and if anything relaxed a population, it was a rainbow.

Naked in the window, there was no one to see me but chickens. Across the way, in the farmscraper – where mesh walls harvested water vapor and solar-motion shade-sails enabled open-air vertical growing without the danger of scorching – grew white greens and cow beans, chard and stemless blue corn. But somewhere inside were incarcerated poultry: cocks, capons, pullets, hens, chicks and cockatrices. Or were cockatrices a myth? Whether or not they were cockatrices, they were silent and featherless cannibals.

I tapped at the glass, as if the birds might hear me. I would have liked to call to them. But the only way to open a hotel window was to blow it out.

"What do you think?" Joel asked from the bed.

"I thought you were interfacing."

"I can't concentrate when you're tapping."

"What do I think about what?"

"About Ulysses."

Impressive. Productive. I hadn't said it aloud. And I didn't say it now as I watched the Sacrifice searchlights, like an agitated beacon, visible in the distance. Forty miles west. "I never objected to Ulysses," I said.

"You hate it," he corrected me.

"No more than I hate most cities."

"You hate it more. You hate it particularly."

"I'll tell you what I hate. I hate the tourism idea that goes with it."

"Goes with what?"

"Ulysses."

"It doesn't go *with* it."

"You know what I mean, Joel. Whatever it does. In conjunction with it. After it. Second part of the two-part plan. I thought you were interfacing. Are we going to get rain or not? I'd really like to see a lullaby."

"Storm Song."

"Whatever it's called."

"You never say what you mean."

How well did he actually know me?

I was willing it to rain. Rain would cover my scent and traces. And I wanted to feel myself again: water poured into water.

"Did you know," I asked, "*monsoon* comes from the Arabic word *mawsim*, meaning *time of year for a voyage*?"

"So what?" he said, always pained by my non-sequiturs and etymological obsessions, though you'd think he'd have gotten used to them by now.

"So everything," I said, louder than I meant to.

I could have said so much more. I could have gone on and on about how *persimmon* came from *putchamin* or *pasiminan*, meaning *a dry fruit* in Algonquian, and how *lieutenant* harkened back to the fourteenth-century Old French for *one who took the place of another*, or how the verb *to be*, as in Hamlet's question, served as the pivot in English, but in Navajo, the linchpin was *to go*, with over one hundred thousand conjugations. But I didn't dare say too much. So I leaned my head on the window, which was sweating in the battle between the cold interior and the heat outside, and I said nothing.

That it *might* rain, that it *might* storm, was a cause for hope. Decades had passed since Govcorps had detonated the key mountain peaks that, as weather siphons, had historically channeled the American Monsoons into the West. Because precipitation had been needed to sustain the New Eastern domes, where the preferred population lived, Govcorps had blown the tops off the mountains and turned the monsoons eastward.

Yet slowly, patiently, the monsoons kept inching westward. They'd been inching homeward for years. Govcorps was divided as to the cause, but in the time of the Sacrifice Wars Outsiders had felt certain that, as the first raindrops fell on the thirsting desert sand, the Twins commanded not just armies but the sky. A cold front had wedged a warm cloud upward, and droplets amassed to saturation point around an airborne pool of dust; the sky had succumbed to gravity at roughly the same time that the Twins had arrived on the front. Roughly. Perfect synchronicity wasn't mandatory, because the wonders of natural systems can't compete with a tale of heroes.

I was standing there, still holding my slip. Standing there, still naked. I was leaning on the glass, motionless but not entirely frozen, vaguely quivering, like dew about to vanish. I was as slim as the origami paper that was being folded by hundreds of street children, thirty-three floors below me, into little cranes. Juvenile Outsiders who swarmed the cars at barricades, begging a dime in exchange for a paper bird.

I hadn't lied about Ulysses. It wasn't more hopeless than other cities; it was, in fact, more honest without a dome. The desperate were down there, if you looked. You sped by them in your car, or they banged on car windows that couldn't open and drivers slid their money through the charity hole that Oxfam had paid Nissan to design, because after opening the door, too many would-be philanthropists had had their heads smashed in.

But white cranes would never float in a crimson pool of my husband's blood, because Yácorp's darling was no do-gooder, and he didn't carry cash and would never have considered opening a limo door. Also, were there such birds as cranes anymore, or were they only depicted on Greater Chinese wedding kimonos as symbols of fidelity and hawked as paper miniatures in the street? Were there only ravens left? *Raven* is Old English, meaning *black and shiny*, but *to raven* derives from French and means to *plunder*, *prey*, *devour greedily*, and *seize by violence*, and it can be used as an adjective, as in *the ravening wolf*.

I must have been visibly agitated, for Joel suggested a technique he'd learned at a mandatory anti-PTSD workshop. "Take three, long, slow breaths," he said. "It'll help –"

"Rain will help," I said.

"– because whatever's wrong with you, Dorothy," he said, "has nothing to do with me."

He looked to his palm-reader for affirmation while I ignored the bait and offered some myself: "If it's monsoon season, there won't be twisters."

I waited for him to contradict me. We both knew freak weather was the norm – everything fiercer, shorter, longer, out of order or out of place – and when everyone's a freak, you should give up calling them names. Seasons meant nothing other than 'expect anything'. But this time, Joel was too preoccupied with interfacing to feel the need to correct me.

Outside the wind was blowing, and inside, too, the central air enlivened my slip, my lipstick, Joel's palm-reader and wallet, and the Gideon Bible inside the bedside table drawer. These were too heavy to be blowing here and there, but on some level, as time passes, everything is in motion.

I was standing in the window by the curtains and nestling among the scentless roses when I remembered the first such flower I'd ever shared with Joel.

It was back in the very beginning. Newly married, we'd bought a Chicago brownstone with leaky windows, dry rot, a carpenter ant infestation and a problem for every so-called season. "A historic house for a historian," Joel called it, proving how much he loved me. It was a house like we might have bought a hundred years before, except that the yard was hardpan. Chicago was equipped with an early-edition dome that had a typical failing: the membrane that allowed for rain was impermeable at the seams. All up and down our east – west street, our microchip-sized yards were desert.

When at the garden gate a rosebud blossomed, I saw it as a sign of spirit rising again from the dust. To test the strength of my husband's observational skills, though I longed to tell him about it, I determined to wait impatiently for Joel to notice the rose all by himself. But when the petals began dropping, I couldn't take it anymore.

"Did you notice the rose?" I cried the moment he placed his briefcase in the hall and, as if he were a blind man, led him by the wrist to the diminutive bloom.

Its pale yellow hues, viewed under the streetlights, had defaulted to a shabby white, but beneath the pavement, its determined roots were active, dowsing for covert water.

"It's barely a rose," he said.

"It grew without rain."

"No one but you would even have noticed it."

The tiny word *even* was the lever between meanings. One meaning: he loved that about me. The other: he loved me not. At that moment, anyhow, he loved me. And love isn't simply blind, it has had its eyes gouged out.

It's fair enough to ask why I'd shown him the rose at all. As he had already failed to see it, all ulterior motives were spent. Yet the determined rose had been hanging on, fighting every day not to drop, offering Joel another chance, every single day. His admiration was the least that I could offer it.

"If it were a snake, it would have bitten you," I said as I glanced into the darkened hallway – his steel briefcase on the scrubbed floorboards.

It was a quote from my Brigader mother, who'd been both amazed and concerned that her daughter displayed no fear of snakes.

I suddenly missed my mother, who'd been killed by the memory of a snake. Not the reptilian kind but a type of cyclone locally called a "snake", due to its coloration, which was red and black or red and yellow depending on the soil in its vortex. My mother's memory of a snake, combined with late-stage Alzheimer's, precipitated her move to an End Facility to receive the final injection. Forgetting that such monumental natural forces were pacified by a dome, when her teakettle whistled, she mistook it for a weather siren. Terrified and confused, she took off for the basement, leaving the kettle boiling till it melted. When a neighbor found her in the cellar crouching in her urine, a Transition was promptly mandated.

Joel claimed he could do nothing to stop it. But hating to see me cry, at least he used his influence to postpone the injection long enough for a limo to speed us to Wichita to say goodbye.

Rain fell through the Wichita dome as the Yácorp limo dropped us at a cinder-block facility with barred windows and bleached walls, through which passed the breathy sound of hushed voices under a perpetual buzzing, whose source I could not ascertain.

Knowing how my mother liked the Raindrop Game, I'd brought along a jar of coins, which I'd found in my old bedroom while closing up the pious house where I'd been raised. It was a simple, wholesome game in which you chose a raindrop at the top of the window, and if your drop hit the sill before your competitor's, you won a coin.

"Shall the three of us play?" I asked.

When she smiled and nodded, I saw she had no teeth. (Whether or not she'd been aggressive, teeth removal was policy.)

I thought playing would make her happy, but although I was briefly right, I was ultimately wrong. The first round didn't go as hoped. My raindrop hung on the window, and hers quivered and turned aside, dissolved in the wet and vanished, while Joel's alone sped on. Something similar happened in the second round. Then it happened over and over, and Joel won all my coins.

My mother became uneasy. Her eyes flicked from the prayer ring on her finger to the steel equipment cupboard. Caught on a security camera, she appeared to be contemplating her imminent death. In fact, she was worrying about me losing the game because, though she was not my blood mother, she felt herself to be a part of me and experienced the loss of my coins as her own. She did not want me to lose to Joel.

Alzheimer's never erased my mother's dislike of my husband. Although she believed a husband was the head of his wife, as Christ was the head of the Christian Brigade Association, and that any woman, especially an adoptee, should be grateful to marry into Yácorp, she never understood what I saw in him. At the big news of his proposal, she had even asked me, "But does he really see you, Dorothy?"

Now, stepping back from the hotel window, I appraised the mark my forehead had left on the glass.

Rain fell across the city of Ulysses.

But it did not fall so heavily as to make the rainbow lights strobe to Ulysses's lullaby. The gentle rain dissolved beneath the hotel window into the intended invisibility of the city streets.

Murders were happening down there. In Patriot Plaza, the Coca-Cola logo flashed across a smashed-in skull, while darkness and the glaring light from the skyscrapers sealed the lower world away. Outsider violence had become self-consuming.

Joel wasn't working anymore. His will to overprepare had slipped. Having left his palm-reader open on the bed and live to Central Hub, he was fishing about in the bar cabinet, trying to find the oak-aged whiskey the hotel offered its most distinguished guests.

His voice muffled, head in cabinet, he said, "Where's the good stuff? There's supposed to be good stuff."

I came to him as if to help.

Crossing the room, my feet were sweaty in the shag pile carpet. I was hot, then cold, then hot again, though the seesaw of menopause was only partly to blame. I was quick to anger and equally quick to make up for no discernible reason. But Joel was long accustomed to my contradictory nature: *half housecat and half wolverine*, he'd called it, a combination that I'd pointed out should have eaten itself.

"There better be good stuff," he said. "Yácorp didn't fight the CBA for a liquor license just to drink plonk."

As I peered over his shoulder, I did not intend to speak aloud, and unless you were in my brain, it didn't make much sense. "It's like reciting an alphabet backwards. It's strange," I said.

"Temperance isn't strange; it's stupid," Joel said, his own brain buried in the bar cabinet. He knew I hadn't meant the antiliquor lobby, but he was demonstrating just how difficult it was to follow my train of thought, which moved about in time as if the calendar had never been invented.

Explaining myself to the back of his head, I said, "Not the antiliquor lobby. The *alphabet* is strange. CBA is ABC but backwards, and the alphabet moving backwards behaves differently from numbers counting backwards. With numbers, you get to zero, but zero is only a pause, because after you get there you hit the negatives, which can go on forever.

But alphabetizing backwards, after A you get to silence, and there's nowhere to go from there."

I should have stopped at that, but somehow I couldn't. I said, "Zero isn't the end, Joel. Ground Zero, Sacrifice –"

He quickly pulled his head out, assuming I was about to launch, yet again, into a defense of the MacAllisters.

"I'm sick of this," said Joel.

"I'm trying ..."

To what? To warn him? I have no idea what I intended to say next or why I'd dream of warning him of anything. I can't be expected to understand all my own motivations.

"You're not trying," Joel cut me off. "You haven't tried in years."

"If you loved me –"

"Like *you* love *me*? Who the hell do you think you are, Dorothy?"

That was the one question I would not answer yet. I opened my mouth and closed it and opened it again and snapped it shut and cracked it open as if I were a baby bird. Did you know a caged bird will ruffle and twitch her wings for the length of her thwarted migration?

When I finally spoke, my words were small and quiet, with only the faintest meaning. Not like a baby bird, which has a disproportionately loud squawk. But I could have been a bird of paradise, the very last one surviving, and it wouldn't have mattered to Joel, because he had stopped loving me. And whether or not I felt the same, I hated him for it.

I placed my hand on my neck, held my ear and pulled my clip-on earring off, realizing that all this time I hadn't actually been naked, because I was still wearing earrings. And always wearing my wedding ring – in a way, I never was naked.

I was standing over Joel, hovering there, pretending to help him find the whiskey. I wasn't doing *nothing*. I was busy, like a pregnant woman is busy even while she's doing nothing. Except I felt the opposite of pregnant.

Crouching down beside him, I looked harmless as a scrawny lab rat. ("Do rats eat baby birds?" I'd asked the Biogenetics expert as Joel sat in the eye scanner and carolers in Santa hats roamed the university halls.)

"There it is," I said, "hiding in the back."

The whiskey was the color of quarried amber, which was also, disconcertingly, the color of dehydrated urine.

Joel stood up. So I stood up. And when I stood, my slip, all this while draped over my arm, swished to the ground. The quiet sound was the fantasy of snow escaping the grade of a roof.

Moved by some admixture of loyalty, guilt and rage toward a man I swore I didn't love, I'd almost said too much. But Joel had failed to notice. And now he set me back on task.

As if no cruel words had passed between us, he asked, "Do you want some?"

The mood, as it does, had changed.

Whiskey tumbler in hand, I was pulling my slip over my head when the spaghetti straps caught around my ears. The lacy fringe hovered above my pubes. This had happened before, for after so many years of marriage just about everything except the end will have happened before.

"Joel," I said, "I'm stuck in my slip, and I don't want to spill my drink. Will you help me?"

And because he was still my husband, he did. But he no longer kissed my ears and said, as he untangled the straps, "Your ears are bookends holding secret diaries."

I didn't like his clichés any more than I liked Govcorp slogans or Brigader aphorisms, yet I'd liked those silly words, because my subject, my expertise, *my* Connie, *my* Connie MacAllister, had kept copious diaries, and if the MacAllister ranch still existed, the diaries probably did as well. But the hour for liking and disliking was past.

How far in the past was hard to say, because history is buried by relentless overlay: past over past. In a canyon, you could point to the present and compare it to the Paleozoic, but in a hotel room on the thirty-third floor, you had nothing to rely on except the retro radio alarm clock. Outside, Yácorp purged the land of time, but in the mall beneath the Grand Hotel, consumers enjoyed late-night shopping in late-twentieth-century interiors. It was 22:40:15, and I had much left to accomplish.

On the Nikwaxed cowhide chesterfield, Joel and I sat side by side. Clinking glasses, I said, "To the future."

"Isn't it bad luck for a historian to toast the future?" he asked.

If it was, I was unacquainted with the superstition. But it definitely was bad luck not to look a drinker in the eye while toasting. So I amended my dedication – "Okay, to the past" – and stared at Joel.

To walk a mile in a man's shoes, as the saying goes, amounts to much the same as spending a year behind his eyes, for whatever reason. And so I felt close to my husband that night as we drank together on the chesterfield and amazed each other with tales of once-ubiquitous leather handbags and cowboy boots. Genetically modified cattle, wired up in the milk factories, had skin like disposable plastic bags, and a real leather sofa was a near-impossible luxury, for which Joel could take the credit.

"To cowhide," I drawled and clinked and eyeballed him again. I ran my free hand down the chesterfield's arm, and opened my mouth wide while Joel looked inside, as if there might be something in there that he wanted. I said, "When I was four, I ate a Barbie head."

"Isn't a Barbie head too big to eat?" he asked.

Wrong question. He could have asked how I'd remembered, having previously claimed that the traumas of the Migration Era had evicted every memory from before my adoption.

"Not a *Barbie* Barbie," I said, holding the icy tumbler to my cheek. "One of Barbie's friends, or sisters or cousins or something. A preteen Barbie. Its head is smaller."

"It's called a Skipper," he said.

"How did you know that?" I asked.

"I have no idea."

Sweat shone under my eyes, making them appear even bigger. And beneath my breasts, damp marks stained my slip, which clung to me like a skin graft. Occasionally, I liked to sleep in my slip, prompting Joel's somnambulant hands to roam back and forth between the silky fabric and my flesh, unable to tell the difference. Awake, he seldom touched me. But he still held me when he slept, for marriage, particularly its ending, stutters between realities.

The night was gearing up to storm. Soon a downpour would begin, and in no time there'd be lullabies. I leaned forward, clasped the neck of the bottle, refilled his glass and said, "Should I feel guilty, Joel?"

"For what?" he asked.

"For everything," I answered.

Recorded, it sounds facile. But it was in fact vital, for the future depends on the prefrontal cortex, in conversation with the amygdala, discussing the subject of guilt. A psychopath's amygdala is incapable of registering guilt and barred from fear as well as empathy. And it's important to know who you are.

"It doesn't matter," Joel said, presuming *everything* meant my getting him drunk and stopping him from working. Finally admitting that dispensation from the CBA was really a done deal, he used a Brigader motto that referenced predestination: "Tomorrow's already history."

I ran my hand down the sofa arm again. "Cows are blessed," I drawled, stretching my mouth around the diphthong.

It was another Brigader line: cows are blessed, goats are cursed and dogs are either man's best friend or witches.

Because I was feeling close to Joel, I asked, "Did I ever tell you how my mother's golden retriever mated with a wolf?"

Joel managed to smile and drink at the same time. He said pleasantly but firmly, "You didn't, and the dog didn't."

"The dog did, I swear," I said and relayed the story.

Wichita, a late dome city, had been in bad shape before its dome, and among the many sites abandoned and collapsed was the city zoo. On the hunt was a lone wolf, who was starving and emaciated. My mother's golden retriever – who was specifically my mother's and who lived in the backyard chained to a pole – didn't stand a chance. The wolf could have easily killed and eaten her, only he didn't. He didn't, because he was playing the long game.

"What long game?" said Joel.

"Genetic preservation."

"I don't believe this story."

"You should, because it's true."

"You saw the wolf screw the dog? You saw it with your own eyes? Or did someone tell you?"

"I saw him hump her in broad daylight. It took all the energy he had left, and, afterwards, he circled round, lay down and died. I wept for them both, the dog and the wolf, but I was happy when the puppies were born, and my mother gave them to the neighbors, pretending they were a golden–German shepherd mix. Mom called it a white lie. She said it was forgivable."

These last details made Joel twitchy, and he glanced about the room, as if Central Intelligence planted recording devices where they could actually be seen. But he didn't need to worry, because, at that moment anyhow, no one was paying attention to a domestic interlude between Joel and Dorothy Saunders. DNA storage technologies allowed for second-by-second country-wide surveillance, but the overkill of information buried itself under its own abundance. Knowing you were seen or heard, not the knowledge thereby derived, was what paralyzed the population, including those in the upper ranks of Yácorp.

"If anyone had found out ..." he whispered.

"Which is why I never told you," I said.

"Why are you telling me now?"

"Because everyone involved is dead."

"You're not."

"I was an innocent child."

I did not look so innocent now. I was welcoming, available, as if I were an exemplary wife in a CBA manual, and all he had to do was reach for me, but Joel remained indecisive.

He dropped his eyes from my breasts to his glass, out to his city, back to his glass, to my breasts again, which in some respects he regarded as belonging to him. He put his tumbler on the coffee table and picked it up again and put it down again, and in every location, like the graffito of a ghost, it left a fading ring.

Joel hadn't always been so tentative. Just the opposite. In the very beginning, he was easy. Chatting at the Futures Symposium, he'd even made the first advance and, already certain he understood what I would like and dislike, suggested a February picnic in Chicago's Grant Park.

I admit to having enjoyed the picnic. The domed weather was obliging, providing the kind of day when, if a bomb doesn't go off, a city forgets itself. The righteous had loosened their ties, and some had even rolled up their sleeves. Nonbelievers had quit their footwear to wade in the rococo fountain. An elderly couple, putting off their inevitable end, lay in the grass with their bellies exposed, tracing each other's wrinkles. Dragging their insignia jackets through the lawn, adrenalized schoolboys chased sister-school girls who had already graduated to wearing mandatory bonnets but who, all the same, hiked up their kilts so that their legs could freely run. A road crew on lunch break had discarded their hard hats, which colonized the ground like giant yellow mushrooms. On the modified breezes, enormous soapy bubbles from a birthday party floated by and burst against the trunks of inoculated maples. In the leafy shade, a new mother tended her baby, believing him the hope of the world, and the baby played with another baby, who was also the hope of the world. A well-groomed dog sniffed at a picnic and, just as eagerly, another dog's butt. It was a perfectly formed day until 12:04:13, when a bomb blew forty miles east in the industrial dome of Gary, Indiana, though it wasn't called that anymore.

The brass ensemble on the bandstand stopped playing "A Day in the Life" and, mid-stanza, switched to the "Battle Hymn of the Republic." The change was not incidental, and like everyone else, Joel and I should have checked our phones to see what had occurred. But I was too absorbed in the task at hand, and Joel in me.

"I preferred the Beatles," I said.

Because Joel was wearing shorts, I knew he wasn't a Brigader and would not be offended by my musical preference. His shorts revealed a white, reptilian scar on his lean left thigh, in the same location as my own but smaller, mine being the size of an expanded palm-reader.

I took the scar as an auspicious sign. The day was going well. I removed my sandals, held them dangling by my side, aware of the effect of my thighs, long and firm and dark. He was dying to see above my skirt, where the flesh was particularly smooth. I tossed my shoes on the grass, took a thermos of coffee from my tote. I filled the faded pink-red lid-cup, its handle deformed by the sun, and Joel blew little ripples over the top to cool it down.

As he blew on my lid, I told him how, in the twentieth century, everyone had loved the Beatles. "It isn't my period," I said, "but you can't understand the twenty-first century without knowing what came before. It wasn't *real* love, of course. More like mass hysteria. Or post-traumatic stress. Violence needs a soundtrack. World War Two had 'Lili Marlene.' Vietnam had the Beatles, or Hendrix singing 'Machine Gun.' Iraq had the Smashing Pumpkins. Gaza had –"

"Did the Sacrifice War have a song?" he interrupted.

"The Outlaws had a thousand of them."

"And our side?"

"If jet fire is a kind of song."

"Do you know any Outlaw songs?"

Surprised he'd go so far, I poked at one of the floating bubbles, weighing the possibility of a trap.

"You like to live dangerously," I observed.

He took some time to answer, and when at last he did, he began by using my name. In the beginning, he used my name a lot, which is a common strategy for influencing people.

"Dorothy," he said, "I can do whatever I want. It's a perk of being Yácorp."

"But can *I*?" I asked.

"When you're with me," he said.

But a song is a serious issue, even when it's permitted. So I suggested a nursery rhyme instead. I recited the medieval rhyme that Connie MacAllister had chanted to her twins, and which she'd repeatedly updated to reflect the current events of the time.

"A was an archer who shot a stray dog; B was a Brigader who demonized hogs; C was a corp with siren and gun; D was a Drifter without hope or home; E was an Eagle strafing the crowd; F was a farmer who gave up the plough; G was Govcorps, whose coup was successful –"

"*Coup*?" Joel whispered. The coup could not be called a coup. Incorporation was a retrospectively legal merger between legislative, executive and judicial branches, orchestrated by multinational-sponsored congressmen and supported by Christian lobbyists, the Brigader cult in particular, with its fishes and fear of witchcraft and long-sleeved modesty in the heat.

I whispered back, "It's an *Outlaw* rhyme. Should I keep going?"

"Yes, keep going," he said, not wanting to appear anything less than all-powerful on our first date.

"G was Govcorps, whose coup was successful. H was a manhunter, cruel and unmerciful; I was AI recording it quick; J was Justice, deaf, blind and sick. K were the kids with rickets and lice; L was the land renamed 'Sacrifice'; M was a mountain, its peaks blown off; N was a nation at war with itself; O were Outsiders expelled from the domes; P was a prisoner dreaming of home; Q was a quarrel that could not be won; R was a rancher, impoverished, alone; S was Satan, who did all he could; T was Tom, who did what he would.

"Or T was for Tam," I explained, "though it didn't really matter, because the Twins believed the one name could stand for the other. T was also for Twins."

"And after T?" asked Joel.

"Nothing came after T. The rest of the alphabet was moot."

"So T is the end?"

"Till the sequel," I said.

Through the magic of transgression, Joel and I had become intimate. To the sound of the "Battle Hymn," I chased a floating bubble while Joel watched and smiled, his teeth as perfect as silicon chips.

Oblivious to the crowds sutured to their phones and scrolling through the updates, I introduced Joel to my scattershot sense of time by returning to the subject of the Beatles: "How many holes *does* it take?"

"How many holes does *what* take?"

"That lyric about filling the Albert Hall. The Beatles never told us. According to the records, they meant potholes in a road. But no one can trust the records. Maybe they meant black holes or bulletholes or holes in the ozone, or holes in a head or a heart, or holes in an alibi. How many holes does it take to fill the Albert Hall? It's sad that we'll never know."

"It's life," he answered banally.

"Great Britain was great," I said, and the two of us paused, resting in the first true moment to pass between us, both of us grateful to be alive.

"You're painfully beautiful," Joel said, lying down in the grass.

Then we rolled back and forth. I liked the cool underneath and the heat on top, Joel smiling down on me or up at me. Between mouthfuls of him, I drank the coffee, before resealing it poorly and knocking it over and spilling it. Then Joel said, as if it were his idea, "To hell with it," and he took me by the hand, and we crossed the park, and he paid for a tiny hotel room where the shower flooded the toilet, and the bed wasn't even a double, and the room was so hemmed in by the roofline that a window had been wedged at an angle underneath the eaves.

We made love three times. Sex would never be our problem. But I didn't like the way he closed his eyes when he touched me, because what I needed most from love was to be seen. My intentions didn't change that.

"Look at me," I said the third time we had sex.

Joel was on the verge of orgasm, and as he opened his eyes and came, he looked into mine and said, "I love you."

I think *love* was an overstatement: later he'd ask me to remind him of my last name. But the rush of sentiment was true in the moment: orgasm can do that to a man.

While Joel slept the dead sleep of intercourse, I took out my phone and saw the headlines. Bombing at 41.59516/–87.356934. Gary, Indiana. There was only one media source, but like Medusa it had many heads, and each one reported identically.

The go-to suspect for every act of terrorism, the girl-who-got-away, was already being blamed. The last remaining MacAllister – granddaughter of Connie, daughter of Tam, or of Tom and Tam, depending on the version of the story you believe – hadn't been seen since the Ambush at the MacAllister Ranch. Nonetheless, Govcorps Central Intelligence credited her with everything from animal-rights arson to intercorporate hacking to industrial bombing. Privately, she'd been rated as inoperative – deactivated, amnesiac, converted or deceased – but, publicly, she kept popular fears alive and enabled Govcorps' self-bombings to produce unifying hysteria. It was one of life's little ironies: alive, the-girl-who-got-away was fundamental to diversionary tactics and monopolistic control – but only if she were dead or in some manner decommissioned, and posed no imminent threat. She was such an effective weapon against the public imagination that schizophrenics believed themselves to be her more often than they believed they were the Second Coming of Jesus Christ.

A message pinged in from my mother, who was forever worrying about me. Like spouses, mothers have ways of knowing things, but only particular things. They know how close you are to danger, or who you were before adoption. Mine, I think, knew much, but she believed that when a person finds Christ, history is washed away.

Don't worry, Mom, I pinged back. *I'm safe in the arms of a Yácorp man, and Gary's far away. Love you too.*

Lying on the recently stained sheets beside Joel, I was staring at a dot on the ceiling. Standing on the bed to see what it was, I found it was only a squashed mosquito. I thought about the serendipity: a bomb on our first date. Was it a good sign or a bad one?

I woke him up by climbing on top of him. Though we fucked a fourth time, it was one too many: we were both exhausted, and neither of us came.

In a hotel room the size of a holding cell, we'd had as much sex as we could muster. By contrast, our present hotel room was cavernous, and it was as cold as a meat locker. Joel sat on the luxurious sofa, picking up and putting down his whiskey tumbler and continuing to waffle over what he wanted to happen next. That I wanted to make love one last time didn't mean I loved him, and he knew it. That is why he waffled.

My intentions couldn't have been clearer, but if I wanted the night to unfold the way I needed it to unfold, I had no choice but to assert myself. From the perspective of the CBA, to initiate sex was to transform myself from a wife into a prostitute. But by tomorrow they'd call me one anyhow, and not entirely without cause. I prefer the Japanese term for the profession. *Yă something* or *yă something something*. (Even a historian is reduced to fragments, but I do know the literal translation: *an open country flower*.)

I removed the whiskey tumbler from my husband's hand and placed both our glasses on the coffee table. I drew my knees up under me. Leaned over him. My internal temperatures normalizing, I was cold again. I'd been dripping hot a moment before, and now the sweat had cooled. I buried my face in his trousers, as if only my face were cold. I unzipped his fly. I stretched my free hand around to the wallet bulge in his back pocket and dragged off his trousers. I briefly admired the scar on his thigh, which was so like my own. The years had amassed: there was gray in his pubic hair, which once had been a mat of solid frazzled brown.

Touching him, I tried to stay present, but though intercourse is the thrust of the future, everywhere I saw the past. The archives of my mind are jumbled and I don't know where I first heard the story, but in certain underground circles the moral is still spoken: "If you want to know a secret, screw the secret keeper."

I believe it was a Navajo story: how Coyote accidentally revealed the secret of fire to the Earth Surface People by screwing the chief's daughter. The transfer didn't occur by whispering sweet nothings or talking dirty. Nor was the chief's daughter a witch or Mata Hari lying in wait under a buffalo rug. Nor did Coyote prattle on about flint or mirrors in the sunlight or rubbing two sticks together or any other incendiary technique. So how? Coyote ejaculated. End of story. Why? Because each of the eighty to three hundred million sperm in a single ejaculation carries half the male's genetic code, suggesting that a single burst contains the majority of its maker's physical, mental and emotional attributes, not only inborn but acquired, because genes, like everything, change, and they do so in a single lifetime. Understood in the light of epigenetics – according to the Biogenetics agent at the university – Coyote's pyrotechnic know-how was encoded in his DNA, and the secret of fire was gifted to his lover with his sperm.

The transmission was not a miracle, but there remains a mystery. Coyote lived in a simpler world, before the Newborn Screening Saves Lives Act of the early twenty-first century in the former USA. Adopted and extended by the RUSA, the Act was applied to all new births after the Migration Era, during which chaotic period only high-profile captives and corpses, like the MacAllisters, were mapped. The Gotcha Act, as it's covertly called, has enabled health-screening eugenics, identification of latent Outlaw sympathizers, selective Sacrifice extradition and hiring, and the identification of missing persons through postnatal encoding or relational links. But no such technology existed in Coyote's day. DNA

Total Recording Systems were yet to encrypt, and afterwards ban, Shakespeare's plays and Martin Luther King's "I Have a Dream" speech, or to make possible total-scale Govcorps surveillance. Chromosomal-extraction science and molecular photocopying were as yet unheard of. So, though sperm can be credited for transmitting Coyote's genetic code, we don't know how the chief's daughter read it.

Back in the queen bed, in strobe-lit Ulysses, the sex went on and on, but I really had to get going. And after the deed was done, I absented myself to the ensuite steam room at 23:28:00, reemerging at 23:39:16.

"I'm going out," I said to Joel.

I was wearing the hotel's complimentary bathrobe with warm deep pockets. He was lying on his bed, naked except for his socks, his hand cupped over his newly shrunken jewels.

"Now?" he asked, astonished.

By way of an answer, I leaned my knees against the mattress, stooped and kissed him one last time. Then, at the dressing table, I applied red lipstick, rubbed my lips together, blotted them and tucked the soiled tissue in my handbag. As was the fashion, I drew down the lower lid of my eye and ran a thin black line along the small horizon. My big eyes had grown bigger as my face had grown thinner, and the horizon appeared to go on forever. I looked all eyes and makeup.

"Fuck," I said quietly, when the tip of the liquid eyeliner touched my eyeball.

In the mirror, I examined the damage: a tiny black ink spot dotted the white of my eye, but my contact lens was unaffected. In the mirror I saw Joel. He was crawling over the bedsheets.

"Where's my palm-reader?" he asked.

"Probably on the floor."

"I left it on the bed."

"I'm pretty sure I heard it drop."

"I don't see it," he said.

As I had a thousand times, I left what I was doing to use my 20/20 vision to help my husband find a thing that was directly in front of him. While he searched under the bed, I produced the tiny retracted palm-reader from underneath the sheets.

"But I looked there," he objected.

"If it was a snake …" I said.

The small dark screen rebuked him. Abandoning a live interface, he hadn't even said goodnight to Central Hub. And now it was too late: Yácorp was off Human Interface.

"Nothing to do but sleep," I said.

He looked at me unkindly. He rolled over on his side, then over on his other side, and back again, demonstrably incapable of getting comfortable. He didn't need to say it: he blamed me for the late hour, for his unprofessional interface lapse, for the inevitability that I'd wake him upon returning (for he assumed I was going night shopping in the mall on the lower floors), and for his future failure to fall back to sleep, due to having been saddled with the lesser of two queen beds. The fleeting harmony of lovemaking had vanished.

I knew Joel's thoughts, though I don't know how I knew them. I don't know how thought travels wordlessly between intimate bodies, even after the act is over, and even after the love is done. I only know, like breath, it does.

"Don't worry," I said. "I won't wake you."

"Pull down your sheets before you go," he said, "or you will."

Expertly made-up, I did as Joel asked. I slipped between the beds and prepared mine for sleep. The thinner I got, the more translucent; I almost slipped through walls. I disappeared into the walk-in closet to hang the bathrobe on a hook and, lastly, I dressed, as the clock silently ticked toward midnight.

I reemerged wearing a large azure gemstone plunging into the cowl neckline of a gray Heatwick frock. I was not sensibly dressed, because Yácorp wives did not wear trousers and flats.

As the moonlight blued my dress, I appeared to admire, once more, the city outside the window, though most things are not as they appear. For example, moonlight is not blue. It is as white as the beams of the sun, which, having set over the ocean, strike the risen moon and return to Earth in a lunar guise. But you see what's put before you, and artists and writers throughout the centuries have made you see blue moonlight.

Behind me, Joel looked so pale in his thin white sheet, I imagined his dry bones blanching. As a child, I had blanched blue corn with my grandmother, dipping the cobs in boiling water to preserve their crispness before canning. Two very different meanings of *blanch*. One conjures demise and the other preservation. We have a choice between the two.

Suddenly, the shawl on my shoulders dropped to the floor, and static electricity held it to the carpet. I bent down and peeled it off, and the shawl sparked a little. I returned to standing, and the hem of my modest dress slipped back over my naked knees.

"It's too hot for nylons out there," I said, not intending to speak aloud. I'd been so careful for so much of my life, yet now on the verge of another life, I couldn't keep myself to myself, and I struggled to find where I ended and my husband began.

"You're going *out-out?*" he asked, utterly astonished.

Nobody went out-out. Ulysses was not Chicago. In the mall, I'd find no vast and airy atrium where automatic doors slid open and shut on holiday shoppers who carried gift bags with bloodred bows. Without a dome, consumers walked between bars, banks, restaurants, government offices and spas, while never stepping outside. There was no need for a pedestrian entrance: Outsiders didn't shop. No one went out-out except in an automobile. Outer Ulysses was dangerous.

Dorothy is dangerous, Joel thought, and in so many years of marriage, he'd never had that thought before.

I could read his mind. Such is one of the sorrows of marriage that makes the end excruciating, regardless of how it started.

I thought again of the Coyote story. Was the chief's daughter plagued by guilt? Did she self-accuse when she robbed him of fire to light the way for her people? Probably not.

But Coyote was a supernatural being. Joel was not. Coyote survived the breach. Joel would not.

And when a secret is passed through sex, along with it comes much of the blueprint of one's self. Joel was the person I knew best, and whether I hated him or loved him didn't matter: the fact was I *knew* him. I wished him no nightmares, even if tomorrow would bring them like a Christmas gift bound with ribbons.

"You're kidding," he concluded, and as I turned to leave, gave a short, mirthless laugh. As I closed the door behind me, Joel returned to seeking a comfortable position in what he was now sure was the dud bed.

Some tomorrows are easy to predict.

In the morning, he'd find me gone. With the dial on the radio set between two stations, the alarm clock would crackle to wake him, and Joel would hit the snooze, until it crackled again and again. After the third hit, the magic number, Joel would finally open his eyes, and seeing my untouched bed, his stomach would slam into his heart.

He'd check the steam room and the walk-in closet, just in case, and soothe his fears with unlikely scenarios: his wife comatose at the hotel bar or in another man's arms. He'd hurriedly dress. He'd yank on his socks – his feet freezing – but rush out the hotel room door without his shoes.

He'd peer into the ice room. Nothing. He'd accost a maid, her trolley of lemony disinfectants squeaking down the carpeted hall. No, she spoke no English, though he thought all Non-linguals had been deported long ago. In the twenty-four-hour Paradise Lounge, he'd describe his wife to the mixologist, who'd offend him by pointing to a middle-aged prostitute draped over a businessman's lap.

Down in the shopping mall, stocking-footed, he'd stand beneath an enormous Santa, with blowers waving a gloved hand and joggling a crimson belly, while cooling the back of his neck. He'd be sweating again by the time he rode the elevator up.

Back in the room, he'd sit uncertainly on his bed and stare at the faux-rotary phone while fending off a premonition. Finally ringing the corps, he'd feel sick for numerous unnamed reasons.

As he waited for their arrival, the flipping sound of his slippers made his pacing up and down the room ridiculous to himself. But the voice on the phone had told him, "Touch nothing," and somehow this command had seemed to include his shoes but not his slippers. And what else was there to do but pace and watch the numbers? 108°, 412.90 ppm by the Climate Tower, 09:45:21 by the clock. And only five hours and under fifteen minutes until his all-important sit-down with the CBA.

A missing wife was a horrible thing, and, in comparison, worrying about work felt good, like an air pocket in the horror. But if I didn't materialize soon, he would have to inform Yácorp, who, he felt sure, would opt to delay the meeting. They couldn't expect him at his best when his other half was AWOL.

"Have you touched anything?" said the head corp after a team of them stormed through the door. He wore a chainmail vest, obviously designed to intimidate.

Joel shrunk at the corp's tone, which implied they'd find me dead under the bed because he'd murdered me in my sleep. He told himself to get a grip and warned himself not to feel guilty.

DNA identification was the first point of action, but my hairbrush and toothbrush were missing, and the basket by the dressing table was empty of cosmetic trash. The flip-top bin by the toilet proved useless: I wasn't menstruating – hardly ever did anymore, my internal clock breaking down – and the previous night, we'd lived dangerously by not using a condom.

Used to detect bodily fluids, multiple-wavelength FLS from a glove lamp revealed, to Joel's disgust, old drippings of sex everywhere – on the chesterfield, in the deep pile carpet, on the drapes – and only the stains on his sheet could safely be assumed to be ours.

When the head corp pressed the transmitter in his ear, the search abruptly stopped. Surveillance had revealed a purer source of identification, Touch DNA, oil from my fingertips on the whiskey tumbler.

10:21:45, the specimen was dispatched. In the meantime, no wife had walked through the door after an unfaithful tryst, and Joel felt obliged to warn Yácorp, which he'd do by secure interface.

He looked for his billfold in the trousers he'd been wearing the previous night. Not there. In the bedside table drawer, there was only a Gideon Bible. He pulled apart his bedclothes and discovered a small box of matches, which lit his stomach on fire.

The Corporate Regional Police, otherwise called "corps", who were busy speaking in acronyms into their ear transceivers, no longer seemed to care if he touched things. And when Joel asked, "Have you seen my wallet?" the question didn't alert them. A corp pulled it from the bathrobe, which was hanging in the closet.

Confused as to how it got there, Joel wondered at the reliability of his memory, but not for long. He sat on the unused bed – *my* bed, by default, though I had never claimed it – and sorted through his cards. Then he did it again. Then he upturned the wallet and emptied it on the bedspread. He shook it so hard that even the lint fell out. Finally, his voice elevating a full octave, he asked if the corps had seen his Yácorp security chit.

He spent the rest of the day at Ulysses Law Enforcement Headquarters, where they offered him nothing to eat but old sandwiches from the vending machine with tasteless cheese and soggy cucumbers. He was furious, on top of everything else. Hadn't he phoned the corps in the first place? Didn't that make him a client, not a suspect?

In the evening, they transported him to Ulysses Number One Security Base, and the military was no better, serving him stale coffee. His tailbone hurt in the hard plastic chair. He felt angry, frightened, bored, excited and shocked, all at once, and absolutely alone. Married for so long, he wasn't accustomed to being alone. And though Yácorp had sent a lawyer, the man offered no advice, no private consultation, not even a whisper in Joel's ear.

No one would tell him anything. And Joel was sick to death of saying, "I don't know" and "I didn't know." Had said it enough to stop believing it himself. It was a bad dream, or it should have been.

My DNA had at last been processed. A close match had been found, for my parents' genetics – or my parent's genetics, the two words sounding identical – had not only been encrypted at death but banned.

That's all his interrogators told him, and yet his lawyer asked, "Do you understand the severity of it all?"

Joel assumed the guy was his lawyer.

"What 'all'?" Joel asked.

Now the grilling began in earnest. They came at him like the deep monsoons, which despite all human interventions, having a mind of their own, had resumed hopscotching north on the Sierra Madre and zigzagging sidewinder-style to spit on the dry Southwest.

"How did she steal your chit, Joel? When did she steal your chit, Joel? While sucking your dick, Joel? That's no mystery, Joel. The security chit was the easy part: you hadn't fucked in months. Don't like that language? Well, fuck you. You hadn't fucked in months, so why suddenly fuck last night? Why fuck her when your chit was in your pocket, and your Human Interface was as open as her legs? Don't like that talk? Don't play prude. How else did she get your security chit? How else did she access your Human Interface? She had you by the balls, Joel. But what we want to know – what we really want to know, Joel – is how she got your fucking eyeballs? She couldn't get clearance without your eyeballs, Joel. So how did she get your eyeballs? How was that fucking possible? It wasn't possible, was it? Unless of course you were in on it, because it sounds to us like you just agreed that it wasn't fucking possible. How many years were you married, Joel? It's not a trick question, just answer it. You were married forever, Joel. And never suspected just once or twice? Too busy thinking with your dick? So when the dark-haired hottie targeted you at a Futures Symposium, you thought it was your lucky day? Didn't notice she was out of your league? Just thought she went for runts? What exactly did she say, Joel? Don't remember? Why don't you remember? Have you got Alzheimer's, Joel? Don't fuck with us, Joel. Why do you say *you* picked *her* up? We've looked at the feed. *She* picked *you* up, Joel. She fucking picked you up, Joel. What else are you getting backwards, Joel? What exactly did she reveal to you, Joel? Nothing, in all those years of marriage? You're lying, Joel, and though everyone knows you're a good idea man, you're a fucking bad liar.'

Their questions made him nauseous, and the emptiness in his stomach only acidified the nausea. Holes spun around his head. All those years of marriage, and the hours were full of holes. He understood he was missing something, he understood he'd always missed something, but he didn't know what.

Whether good or bad he couldn't say, but eventually, like a hive swarming, they arose as one and departed the interrogation room. They'd never introduced themselves. Some of them were corps, others Govcorps. All were gone. Even the Yácorp lawyer left – he'd come and sat and said next to nothing and gone with the rest and promised to come again, and yet no sign of him.

Left alone for hours, Joel suspected he was meant to miss his captors. The clock ticked in its cage. A secretary with thick heels and a submachine gun across her breast brought him another beige coffee. She spoke not at all and departed.

When at long last there appeared a corp – minus his helmet and with an enormous matte-black mole on his forehead – Joel felt a wave of relief. That the guy's forehead might hatch didn't even bother Joel. As his inquisitors intended, he was just glad not to be alone.

"Coffee here is shit," said the corp.

Joel's relief was cautious. He recognized the strategy: share a common distaste for the coffee, then spill your heart out.

But he was taken off guard when the corp said, "Go back to the Grand, order room service and get some sleep."

Behind his jailor, his prison door hung open.

As his hard plastic chair pushed back from the table and scraped along the cement floor, Joel concluded that, in a back room, his Yácorp lawyer had come to his rescue and worked some magic on whomever was responsible – no saying just how high this went – for detaining him all day. There was no other explanation.

The corp, having turned to leave, stood with his hands on the doorframe, as if about to push the wall down. He said over his shoulder, "And report at 0800 tomorrow, prepared to accompany the next labor unit into Sacrifice."

Joel stopped dead, like a deer or a bird or a snake or a rat or any variety of creature who knows it's being watched. He spoke slowly, carefully, an awful knowledge, stagnant all day, stirring in his guts.

"Why?" he asked.

"If it was up to me …"

The corp patted his gun.

Joel looked about him at the cameras in the corners of the cinder-block room. He'd never know who gave the order, but suddenly he got it. The severity of it all. The severity of it all that Joel Saunders, Yácorp darling, had married Dorothy, adoptee from Wichita, Kansas, who claimed she couldn't remember her life prior to adoption, and he had given her access to data west of −101.35 and clearance to cross the Fence. The severity of it all that the girl-who-got-away had gotten away again, and her first name having been verified, she would hereafter be known to history as Dorothy MacAllister. The severity of it all that the Sacrifice War was the Sacrifice Wars, because though time may take a coffee break, life and death and death and life are never-ending stories.

"Still pretending you don't get it?" said the corp.

The story of forty-six million Americans is best told through a few, but one of them will not be Joel Saunders, for the story does not belong to the darlings of the hour, who, for all their privilege, vanish with their usefulness. The story belongs to the ordinary, who sometimes are also the very rare.

Repeatedly captured on camera as I exited the mall, my blue gemstone necklace, tailored suit dress, open-toed heels and Gucci handbag would soon identify me, though other than the gemstone, found in serpentinite and mined in the Diablo Range, they did not describe me at all. Zooming in and adjusting the resolution, the ridge of my contact lenses, manufactured by our agents at Cognoptix after the previous year's Christmas fête, would be discernible to Central Intelligence. But the Biogenetics operative would never make himself seen again. He too had not attended the university party, and soon holiday trimmings and orange crime tape would cordon off his lab.

The phone in my purse contained geological maps and extensive cave surveys, but these did not help me to navigate the mall, and I struggled to find the exit where the limo would pull into Departures at the stroke of midnight. Yácorp drivers were punctual, and I was racing against time, as I had done all evening. Only minutes before Human Interface had closed – while my husband luxuriated in the aftershocks of his little death – I had squatted in the steam room, changing his mind about a late-night tour of Sacrifice. I was grateful to the Grand Hotel for providing fluffy robes with giant pockets, in which to return the palm-reader to his bed.

I'd expected navigating the mall to be the easy part of the journey. Stepping out of the elevator, I was met by a popular song, orchestrated and stripped of its words, which was not a Christmas carol but resembled one nonetheless, and a massive airbag Santa waving his fat hand in the fabricated breeze. He pointed this way and that. One exit sign led to another, then back to where I'd begun: back to the overweight gift-giver, where only the music had changed.

Whatever song was playing, it was the wrong one, for we've been singing the wrong song for a very long time. We have been singing wrongly, words moving counterclockwise, downgrading Earth's bounty to a resource that is extracted without prayer or any reciprocal gesture, and if time is linear, it's too late to change the lyrics. But God can do what He wants, according to my CBA mother, and, as a historian, I know that when you change the past, you also change the future.

My job is to blow on corpses and bring them to new life. It is a dangerous undertaking, and at a glance the story of the MacAllisters is not a hopeful one, but little is as it looks. I am the last of my ancestors, and this story is mine to tell.

II

CONNIE

Age fifteen was a stutter, and history has not recorded the date. As if time were her body, Connie MacAllister's diaries offer only her age. *Again*, she wrote, *I'm going to die of boredom.* And if she had – in solitary confinement it has been known to happen – history would have forgotten her, like any other teenage girl.

But Connie MacAllister wasn't dead, nor was she alone in the year two thousand and something. At the annual grandchildren's gathering, held each spring vacation at her throwback grandparents' cattle ranch in Southern California, her cousins had already arrived. They too had come, as was the custom, without parental chaperone.

But ocht is better than rain, Connie wrote in a Scottish dialect, because, in the ping-pong of generations, on the run from American politics, her parents had repatriated. It had already proved a mistake: Scotland no longer rained, it poured, while the USA stayed dry. And, as always, Connie's cross-Atlantic journey started with a deluge.

She'd made the trip repeatedly, an unaccompanied minor, clutching the hand of a flight attendant and singing *over the river and through the woods to grandmother's house we go,* though the ranch was historically snowless, and the cottonwoods were dying back from the tips, and the holiday was always torrid Easter, never Thanksgiving or Christmas, and her grandparents were flint.

By age fifteen, no flight attendant and no singing. She flew the Atlantic solo and braved the stratospheric dervish-storms with earphones and inflight movies. Landing at Los Angeles International Airport, she dragged her burden off the carousel and wheeled it out the exit.

High noon. Sweat pooled behind her elbows. Every year was hotter. Yet the City of Angry Angels, murder capital of America, was peaceful compared to Edinburgh. And if anyone could conjure the illusion of changelessness, her grandfather could do it. The annual spring vacation meant retracing the hours westward and stepping back in time.

His pickup rattled to the curb. Windows down, a cardboard pine-tree deodorizer and a rare condor feather hung from the rearview mirror and twitched in the hot wind. He was ruminating in the driver's seat. He wore a tawny Stetson and sucked on a matchstick and raised a rutted hand hello.

He stepped out of the cab and said, "This your bag?" as he took her giant suitcase and threw it like a feed sack into the truck bed.

She could smell the horses on him.

"Long drive," he said, as he always did, as if each year were the first, or as if the drive had lengthened since the previous year.

The door handle burned to touch. She pulled her sleeve over her palm. She squirmed to avoid the metal coil poking through the vinyl seat, slashed open in a routine stop-and-frisk. The old, white sheepskin rug covering the damaged seat was itself covered with dog hair, each strand bearing the genetic code of generations of night-black collies and one albino, its fur undetectable in the snowy hide.

Her grandfather pointed with his chin and said, as if there were some other option, "You okay sitting there?"

"Uh-huh," Connie answered and leaned under his Stetson and, dodging his toothpick, kissed him on the cheek.

She locked the door because it was the law, but at least the open window felt like freedom.

Pulling away from the curb, her granddad said, "Your cousins got in last night."

They invariably got in before her. The twins, Carol and Billy, flew from Dallas, Jacob from Chicago, and Arnold and the doorsteps – little Tatsie and littler Quentin – from DC, each in the care of a flight attendant wearing a jaunty neck scarf and epaulets. Connie, the eldest, traveled the farthest, and hers was the most dangerous trip.

"I didn't get sick this time," she said.

Her granddad nodded.

She had a stomach as strong as a terrorist's holding cell.

There is no more to report about the inaugural year of her diaries, and the next year, age sixteen, began much the same: earphones, LAX, Ford pickup, heat. But a human fetus resembles a fish until the fingers sprout.

Connie was feeling very grownup when her parents, as usual, drove her to the airport in Edinburgh. That it was raining goes without saying. Rain had become as unequally distributed as wealth and populations. Like worms in puddles (so went the expression), Scotland's population had boomed. With Scotland better off than England, and England better off than other neighbors, the Migrations had begun, and the displaced crossed the Channel, overran the checkpoints, then headed north.

Connie's father slowed the car, trapped behind a fleet of vacuumers – monstrous eighteen-wheelers sucking water off the motorway and spraying it over the safety fences into a no-man's-land where migrants camped by the flood canals. Connie's mother told him not to tailgate.

"I'm not," he said, though he was.

"You can't get around them?" she asked, her sharp American twang made sharper by nerves.

“Don’t you think I would if I could?”

Over her mother’s lily-of-the-valley perfume, Connie’s parents stank of fear. And when a stone, thrown from beyond the fence, dinged off the hood of a vacuumer, her mother begged her father, “Get around them!”

Now her father did the thing that a moment earlier he’d sworn he couldn’t: he veered onto the shoulder, scraped the chain-link fence and careened around the fleet. Just in time, for suddenly everyone was at it, digging rocks out of the knee-deep mud and lobbing them at trucks.

While Connie pressed her nose to the window to see, her mother dragged on the door handle as if it were a brake. Connie banged her nose on the glass as the car sped off toward the airport, leaving the displaced behind.

“Don’t I get a kiss?” her mother asked before her daughter vanished into airport security.

But Connie was in no mood. “I look like a twat,” she said, gesturing to her high-school uniform (though Scots didn’t call it “high school”).

She was wearing the same white shirt, black tie and tartan kilt with matching knee socks that she wore every weekday to school. Her mother had insisted on it, because this year her granddad wouldn’t be fetching her from LAX. Some cowboy named Henry needed the help of her uniform to pick her out of a crowd.

“It’s cute,” said her mother.

“A total twat,” said Connie, as she stepped into the body scanner and spread her legs and lifted her arms above her head.

The moody sweet-sixteen-year-old, who, unbeknownst to her parents, smoked and drank and indulged in detailed fantasies about quitting the virgin condition, disappeared into security. And as punishment for the twatty uniform, her mother didn’t get a kiss.

The flight was long and anguishing, but with the exception

of the awful kilt, neither longer nor more anguishing than the previous year's flight. At the luggage carousel (no rolling blackouts in LA), Connie flipped over her waistband to shorten her skirt to above her knees, and she unbuttoned and scrunched up her sleeves. Removing her tie, she twisted it around her wrist, as if to demonstrate her experience of bondage.

Leaving Arrivals, she pushed through the crowds, as twenty-four-hour breaking news announced the latest closure: no one without an American passport would be cleared at customs. She felt lucky to be American, even luckier to be a dual-national – neither country defined her, but neither could keep her out. She collided with a limo driver holding a sign that said YESCORP, and then with another driver holding a sign that said TESLA. The automatic doors opened, and Connie dragged a hoard of hard-shell luggage into the cruel sun.

Her granddad's truck idled at the curb, heat rippling off the hood, but it was a young cowboy who leaned out of the window.

"You Connie?" he called.

"Must be," she said, dropping her luggage and opening her arms to show off her modified school uniform. "You Henry?" she asked.

She was pleased to see he was hunky. But he wasn't Instagram-handsome. He might not have been much older than her, but like most indigent ranch hands, he'd been an adult since he was ten. His legs were already bowed, and dark spots marked his face, because measles hyperpigmentation doesn't fade if you do not pamper your skin. A white scar on his brown neck revealed where a bull had gored him.

"Throw your bags in the back," said Henry, and Connie found it wasn't as effortless as her granddad had always made it look.

The truck sat in sunshine and traffic. Henry's snap-down

shirt was sweaty. He draped his long hands over the wheel and steered with his wrists, which were strong from roping cattle. When the highway came to a stand still, he pulled his clutch foot onto the seat and rested his elbow on his bent knee, where a tight thread stretched over his torn jeans and his skin whitened with the pressure.

He said, "Traffic makes me hate people."

She said, "I'll drive if you want."

"You got a license?" he asked.

"Kind of."

"How 'kind of'?"

"Granddad lets me drive at the ranch."

He ignored this and lit a cigarette. Smoking enhanced his full lips. He wore a relaxed, unworried frown that made his jaw protrude. Whether he was ugly or handsome was a coin toss.

The dash radio, tuned to an AM station, played what the DJ called Classic Country. Johnny Cash's "Ring of Fire" was genius, but next up was "Butterfly Kisses," which was just insipid.

"Can we listen to something else?" asked Connie.

Henry flicked the dial. He couldn't find anything but talk, and the talk was mostly ranting, a litany of grievances about immigrants and liberals, and the virulent praising of Christ, who had risen as a bully. Henry continued to flick the dial.

Now a man with a flat accent spoke over beating drums. Native American broadcasting had somehow survived the cuts. So Connie leaned her head against the open window and listened to the man on the radio recount his rendition of a Navajo tale.

"There were many worlds," the man said. "Our people came up through the worlds. The first world was red. Red ants lived there. Yellow beetles lived there. Black beetles lived there. Coyote-dung beetles and bats. The world was small and dry and bad and spinning fast, and the people who lived there were dizzy. So our people climbed up through the hole in the sky. The second world was blue. Bluebirds and blue jays and blue-tinted swallows lived there. It was a bad, small, dry world. The world spun fast and made the people dizzy, like drunks. There were no plants, rivers or mountains. So our people climbed up through the hole in the sky. The third world was a yellow world. Yellow grasshopper people lived there. The land was bare and made of cliffs. The rivers were dry and thin as spider legs. The spinning made the people dizzy and angry, and they fought with each other, because the world was small and dry and bad. Then they crawled up through the hole in the sky. The fourth world was every color. Red, blue, yellow and black and white, but no sun or moon or stars. First Man and First Woman were born there. There was water, but too much water. Floods came, and our people crawled up through the hole in the sky. This is the fifth world. The last world. Here there is light and darkness as well as every color. This world is good, and it does not spin too fast. The hero twins were born in this world. They were the children of the sun. They traveled to the sun's house. They rid the world of monsters. You can still see dead monsters lying on the ground. Maybe you think these are mountains. You can climb the mountains and feel very near the sky. But you will not see a hole in the sky. If this world goes bad, there are no more worlds. We are ordinary people and cannot get to the sky."

As the pickup moved out of range and the man's voice crackled and splintered, Connie asked Henry, "You think that story's true?"

"You think it ain't?" he asked.

"How would I know?" asked Connie.

If traffic made Henry hate people, he probably already hated her, but her question was a real one. How was she to decipher the honest-to-God truth from the fictions of hope and despair, or the chemical seesaw between them, when true and false had been weaponized and reality had paled like the aerosoled blue sky? In a world of increasing uncertainty, lies proliferated and everyone grew dizzy. Even Scottish sheepdogs had to be prescribed downers.

The radio continued to crackle, but Henry left the static buzzing. He didn't feel the need to talk. He smoked, and smoking was enough.

Her own cigarettes in her suitcase, Connie willed him to offer her one of his, but he didn't, either because of her age or her grandparents' rules or just because he didn't. The nicotine urge was excruciating.

Eventually, the traffic moved freely. The air-conditioning busted, Connie kept the window open despite the wind and traffic roar, the din of sirens and army helicopters shadowing the city, and the wars between car radios from other clunkers with their windows down. No silver-screen blondes sped by in topless convertibles combing the wind through their perfect hair. The wealthy drove steel-roofed Cherokees, with security-sealed windows that popped out in emergencies, and the only open-top car on the highway was packed with tattooed henchmen in A-shirts.

Connie stared at the road as if her gaze would help Henry to drive. She said, "You can't ride with the windows down in Scotland. Even if they open. It's illegal."

"I seen that on the news," he said.

"You have a signal at the ranch?"

"We got a TV in the cabin and tinfoil on the roof."

"Cool," she said. "That's allowed?"

"What your granddad don't know won't kill him."

Connie smiled. Maybe he didn't hate her after all.

"He's got some backwards rules," said Henry.

"Gran's got even more," she said.

Both grandparents were inconsistent: they shoveled and

tilled by hand, refused to use an electric brander and washed their laundry in the sink, but, like any modern American, they had a wide collection of weapons, including a crossbow, two muzzleloaders, a Henry Big Boy Carbine with walnut stock and brass bead front sight, a Chinese lookalike AK-47 and a 3D-printed semiautomatic. And they had a phone, though it was a landline rotary phone, which they never traded in or traded up, and which had cost them a fortune in a lifetime of monthly fees. They'd never have approved a television, not least of all because the house was solar-powered and what electrical equipment was necessary in the daytime was forbidden to use after dark.

"I won't tell on you," said Connie, "You can do whatever you want."

"Can I?" Henry said.

Whether or not he intended it, the way he said it reminded her that she was a pretty girl. But he still didn't offer her a cigarette. And if he had something more to say, he lacked the need to say it.

Driving in silence, Henry was as self-contained as the fossil-wood that Connie's granddad had spirited home from a trip to the Petrified Forest. (*Spirited* was her granddad's word, the more regular one being *stolen*, but he claimed he hadn't stolen it, couldn't have stolen it, any more than the wind could steal the dust. "But don't tell your gran.")

The city backed out of view. Farmland idled in the wind. Irrigation systems, like skinned vertebrates, straddled the sterile furrows. The city lights receded with the sun, which went down as if it were innocent: an orange bauble in a rearview mirror.

Soon the stars topped the roof and filled the windows. The moon not yet risen, and too early for anything but Venus and Vega in the sky, the view dissolved. It was mostly emptiness anyway. The night snuck close as if to peer at a curiosity.

Connie strained to see the mountain ranges, which her granddad called the Saints: the San Bernardino Mountains that became the San Jacinto Mountains that became the Santa Rosas, running north – south to divide the Pacific Ocean and Salton Sea watersheds. Powerful arbiters, the Saints directed the weather wherever they wished, and they created a rain shadow that kept the MacAllister ranch drier than its neighbors. The ranch stood on the crest of a hill, but the hill sat in a trough beneath the jagged peaks, which even the powerful American Monsoons didn't deign to cross without the permission of the Saints. The Saints were the deciders, according to Connie's granddad. Not that he was a Christian. Not that he was anything but the place that he was from.

If with his hat, white shirt and jeans and his economy of words Henry resembled her granddad, he obviously didn't in years. Also, Henry wasn't a white man whose roots went back to Scotland. If, somewhere in his DNA, a pasty colonizer could be located, the gene was buried and recessive.

"Where are you from?" Connie asked.

"All over," Henry answered.

"Mexico?" she guessed, wondering if his turquoise ring was a clue or just something he'd picked up along the way all over.

"Sure, sometimes," Henry said, because he wasn't from Mexico any more than the monsoon rains were from the Sierra Madre, where the high-pressure winds originated before traveling north in the summer heat till low-pressure troughs reversed them so they blew wet off the ocean, producing torrential rain. Like the wind itself, Henry had been a Drifter well before the word was used to describe half the displaced population.

"Sometimes where else?" asked Connie.

"Oklahoma. Montana. New Mexico. Dinétah. Other places too."

Because Dinétah was neither English nor Spanish, she assumed it was far away and said, "You're a long way from home." Her pasty arm, stuck out the window most of the day, was turning pink in the night.

"Not really," said Henry. "You're a heck of a lot farther."

The wind gusted and the truck jittered, pushed to the far edge of the shoulderless road. No highway fences this far out, there was only an irrigation ditch between the truck and corn.

"I hate the wind," said Connie.

"Can't hate the wind. It's in you. You hate it, it'll leave you. It's what keeps you standing upright."

He pulled hard on the steering wheel and drove a straight tight line, then turned up a steep dirt lane, rutted and pocked by the hybrid destruction of rain and no rain, predominantly no rain.

Isolated on twenty thousand acres, the family homestead emerged. Built to look like its Victorian architect, it was ruddy, stocky and broad, only one and a half stories, and roofed at a sharp angle to dispel winter drifts, though snow had never come. With no special twists or flourishes, it was as plain as the steppe it sat on. One front door and two windows on either side looked like a square-eyed emoticon, but the symmetry stopped there, and having only a single dormer, the house more resembled a Cyclops. The roof sloped sharply toward a lopsided porch, and addition tumored off of addition, with each new roof pitched lower than the last, till the lowest was no more than a lean-to piled with reusable trash. It had stretched through the generations, sprawling with New World optimism and upturns in the economy, because a house, like everything else, grows before it disintegrates.

But its hour of demise had not yet come. Clean red paint brightened the clapboards, and the windows glowed with oil lamps, and a purple bougainvillea and pale lilac whited-out in the high beams as the Ford pulled up the drive. As far as anything is, as far as rocks are, even, the MacAllister homestead looked permanent. Like Scotch broom, it had put down its roots and stuck. Had it been better adapted to its environment, instead of four-by-fours and clapboards it would have been made of dirt and would have had deep-set windows with heavy overhangs, like the brow of a desert hawk, or at least it would have been painted white to chase the heat away. But ill-suited it stood, solid and resilient.

Stalwarts of American history, in its several bedrooms Connie's paternal forebears had been conceived in love or violence. There they had been born or given birth or died, some even dying while being born or giving birth. No moral had marked their end, for the good had often died young, and, defying all hackneyed rules of justice, those who lived by the gun had died upright in a chair. The ghosts of the good and the bad, and the majority in between, still dwelled in the ranch house walls. Their spurs marked the floorboards. Their blood had hardened in the varnish.

"Granddad's okay?" Connie asked as the truck skidded on the dirt and the headlights strobed across the house. "I mean, I know, I was told," she said. "But he's more or less okay?"

She couldn't imagine her granddad going blind. And it was scary to imagine him anything less than strong, recalcitrant and capable, because if her granddad could change, anything could.

"Depends on what ruler you're using," said Henry, "but according to himself, he's right as rain."

The two stepped out onto the hardpan. Though the ground felt rough and flinty, it was firm beneath the feet. On the dark horizon, no cattle, but on so many rolling acres, even a monster might go unseen.

As Henry dragged the bags from the back for Connie, she took the opportunity to interrogate the illimitable stars.

Could a hole in the sky, like the draw of a chimney, take

the clouds away, and all her people too? Was this, in fact, the final world, as the Navajo man had said, and ordinary people couldn't reach the sky? But you can't prove there are no more worlds, can you? And not everyone is ordinary. Why tell a hopeless story? In the end, isn't it true that, given the earthly accretions of time, the sky comes to us all?

"I think so," she said aloud.

"You think what?" asked Henry.

"Never mind," she said, because he was still a stranger.

He left her at the door, and now Connie stood in the hallway while one black collie and six young cousins who had stayed up beyond their bedtime to greet her bounded down the stairs. Little Tatsie, in her princess dress, tripped over the dog and banged her knee but felt too excited to cry. In an instant, they surrounded their oldest cousin.

The girls and Quentin wanted a kiss, and all of them wanted acknowledgment, and Connie both begrudged and coveted the giving and getting of attention. She felt obliged to complain, hiding how much she loved them.

"Were the winds bad?" they asked. "Were you forced to wear your seatbelt all the way?" "Did they make you make an emergency landing in Idiquarta–" "Idiquartamormit–" "Ittiquorrtimorti–" None of them could pronounce it.

Their grandmother announced five minutes to bedtime and, being parsimonious, gave them only three. Then, when the children skulked off to their rooms, she said to Connie, "You get to bed too." And she disappeared into the kitchen to bring her an ice water.

Connie sat slouched on her giant wheelie bag, with a smaller version at her feet and a matching carry-on still dragging at her shoulder. It was an excessive amount of luggage for a two-week vacation, but she had brought doubles of everything, considering the overkill to be a mark of her maturity.

Her granddad asked, "Winds awful?"

"Bad enough to make me throw up. I didn't though. I never do. But the fat guy next to me did. And not just once. And there was a baby who wouldn't stop screaming. They shouldn't let babies on."

"You got here prompt. That's something," he said, because, more than once, Connie had sat in a monochrome landscape of asphalt and glaciers, forced to wait out a storm at the Ittoqqortoormiit airstrip in Greenland.

"They don't let dogs fly," she said as she pet the collie. "Why do they let babies?"

"Drink up," said her grandmother, who had returned from the kitchen with a teacup of ice water tinted brown from the iron in the pipes. She eyeballed Connie's disheveled school uniform and said, "You look like what the cat dragged in."

But the old man said, "Nothing sleep can't fix."

Watching him carry the big bag to her room, you wouldn't know he was almost blind. He didn't clutch the banister or run his stained fingers along the walls that had yellowed with nicotine. He didn't read, like Braille, the old bullet holes in the plaster. The only sign of his infirmity was that his wife followed close behind him.

"Coffin room?" asked Connie.

"Nothing's changed," said her granddad.

Wedged into the diagonal in the gable-end wall was a coffin window, so named by the Victorians because, in such a confining room, it could be used to maneuver a casket out and down the roof. Whether anyone had actually died in the room, Connie did not know.

The room was too tiny for a big man, a wiry woman and a teenage girl plus three pieces of luggage. So, while her grandmother adjusted the flame in the oil lamp on the bedside table, Connie sat cross-legged on the twin – a weird name for a single bed, unless the other twin died at birth.

Her granddad stood in the doorway, his hand on the doorknob with its pressed-tin lock plate of little ivy wreaths.

"Don't lock the door," her grandmother reminded her as she stepped back from the flame.

"But I have jet lag," Connie objected, knowing her cousins would pounce on her at dawn.

"You know the rule. It's dangerous," said her grandmother, but why and how it was dangerous she did not explain.

And if anything was dangerous, it was driving through riots to the Edinburgh airport. And now – fuck! – no locking the bedroom door! Connie rolled her eyes.

Her granddad couldn't have seen her roll them, but he might have sensed it. He said, "It may not be dangerous, Connie, but this is still our house, and it's the rule."

It was both irritating and comforting that, while the patterns of the world imploded, life at the ranch refused to change. Tomorrow's petty pace was utterly predictable. First thing in the morning, her granddad would bury an entire cow in the firepit, where it would slow-stew in prickly pear syrup throughout the day. Her grandmother, meanwhile, would bake cookies and a House Burning Cake, which had earned its name when its first iteration caught fire in the oven and almost burned down the kitchen. Connie's cousins, as they invariably did, would tackle her at dawn, then run away laughing, careening down the hallway, past the small door to the crawl space, where, once the sun set, a hunted child would disappear during a game of Murder in the Dark.

"We're glad to see you," said her granddad. He said it every year. The only difference this year was that he did not really see her.

As he left the room, his watchful wife, close behind him, completed the annual ritual. "We're always glad to see you," she said and closed the unlocked door.

Connie rolled into the mattress's dip, which her granddad blamed on lodestones far beneath the house.

"Magnetism," he'd explained to his granddaughter before the other grandchildren had been born or even imagined.

"What's magnetism?" she'd asked.

"The thing Jesse James had," he'd said.

"Do I have magnetism?"

"You do," he'd said and, picking up a bedtime book, resumed his reading. Then, skipping the part where the gunslinger scalped the unarmed soldiers, he'd said, "And then they did bad things."

"What bad things?"

"Things like not going to bed on time."

The dip in the mattress remained, but those childish days were over.

She listened to the familiar clomp of her grandparents' boots receding down the stairs. Lying in her twin, with its starched white sheets rinsed in blue moonlight, she watched the night sky. She hadn't drawn the curtains, because she wanted to see the stars, invisible in the Scottish rain. A surveillance satellite passed Venus. A meteor burned up. A bright star pretended to be a planet, then twinkled and gave itself away.

When Connie tried to sleep, her eyes refused to shut. She stared a while at the royal blue bedside table, where an earlier coat of red peeped out at the legs. Then she stared another while at the diminutive wall mirror that bounced a beam of moonlight back whence it had come.

Her breasts sweated and her armpits stank, a sign that childhood was over. Her young cousins didn't stink. Even Jacob and Arnold, who were always dirty, didn't stink. She envied them. They still slept the easy sleep of children.

The thought of them waking her kept her awake. Or perhaps the heat did. Or the fact that she was now sitting up in bed and writing in her diary, and when her fountain pen ran out, she pawed through her many bags to find more ink. When at last her head returned to the pillow, the origin of her insomnia was no longer in doubt. Why was it still so hot? Heat was supposed to skim off the earth in the desert's cloudless nights.

She hiked her t-shirt up to her collarbone, until it was uncomfortably bunched behind her back. She spread her naked legs wide on the mattress and stuck her feet out either side of the sheet. A click-clack of undercut bootheels ascended the stairs once more; then, beneath the door, the band of light vanished. Her grandparents had gone to bed.

Connie rose and looked out the window.

Silence. Nothing out there. Nothing except a lonesome firefly, the first trailblazer of its kind to migrate west of Kansas.

No sign of cattle. As if they were special ops, they were hidden in the vastness. And though a cow moos for many reasons – from labor pains to hunger pains, to anger, danger and loneliness – nothing mooed in the dark.

Connie sprayed deodorant under her t-shirt, slipped on a pair of shorts, took a pack of cigarettes from her suitcase and felt her way down the shrouded hallway, trying to find a stride that would keep the floorboards mute. She raised her arms like wings for lift, as she tiptoed down the stairs. The steps creaked and she stopped. She glanced up to the master bedroom. No one stirred and she descended.

Outside on the porch, she knocked a cigarette from her pack, but she'd forgotten her lighter.

"Fuck!" she said loudly, then again quietly, as if to erase the sound.

The moon had set and the ranch lay still, in near-perfect darkness. The lamps were off in the house, barn, corral and shed, but one bulb in the henhouse kept the laying hens productive, and down a path, a split-log cabin glowed through shuttered windows and through the gaps in the logs where the shrunken mortar had flaked away. She followed the dim path slowly. The hired hands were still awake.

A long-toothed cowboy in a dirty button-down shirt answered the door when she knocked. His back to her, Henry sat across the room beside two other cowboys, one wearing a white hat, the other a black hat, and neither hat differentiating the good guy from the bad guy. Their necks too gave nothing away: one had a pink, wrinkled neck, the other's skin was sun-black as sugar beet molasses and Henry's neck was hidden behind a blue kerchief, which was sopping wet because he'd soaked it under the tap to try to cool himself down.

They were huddled around a TV the way they would have huddled around a campfire on a colder night, in a time when nights were cool and cowboys still lit fires. The woodstove in the cabin had been reduced to burning hot peppers to drive the scorpions out of the walls. Even at the main house, the firepit in the yard glowed only on special occasions, and the solar oven was favored over the propane one. Fire was out of fashion, though just about everyone smoked.

"It's too hot to sleep," Connie said to Henry's head as she strode past the cowboy at the door. The dirt floor kicked up under her feet, and the wind brought in sand. "What are you doing?" she asked, though it was obvious he was watching TV. "Can I watch with you?"

When Henry took a drag of his cigarette, seeming to swallow the smoke, and moved over in his chair, it was not an invitation to join him, just a way of relinquishing space as he gestured to a vacant recliner stuck on the horizontal.

"Hell," said the long-toothed cowboy who'd opened the door and lost his seat to Connie. "Aw shit," he said as he lay on his cot and crossed his ankles; one boot smacked against the other, and a clod of frazzled earth fell onto the sheet.

Connie felt a little guilty but did not relinquish the recliner. "Can I have a light?" she asked, leaning into Henry.

When Henry held his tip against hers, she sucked till she was lit. Because the cabin smelled of smoke and men who reeked of horses and oil off the tractor, she didn't feel self-conscious about her armpits.

"What are you watching?" she asked.

Henry wasn't sure.

"What are we watching?" he asked the pink-skinned cowboy.

The cowboy said, "Dunno."

Henry said, "A movie."

Good enough.

After that, no one spoke, even during the advertisements. A scratch in the TV screen became a scar across a character's face or a thorn in a landscape of cholla. The film was a Western of sorts but also sort of a love story. And at the part when the handsome young cowboy flattened his hand over his lover's mouth and pushed up deep inside her, it seemed to Connie that the scratch in the glass completely disappeared.

When the movie ended and Henry stood up and silently turned off the sound, Connie was reminded of the reticence of wolves.

Being a topic of conversation her granddad loved to hate, she knew more than most teenage girls about the government's wolf policy. Schizoid bureaucrats had mandated their culling, then their reintroduction, followed by their culling again. The packs had fled to Canada, the less lucky ones to Mexico, where the heat was becoming unlivable. Packs no longer harassed the cattle on the ranch, but a lone wolf might conceivably stalk the range at night.

Connie had almost seen a wolf pack as a child. "Quick, Connie, come to the window!" her grandmother had called, but as if it were their cue, the wolves had sunk back into the darkness, and feeling their absence rebuked her, Connie had burst into tears. Lacking a talent for comfort, her grandmother had patted her on the hand and said, "Things disappear."

"I'll walk you home," said Henry.

"I'm not afraid of the dark," said Connie.

Henry looked at her hard. He wasn't a Christian Brigader, whose ranks were swelling countrywide, inversely linked to the demise of wolves and proportionate to the rising temperatures and seas. But Brigaders weren't the first Americans to believe in witchcraft: many indigenous peoples did too. And only witches weren't afraid of the dark.

"I'll walk you home," he said again.

"Okay, if you want to," she said, trying not to sound too pleased. "But I'm not chicken," she added.

When he looked at her hard again, she imagined she'd used a Scottish expression, though *chicken* was definitely American.

As they retraced her steps toward the house, Connie didn't talk, too busy concentrating on not walking into unknown things in the dark. The stars scattershot in the sky gave little light by which to navigate. Henry and she were walking past black masses of pale cottonwoods. No moon now, and their faces were blank. They smoked. The little light at the end of their cigarettes came close to their mouths, then dangled by their sides after every puff. Only when they'd reached the Ford pickup in the drive did either of them utter a word.

Connie broke the silence.

"I can't go two weeks without a signal. I'll die."

"You won't die," said Henry.

"How do you know? You can't see the future."

"I'm not a witch," he said, "if that's what you mean."

"That isn't what I meant. Can I watch with you again tomorrow?"

"Don't know why not. It's a free country, mostly."

"It's weird I was in Scotland yesterday. Seems like another world."

"You know that fellow telling his story on the radio today? His language don't got a *was*. The Navajo language don't got a real past tense."

"You speak Navajo?"

"My grandma did."

"So how did she talk about the past?"

Henry thought a moment. "I guess everything was now."

It was a full-blown conversation. Henry left her at the porch door, as he had done once already, just a few hours before. He walked away and merged with the dark.

That inaugural night, Connie lay down naked without a sheet, but unable to settle without weight on her body, if she slept at all, she didn't do it well. Outside the window, in the yard, something had spooked the rooster, who, no matter how much she willed it, just would not shut up. His screeching entered her dreams: an owl had arrived in the yard, quiet as a wolf, to airlift off the hens, while an Edinburgh riot-copter chopped and diced the rain and plucked protestors off the Bank of Scotland roof.

She slept and woke and slept and woke and didn't do either fully, and her dreams mingled with a memory. While her grandmother was away at a CowBelles get-together, she'd accompanied her granddad to a housing development meeting at the valley school gymnasium. Too little to grasp the big words, she heard *blah blah blah* and something about water rights or water theft and dollar per acre. As men in suits talked the sun down, the hours inched by painfully on a hard plastic seat underpinned with gum. Clenching his Bronco keychain, her granddad watched the caged clock on the gymnasium wall as if it were a trapped thing that might any minute break loose. Then suddenly he stood up and said for everyone to hear, "I got chickens to coop and other wolves to worry about than those wearing suits." But he had waited too long to act. The wolves had already come down from wherever they came down from, for who knew where wolves came from. They'd come down fast and silent as the dew, and they'd jawed away the four-by-fours used to secure the netting protecting the chicken yard. The carnage showed in the headlamps as the Ford crested the hill. Not much to see: no heads or feet or guts, not even the crown of the rooster, because wolves aren't finicky eaters. There was only one surviving hen, who'd buried herself in a hole and had no wish to come out.

The fitful and interminable night left Connie in a pissy mood in the morning. And when her cousins crept through the unlocked door to rout her from her bed, she knew how that chicken had felt.

"Monsters!" she shouted. But it was her nakedness that frightened her cousins, and they ran screaming from the room.

She slammed the door, and the sound banged against her head. Sleep-deprived. Thirsty. Hot. Probably other things too.

She locked the door. Sipping her rusty water, she glanced out the window, half expecting to see a farmyard scene from a horror movie, but the hens were quietly preening, the rooster looking smug. No owl murder. No helicopters. The cock had squawked all night at shadows.

She found her phone and earphones in her carry-on. Her cigarettes, where she'd left them in the pocket of her shorts. Her lighter, tucked away in her toiletry bag. Connie threw open the window. Neither electronic music nor smoking, under the age of eighteen, were allowed in her grandparents' house, but having locked the lock, she already stood on the far side of the law.

When the cousins returned, Arnold, Jacob and Billy pounded at the door, and Tatsie, in her high-pitched six-year-old squeal, called, "Connie, let us in!" and Quentin, even higher, like the echo that he was, said, "Connie, let us in," too. Carol, who was shy at seven, stood silently by the door, willing it to open, which was a kind of mind control Connie could actually feel and was even more persuasive than the pounding.

But she held her ground. She wasn't a kid anymore. She wasn't obliged to play, and solitude seduced her. She smoked by the open window and examined the grade of the roof. She was thinking of climbing out. But the coffin window – which was sometimes called a witch's window, because the energetic force of the diagonal was said to keep out necromancers – worked in reverse and kept her in.

She plunked herself onto the bed. Over the cousins' banging, Neil Young thrummed in her ears, crooning about nostalgia for his teenage years, his so-called changes, though his privileged generation hadn't understood the meaning of the word. Next up was Billy Idol, pining for a runaway girlfriend, a sweet-sixteen invitation to join the sex-offender register. Her parents hadn't vetted the lyrics before downloading, for her birthday, every imaginable oldie connected to her misnamed age.

Connie scrawled in her diary, *Stop the bleedin' pounding!* Curiously, the pounding stopped. She took out her earphones. Silence. She slid the diary and pen back under the pillow and dropped the cigarette in her glass of water, for as yet she hadn't learned to respect clean and drinkable liquids. Opening the door, she found her cousins gone.

Knowing they'd be back, she left her room and closed the door behind her. As she had the night before, Connie tiptoed down the hallway past a sepia photograph on the wall, where an expressionless MacAllister ancestor mounted on a mustang followed her with his eyes. She crawled through a dwarf door leading to the storage space underneath the eaves and holed up and waited for the cousins' return.

Sure enough. She heard them padding along the hallway runner. As they hammered on her bedroom door again, Tatsie called, "We brought you a cup of tea. Let us in!"

Connie's eyes adjusted to the dark. Her hiding place was stuffed with hard-shell suitcases with unset locks that opened when the zeros aligned. A plastic garment bag held one black dress sock. Two tennis racket holdalls – his-and-hers, one blue, one pink, vinyl creatures overtly gendered – bore a white lightning zap beside the word *Dunlop*. She couldn't picture her grandparents playing tennis in their youth, but then again, she couldn't picture her grandparents in their youth at all.

To her, they were straight out of *American Gothic*: a leathery woman standing beside a leathery man who was holding a pitchfork, though he should have been holding a lasso and wearing a cowboy hat, because only tourists went bareheaded in the desert sun. And, updating the picture to match more recent history, the woman should have been holding her husband's hand, if not out of affection then because she insisted he needed her help. She would take it, he would drop it, she would take it again, because the old man was blind.

Connie heard Arnold say, "Maybe it's open."

He tried the handle to her bedroom door. Bewildered, the cousins talked among themselves as if the elder's vanishing were magic.

Tatsie said, "Should I leave the tea?"

Jacob said, "No, I'll drink it."

And the lot of them ran away to play.

Connie crawled out and cracked her stiff back. Under the eaves it was stifling, even first thing in the morning. She picked off the pellets of rat poison sticking to her ass. They looked like breakfast cereal. She went to her room and dressed. The cousins were gone for now, though they were out there somewhere.

Soon, Connie was lying in a hammock outside while the

mountain peaks watchdogged in the distance. The morning showed no signs of weather coming. Thunder to the east wasn't thunder, it was one of two other options: either a gunnery exercise in the Chocolate Mountains, a delicious name for a military zone cordoned off with sheets of razor ribbon, or a detonation in the Salton Sea mines, where there wasn't a sea at all, but a salt lake with aspirations. The third possibility was unlikely, but it could have been an earthquake, because the green swath in the distance was the San Andreas Fault.

Big sprinkler-drops filled her mouth and slid into her eyes. In the hammock strung between two cottonwood trees, with only five minutes of sprinkler time before the water cut out, Connie was getting as wet as possible. And, once again, she was wearing her school uniform, and most unlikely of all, she was wearing her school's insignia sweater, which she had found packed in her hand luggage in case the plane was hyper-cooled. To wear the uniform a second day, and wet it down in the sprinkler, was an act of reappropriation, empowering but unpleasant.

The water eased her heat rash, but the wet fabric made her itch. The damp sweater hugged her breasts, and the wool released an acrid smell against the scent of lilacs, which hung so drenched and heavy the blossoms touched the ground. Her blouse was minus a button, lost somewhere in the sky over the Atlantic, and her nipples rose like two tiny bottlenose dolphins nudging through.

From under a floppy hat, she peered through the sham rain. In the big morning sun, which was squatting on the mountains, the blue fescue grass looked black as one blade shadowed another. As if it favored chaos, the low sun picked out the choke-weed. A cluster of seeds floated on the air, and the wet crosswise sunbeams showed them bright and silver. A Gila monster scuttled into the determined bougainvillea, beyond which was the struggling orchard of avocado and persimmon trees, which had to survive unirrigated ever since statewide rationing. If they weren't tapped into underground streams, they were not long for this world.

Persimmon was a curious word. *Avocado* was too. Neither sounded like English. But a lot of English wasn't English. English was opportunistic. English was promiscuous. A relative of many languages, it entwined with everyone everywhere without a second thought.

As she lounged in the sprinkler, Connie's mind moved with the wind, and she found herself wondering if dolphins were truly promiscuous. Was it fake news that a dolphin had raped a fisherman off Cape Cod? Was the aquatic mammal really just trying to cuddle? Were dolphins in fact related to wolves, or had the wolf-dolphin evolutionary link, more broadly refuted by the Christian Brigade, been debunked by science?

Her bicameral mind drifting apart, Connie closed her eyes and enjoyed the gentle, sunny drizzle, so different from Scotland's leaden torrents. An eerie sound carried uphill. Black Angus on the range. A cow was being humped. In school, she'd studied the Romantic poets for whom Spring's pastoral horniness was bliss, but was that just propaganda? Was the cow actually lowing with pleasure? Or was it pain or protest? And was the sprinkler water actually flavored with salt, or did she just have a taste in her mouth? And had Black Angus learned to talk?

Connie opened her eyes. Her grandmother was calling her from the front porch, and her voice, as wiry as her arms, did not reveal a woman sentimental enough to water an ornamental bush in a drought. "Don't get burned. You'll get sick. Don't get sick," she called, and as if the hour obeyed her, the timer struck zero, and the sprinkler stopped.

"I never get sick," Connie called back, which was mostly true. She almost never caught a cold, and even more impressive, she'd never contracted dysentery from drinking contaminated water.

"Don't press your luck," her grandmother called again, "and don't tempt the Fates." The old woman covered all her bases, uncertain which of the two she actually believed in.

Connie too was undecided. Flopping onto her belly, she pressed her face into the weave and dropped one hand to the ground and touched the grass, which was tidy on top, but stick a shovel in there and you found the roots were knotted. She considered the question of luck and fate. Was it good luck or divine plan or systematic injustice that her parents could borrow heavily to send her to a private school with an optimal ratio of security guards to students? Was it just rotten luck that her entire world was traumatized and there was no escape, except her grandparents' ranch? And if a life goes on long enough, isn't the assignation of luck, at any given juncture, inherently premature? She pushed the thought away. She didn't want to think about how lucky or unlucky she was, but being sixteen years old, she couldn't help but think about herself.

Suddenly, a force of hands lifted the hammock against her stomach and flipped her over on the ground. The cousins ran off laughing, down toward the parched arroyo.

"Little bastarts!" she called after them, using the Scottish variation with the hope it would go unchastened.

No such luck.

"Connie MacAllister! Mind your language! And take your cousins to the store." Retribution for the dirty word.

Connie pouted and licked at the stain on her arm and rubbed it about with her thumb, which only entrenched it deeper.

But she did as her grandmother commanded. She called to the kids, who were on the verge of vanishing over the hill, "Hang on!"

Carol, Johnny, Jacob, Arnold, Tatsie and Quentin turned

around, the vibrant sun behind them. They awaited her instructions. Arnold shrugged to say, *What*? In tandem, Tatsie and Quentin cocked their heads.

The littlest were so little and even littler at a distance. Hormones rushing up and down, Connie tried not to find them cute. She wanted to nurture a hostile attitude, but even irritated she couldn't help but melt a bit.

"You're going to the shops," she called. "Hop in the truck."

Taking her place behind the wheel, Connie looked about for Henry with the hope of proving to him that her granddad let her drive on the ranch and even drive as far as the Higgly Piggly in the valley. But he was nowhere to be seen. So, as instructed, she took her cousins to the grocery store, where a teenage boy worked a holidays-and-afterschool job in hardware.

That Connie liked him was a slim affair. She mainly liked his square-rimmed shades and the slight black moustache that resembled ants on his upper lip. He was just a boy, the way a hammer is just a hammer; she didn't know which was the best hammer and didn't really care. Many boys had the same shades, though how well this one could grow a moustache was one thing that set him apart. Also, his arrogance was reassuring: as if his jeans were lined with asbestos, he acted like a world on fire couldn't touch him. Meeting him the previous year at the Higgly Piggly, she'd admired his facial hair and attitude from the start. Now meeting him there again seemed like a kind of sign.

The commuter town was mostly empty on a workday. So even driving to the strip mall, Connie experienced the desert's emptiness and symmetry: nothing above meant nothing below, a cloudless sky like a vacant lot, a sun like a burning car. Once in a while, a hawk flew by. A hawk or an eagle or maybe even a condor, each in his turn a loose page from an old book on which the spine had cracked. In such emptiness, signs are plentiful, and, as a result, the boy became more attractive than he really was.

While the cousins bought Snickers bars and candy cigarettes, he pulled Connie into the detergent aisle.

He said, "You're back."

"I am."

"From Scotland?"

"No, not back from Scotland. I live there."

The boy looked confused at this, but it didn't matter to either of them.

He said, "You didn't come over last year. You said you would."

"I did. I do it every year."

Now both of them looked confused, but when the condensation from the air conditioner dripped into her hair, Connie finally got it: the boy had meant she hadn't come to his house. He'd invited her the previous year, but it hadn't seemed a real invitation, though she'd wanted it to be real, and now it was. "I can come over this time," she said.

"I'm done at one-thirty," he said. "Come over after. My parents are at work all day. I've got a Jacuzzi, and it's full."

Connie was impressed. Water laws meant that orchards wilted, but a powerful spa and pool lobby had successfully argued that hot tubs were drought-friendly alternatives to lawns.

The grocery boy didn't give her a kiss or squeeze her hand or any outright signal, but he leaned slightly toward her, and his apron was just a little closer to her kilt than it needed to be.

"What do you smell of?" he said.

She smelled of wet wool. "Lavender oil," she answered.

"I like it."

The tight sleeves of his T-shirt pinched his biceps, and even a Higgly Piggly apron couldn't make him look soft.

The pleasure Connie felt at the interlude didn't last long.

Leaving the grocery store parking lot, she spotted a series of billboards featuring Revelation's greatest hits, which undermined the fun.

He is coming with the clouds, declared the first one.

There was a great earthquake, declared the second. The sun turned black like sackcloth made of goat hair, the whole moon turned bloodred.

Completing the dismal picture, the third billboard declared, It had ten horns and seven heads, with ten crowns on its horns, and on each head a blasphemous name.

And the last billboard made it personal: Do not be afraid of what you are about to suffer.

WTF, thought Connie, who was accustomed to America's roadside testimonies that Jesus saves and Jesus is coming and Unbelievers burn but had never before seen such baroque elaboration. Then, even worse, on the hill to the ranch, she stalled the truck, which embarrassed her in front of her cousins.

Billy opened his mouth full of nougat and laughed at her, his glutinous candied teeth visible in the rearview mirror. Arnold told her that she didn't know how to drive.

She revved the engine and told him, "*You* don't know how to drive. You're only ten. I drove all the way from the airport."

"You didn't," he said. He turned to Jacob, who was two months older, for reassurance. "Did she?"

"No," said Jacob.

"Did you really?" asked Carol, who wanted to be just like Connie.

Connie could count on her loyalty, but Carol had failed to warn her that her mascara had run in the sprinkler, and she'd looked like a fence-walking whore in front of the grocery boy. So even Carol was in her bad books.

"Didn't I just say I did? Do you think I'm a liar?"

"No," said Carol.

"Me neither," said Tatsie.

Connie glanced in the mirror at Quentin. He was pretending to puff on a candy cigarette and was too babyish to know that driving was important.

"You see," said Connie to the older boys, who were her juniors by six years and yet acted as if they were her equals, "Carol and Tatsie ken that I don't lie."

"Not in Scottish! In English," Jacob demanded.

"Know," Connie said, which they mistook for *no*.

When they arrived back at the ranch, Arnold made Quentin sit on the pickup's hot hood or he wasn't allowed any gummy bears.

"But they're mine," whimpered Quentin, trapped between a desire not to cry and the wish to all-out sob. His quivery face looked like a pond where kids skipped stones.

Connie plucked him off the hood, snatched the bears from Arnold's hand and shoved them into Quentin's palm. But he was too small to hold them all, and a couple fell out in the dust. That tipped the balance, and Quentin burst into tears.

Connie said, "You're a bas, Arnold." Then she whispered to her littlest cousin and wiped away his tears, leaving salt dirt on his cheeks. "Don't let them see you blubber, Quentin," she said. "Show Arnold how big and strong you are. You've got to tough it out."

When he nodded and bit his lip, she squeezed his arm and asked, "Are those muscles yours? Or did you steal them from the grocery boy?"

"Mine," said Quentin, very serious, for he was still so young that he only laughed at jokes that were earmarked in advance as funny, and Connie hadn't asked, "Want to hear a funny joke?"

She sent him off to play and stood and watched the cousins leave. Having bravely mastered his sorrows, Quentin skipped over and down the hill, hand in hand with Tatsie. They were the picture of tenderness and trust, fading into nostalgia in the sunshine.

The older kids carried plastic shopping bags full of empty peanut butter and jelly jars and home-canning mason jars and the odd yellow margarine tub, because this wasn't a dairy farm. Supplied thus by their grandmother, they were off to the dry gulch, which cut through the range and made the road to the valley into a jagged and absent-minded thing. There, at the gulch's bottom, their glass and plastic containers were to be used for catching beetles, but would, in reality, be used for trapping scorpions, some as old as Connie.

While the photophobic arthropods baked in the sun, the cousins would forget them, not intending to be cruel but because, being children, they were easily distracted and in a hurry to explore their world. The boys would want to play truth or dare, and the girls would want only truths and the boys only dares, and the boys would rule over the girls and demand that the girls take their share of dares. They'd play truth or dare in the steep-sloped gulch where no one could see them display to each other their small boy wienies and their little girl pee-places, or pee in each other's hands, or some other worser unspeakable dare that could only be performed with the utter innocence of children.

Connie knew what they were like. Not long ago, she'd been one of them. Standing by the truck, the hot motor under the hood making visible heat in the air, she watched them go.

"Can you come in and read a book to your granddad?" her grandmother called, standing on the porch like a grim-lipped daguerreotype, though the earliest photograph from her youth would have been a Polaroid.

When Connie took too long to answer, her grandmother called again, "Can you come in and read a book to your granddad?" for she was a woman who had no trouble repeating herself.

"Aye, Gran," Connie called, studying the horizon. The cousins had disappeared from sight; the shrill sun had blotted them out.

She followed her grandmother into the living room, not a stiff Scottish sitting room but an American living room, which sounded much more alive. Actually, it wasn't. A grand piano sat in the corner like an asphalt pit, and no one living knew how to play it. There were his-and-hers comfy chairs and an uncomfortable couch and a disused fireplace with a knotty mantel in which was carved in Gaelic, *Nuair a nì iad fàsach, canaidh iad sìth ris* ("They make a desert and call it peace"). Above the hard-nosed observation yawned a mounted javelina head.

No TV of course. No snapping twigs in the hearth either. The heart of the room was the eclectic bookshelf, where dwelled *Heart of Darkness*, *Robinson Crusoe*, *The Odyssey*, *On the Origin of Species*, *The Grapes of Wrath*, *Thus Spoke Zarathustra*, *Gravity's Rainbow*, *The Wonderful Wizard of Oz*, *All the Pretty Horses*, *Riders of the Purple Sage* and an assortment of penny Westerns, the most valuable featuring Jesse James, still in its plastic sleeve. There was Nietzsche and Heidegger and Abram (who had coined the term "the more-than-human world") and a mostly complete Shakespeare collection, minus *Titus Andronicus*, whose absence from the bookshelf could not be explained by its extreme, gratuitous violence, for MacAllisters were tough and not known to flinch. There were cookbooks and practical how-to books: *When Technology Fails: A Manual for Self-Reliance, Sustainability, and Surviving the Long Emergency*; an outdated *Encyclopedia of Nature*; pamphlets on water conservation, solar power, sustainable agriculture and natural capitalism. A considerable assembly of American biographies was strongly biased toward the Founding Fathers, and yet there was *Bury My Heart at Wounded Knee* and even Silko's *Ceremony*. There was a hand-cut book on

Scottish heraldry and *The Epic of Gilgamesh* and an abridged *Mahabharata*. There was an antique twelve-volume *Oxford English Dictionary* compiled on the eve of World War II, which was missing important words like *cyberspace* and *bioengineering* and even *fascism*, because there is a lag between current events and language. All of these had been arranged not by title but by publication date, as if to defend against the scrambling epochs that swept as dust through the door.

Beside the bookcase, a display cabinet held a collection of bobblehead dolls, their oversized skulls held on by metal coils. Too precious to be manhandled, the dolls in the cabinet were kept locked away, but Connie knew where to find the key and, alone in the house with her cousins, had more than once flicked the playful bobbleheads to make them nod yes. "Can I lock the door, Gran?" "Can I bum a fag, Granddad?" "Is it going to cool down tonight?" The dolls invariably answered aye.

She didn't, however, expect to be alone in the house ever again, because her grandparents had ceased to ride the range. They no longer hauled protein blocks to the herds, or tagged, weighed and trucked out calves to sell, or rode the fences on horseback, checking for dangerous breaches. The cowboys did it without them. The old man was too blind to protect himself outdoors, and wishing to protect him everywhere, an invisible vector field allowed the old woman to travel as far as the lilac but no farther. Mostly, it kept her in the kitchen, where, like a penitent, she spent her time baking. Having never left her husband's side on the range, she wouldn't leave him now, except by dying.

They'd been arguing about that very thing. And returning to the living room, the old woman picked up the argument exactly where she'd left it. "I'm not going nowhere," she said. "The boys can handle that beefing."

"That bull listens only to you," her husband said.

"Unlike you," she said.

"It'll bust the fence down."

"What did we hire those boys for, anyway?"

"That bull don't like newcomers."

"I don't like them much myself, but I get over it."

"The cowboys need you, and I don't."

"You don't need me?"

"You want me to say it again?"

"Repetition is not gonna make it true." And to prove herself right, she pointed at her granddaughter and demanded, "Tell me who is that!"

Connie was standing in the archway between the living room and the front hall. But though her grandfather squinted in the appropriate direction, he misaimed. He was staring at the hallstand, with its tin drip trays and iron hooks, trying to make out its face.

Macular degeneration had got him. The middle of the backs of both eyes was diseased, the part that reads small details like the shape of a nose or the quality of an eye. He could negotiate space, but he could not know a person in it.

When he waved his hands in the air as if brushing away a phantasm, his wife raised hers, and, as if she were a religious woman, which she probably wasn't but she liked to keep a person guessing, she quoted him yet another billboard erected on the thoroughfare through town. "'The Earth was without form and void, and darkness was over the face of the deep.' Anyway, I can't go out. I've gotta bake some cookies for the grandkids."

Removing herself to make batter, as she passed her eldest grandchild she peered into Connie's face and asked, "What's that black stuff? Spider spit?" Knowing it was smudged mascara, she didn't wait for an answer. At the end of the hall, the kitchen door swung open and shut and open and shut behind her.

Connie said, "Granddad," to alert him she was present. "What book do you want me to read you?"

"Is that Connie?" he asked, not because he didn't know her voice. It was an invitation to play a game, one they had played for years, though it used to involve covering his eyes with her little hands.

Connie smiled. "No, who's Connie?"

He smiled too, but slower. "You sound a lot like Connie," he said. "Who are you?"

She offered her usual answer: "A ghost."

"Connie's ghost?"

"Lady Macbeth's ghost," she said, taking her cue from the books in the bookcase.

"No, you're not. You're not as mean."

"Jessie James's ghost, then."

"He was even meaner."

"Jesse James's wife's ghost," Connie concluded, but she immediately regretted it, recalling that the gunman's wife was a head-in-the-sand denialist who'd convinced herself that Jesse worked in import – export and was not a robber, killer, and gang leader in the chaotic aftermath of the Civil War. Connie didn't want to be her. "I changed my mind," she said. "I'm Jesse James's mom."

As if it were a hangnail, the old man picked at the varnish on the arm of his chair as he ruminated on his granddaughter's newfound identity. Satisfied, he nodded, just as slowly as he'd smiled. "I guess you are. I mistook you for Connie."

Then he chose a book. "The little pink one," he said. "The nineteenth-century little pink one," he added, in case there was some confusion.

Though it was funny to hear an old cowboy say "the little pink one," Connie wouldn't laugh at her granddad. She brought the small book to him. Clearly someone's obsession, its red velvet cover had been fingered with such vehemence it had worn away to pink.

"It's actually red," she told him. Then wiping her runny mascara on her cuffs, she asked, "Why's the sprinkler water salty?"

"'Cause of the Salton Sea. You can see it from the window."

"You can?"

"See for yourself."

Connie looked out the window.

"You can't see the sea," she said.

"Can't you?"

"No."

"'Cause you don't really want to."

Before Connie could decide if this was true or not, he added, "Desire is the progenitor of sight."

Connie glanced at the bookshelves as if they'd spoken. Then she appraised her grandfather in his chair. He was himself some rubbed-up thing of earth and dung and wind. He was something like the wolves that were gone with the heat and culls and subdivisions, and before them the Indians, gone with the gunfights and broken treaties, and right or wrong he felt himself to have as much claim to that dried-out patch of earth as anyone. His cowboy boots were coated in it.

Connie couldn't understand how he could be who he was and yet have read the books he'd read, and even, when the mood came over him, speak their highbrow language. She had as yet the absolutist disposition of a teenager, oblivious to her own contradictions and incapable of understanding that a person is two or three or four things all at once.

"What?" he said.

"I didn't say anything," she said.

"Don't indulge him," said her grandmother, emerging from the kitchen with a bouquet of lilac blooms and a tarnished spittoon in her hands. "You cannot see the Salton Sea."

It was time for more tough love. So the old woman told

her husband to walk up and down the room. "Gotta keep your legs moving."

Connie dropped the tiny book on the coffee table. "So you don't want me to read to him?" But she didn't get an answer, for her grandparents were at it again.

"If I got somewhere to go, I'll ride," said the old man, who'd lived his life on horseback.

"You're not riding nowhere."

"I'm not taking walking lessons, neither. You know the difference between eyes and legs, woman? There's nothing wrong with my stride."

"Suit yourself. Just don't complain to me when you turn into a block of salt."

Feigning indifference at the worst imaginable ending – her husband stuck permanently in his chair – the old woman placed the spittoon on the mute piano and arranged the blooms in the makeshift vase. Then, briefly taking refuge in a thing of beauty, she stepped back and admired it. But the stems were short and the lilac blossoms top-heavy, and they fell out on their heads.

"I'm going out," said Connie.

"Where, out?" asked her grandmother, jamming the blooms back in.

"The valley."

"Why?"

"I feel like going somewhere. Can I borrow the truck?"

"Unlike your granddad, you got legs," said her grandmother. "And your boots are made for walking," she said, appropriating an old song, though Connie was wearing flip-flops.

"Don't go down to the valley," her granddad said.

"Why not?" asked Connie.

"You don't got the time."

"Why? I'm not doing anything else."

"A storm is on its way."

Connie looked out the window. Sky blue, and nothing except some blowing dust. No sign of a storm. But her granddad knew his weather, and if the Saints declined to turn back a storm, especially in the time of the Climate Twins, sudden rains and freak fronts moved in at lightning speed. El Niño winds brought blackflies and drought, and the valley grew too parched to absorb a downpour. La Niña brought mosquitos, ushered in by springtime cold that froze the eggs of insect-eating birds, and with the cold came bitter storms. A storm out of nowhere was rare, but her granddad was firm on the subject. "Rare isn't never," he'd said. "Rare is sometimes. Rare is dangerous."

The window showed the barren sky, and in it Connie looked for a sign but saw none. Just a crow hazing a hawk, their shadows tightening a noose around some unseen creature.

"Can you see your cousins?" her granddad asked. "They shouldn't be out in this weather. Time to call them in." When Connie answered that she couldn't see them, her grandmother said, "Well, where are they?"

"Somewhere out there," said Connie.

The three of them fell silent.

Finally, her granddad asked her, "You see something now?"

"Nothing."

The cousins were gone, the sky was clear, even the hawk and its crow had disappeared.

For no discernible reason – maybe because she felt better with something in her hand – Connie's grandmother picked up the little pink book that was lying on the coffee table. Carrying it to the window with her, she strained to see the distance. "Nothing but nothing," she observed.

When Connie looked over at her grandfather, he must have felt it. "What?" he said.

"You sure it's going to rain?" she said. "There isn't one cloud."

"When cockroaches fly, it rains," he said.

"But there isn't one cloud," she said again. She appealed to her grandmother, "Is there?"

"You know better than to contradict him."

But the old lady contradicted him herself by not instructing her granddaughter to forfeit her trip to the valley and rush off to find the kids. She placed the book in Connie's hand and retreated once more to the kitchen. Any thought of bringing home the children disappeared behind the clear blue sky.

Connie asked her grandfather, "Do you want me to read to you before I go?"

But he didn't answer. He'd fallen asleep, just like that, as old people do. His snoring didn't wake him, nor did the fly that traversed his forehead and traveled a crack in his dry-as-jerky skin.

Connie watched the fly's black palpus moving in and out. Then, gently, she brushed the fly away and, as if it cared about her instructions, whispered, "Go away. He's sleeping."

Then she lay the book on the mantelpiece, beneath the mounted javelina head, and exited the room.

At the hallway mirror, she spat on her finger, rubbed away the smeared mascara, and frowned at her reflection, certain it could have been better. But she had little to complain of. Her chestnut bangs cut sharply over her chestnut eyes, as genetically matching as a pantsuit, and her wide MacAllister nose wasn't so wide as to be unattractive. There was intelligence in her eyes, and she was prettier than most. No one would ever have imagined she'd be depicted as a creature who should have been sterilized.

In the kitchen, her grandmother's hands were thick with cookie batter, but when Connie reached out a finger toward the bowl, her grandmother whisked it away without a word. There are only so many words, as there is only so much precipitation in a desert, and she'd spent hers on her husband.

Connie walked out the kitchen door and into the arid garden. Carrot tops flicked in the wind, and a cabbage stalk nodded its head, and under their mounds, potatoes swelled, sweeter because they were thirsty. She walked past the laundry line, which extended between the telephone poles and was accessed by a rickety scaffold, upon which the cousins had been known to enact mock hangings. She walked past the giant firepit, under whose plywood lid the beef stewed in its juices and slow-cooked in tinfoil.

Not a cloud, hardly a sound, no sign of cousins or cowboys, as if the entire world were asleep on this hill of vanished wolves and peoples, with a hole in the sky watched over by a blind man. At the hammock, she gave it a swing, and it twisted itself, commenced untwisting, aborted and held still, snarled and knotted.

She followed the dirt road downward, kicking away the loose stones that lodged between her toes. She was thinking about the grocery boy when she almost walked into Henry.

"Watch it," he said.

"Where'd you come from?" she said.

"Nowhere," he said. "Been working right here."

His rolled-up shirtsleeves revealed his sculpted forearms, and he was whitewashing a persimmon trunk to protect it from sunscald and pests.

"I didn't see you," she said, recalling how in an eye exam she hadn't seen the middle column on the computer screen until the eye doctor had informed her it was there. His assurance that this was normal in one in three persons wasn't altogether comforting, because what else can't you see until somebody tells you to look?

Tethered to a nearby tree, Henry's mustang was grinding its unshod hoof against a rock. With no need for horseshoes, it had little need for humans, making the bond between a mustang and a cowboy a union of equals. When Connie walked over to pet it, Henry did the same, and the horse quit tending to its manicure and began gumming a patch of trash-grass, yet disdained to eat it.

"Costs too much energy to digest," said Henry, as he pulled the gobbet from the horse's teeth. "Certain cold comfort in burning the stuff. Can't compost it though, or there'll be hell next spring."

Then, with the tip of his boot, he nudged at something that was poking out of the ground. His ratty boots were as a worn as his pony's hooves. The outer edges of the heels were slanted from the slight bow in his legs, and the leather uppers were sun-crazed, but he wore them day and night while a pair of pristine Johnny Ringos lived under his cot, dry-rotting away in the drought. He kicked at the thing in the ground till he excavated a scrap of barbed wire. He added it to his horse's pack.

"Wire on the ground is hardware disease," he said. "Wire on the fence is supplies."

"My granddad says the same thing," said Connie.

"'Cause it's true."

Just like Connie's granddad, Henry told a person how things worked as a way of showing affection.

In the distance, cattle lowed.

"Is the Miscreant Bull still alive?" asked Connie.

"If anything lives forever, it'll be that bull," said Henry.

The Miscreant Bull was the name for the biggest and oldest bull in the herd. The name had been earned when it broke down a barbed-wire fence and returned a full year later, four hundred pounds lighter but with so little depletion of attitude that it had won lifelong respect. As a rule, headstrong cattle were culled, but the Miscreant Bull lived on, because Connie's grandfather admired it. And now it had escaped again.

"Are you going to catch it?" she asked.

"When we find it," Henry said.

"Tomorrow, can you teach me how to lasso?"

"Rope," Henry corrected her, because if she wanted to rope like a cowboy, she had to talk like one. But he liked her well enough to plan to put down his work tomorrow and start to teach her how to do it.

"Okay, rope," she said.

"Okay, tomorrow," he said.

Now Henry shielded his eyes with his hand and looked out across the range, as if he might spot the bull out there causing trouble. The sun, which made it possible to see, made it difficult as well. The drier the earth became, the fiercer was the glare.

Connie scanned the horizon too, disbelieving that the glaring orb of molten plasma, heavy with gold and uranium, could actually give way to biblical volumes of rain. She was about to bring up the weather when Henry touched his hat and got back to work.

Connie carried on downhill. Other than the steep and ashy descent over the range and through the gulch, there was only one way downhill into the valley. As the dirt lane bent and disappeared into a cluster of cottonwoods, Henry and his mustang vanished from view. Squatting against a tree, out of sight of all but birds, Connie stopped to pee; the small stream rolled across the compacted ground, and like every drop of water west of the Continental Divide, took off for the Pacific Ocean. The house with its grocery boy was calling to her, and she unbuttoned the lower buttons on her shirt and tied the tails in a knot at her ribs. As she carried on downhill, there was no explaining why she still wore her sweater.

As the sun flashed through the leafy cottonwoods, she spoke aloud in a singsong voice, "Cottonwood, cottontail, cottonmouth, cotton-pickin' idiot." As she sauntered down the hill, she relished those weird American words, the slavish roots of which she didn't know.

She still had jet lag and felt like clotted cream, but the walk was making her better, and one foot fell easily in front of another. The journey across the angry skies was leaving her. She wondered whether a language without a *was* could change space as well as time. Unable to say "Yesterday I was in Scotland," maybe she would not have been there. Maybe she would always be here and now and forever in America on holiday. The thought made her relax and swing her hips more freely. Though LA had highway fences too, Edinburgh, a walled city, had become a city of walls inside walls, and she was happy to be outside of them. No more military-guarded private school, where she took lessons in cognitive dissonance and sat tests in which, unlike reality, there was always a right answer. She'd read Dante's *Paradiso* while, out in the city streets, the displaced killed for rations and clean water. But being here-and-now in America, she didn't have to think about yesterday at home.

Other than having cowboy grandparents, she could be like everyone else: a typical middle-class kid in a world abandoning hope. In the land of Hollywood and Disneyland, she was going to have some fun. She kicked a stone along the road and experienced a rush. *No boundaries*, she said to herself. *No locks. No fences, except those that keep in cows. No walls. None of that today.*

She bent down and picked up the stone she'd been kicking, and though it wasn't a special stone, she put it in her sweater pocket when the dirt lane turned into tarmac. She was instantly hotter the moment the tarmac began.

It was less than a half hour's walk, yet down in the valley and up on the hill were worlds apart. Seen from the hill, the housing development was a congress of flat-headed snakes, because each cul-de-sac curled to a square end, its corners lopped off by cast-cement planters, in which geraniums and tiny American flags had been planted. The cul-de-sac houses were fat and more or less identical. Street numbers, mounted on faux-Zen lanterns or laser-cut beneath a Jesus cross, were their most distinctive features.

Lifting a grocery receipt to the sun, Connie read the address scrawled on the back. The boy's house was one of the fattest, the kind with a three-car garage, prized by families with teenagers who drove their own cars to school. His street number was black plastic and solar powered, but in the daylight it didn't glow.

He was wet when he opened the door, and he smelled of chlorine and tequila. His swim shorts dripped water down his legs. Like a gentleman taking her coat, or as if she'd come to deliver a pizza, he took the receipt from her hand.

She couldn't decipher his attitude as he dropped the receipt on a console table, on top of which a crystal bowl held lime-colored peppermint candies, and instead of *hello* said, "You want one?"

Connie felt embarrassed by the sound of the wrapper crinkling as she untwisted the ends. "Your house is like a hotel," she said and winced when the acoustics of the white quartzite floor made her voice too bright.

Arctic air blasted through a floor vent onto her bare ankles. It was the first time all day that a sweater made any sense. She noticed how he looked at her, knowing American boys rarely saw a girl in a school uniform except on a porno site.

"Hey," he called to someone out back, "I told you the English girl would show."

She didn't remind him she was Scottish, or that she held a US passport. She was pleased enough to know that he, and whoever else was out there, had hoped for her arrival. But she did say, "Connie."

"Yeah," he said.

The boy on the porch, in the Jacuzzi, had dirty blond hair with a bleached stripe. Other than that, there was not much difference between the boys. One was light, one was dark.

The light-haired boy was facing away and had hiked himself up on the tub's lip to reach the drinks trolley. His skin was marbled by hot water. His waistband had inched down, leaving an imprint that resembled a motorcycle track across his lower back. When he swung around, he held out a glass and asked, "Margarita?"

Not having packed a bathing suit, Connie stepped inside the house to strip to her underwear. She turned her back to the glass patio doors and undressed to the soundtrack of the fridge-freezer producing crushed ice. She pretended her back was a wall, but it remained the half-naked backside of her body. And when she approached the Jacuzzi, folding her arms over her breasts only increased her cleavage.

The boys silently appraised her, and one of them passed her a pale green cocktail.

She sat in her bra and panties, her feet in the tub, the rising steam becoming sweat, and the sun bearing down on any piece of flesh that came close to the horizontal. Nose, breasts, thighs. Then, slipping into the water, her arms drifted out to each side. In her bra as if in a boat, her breasts floated on the surface and joggled with the puffing of the air jets.

She couldn't believe her luck: she was floating in bubbling water without a care. Gone were the armed guards and the vacuumers and the daily doomsday reports.

"Americans just want to have fun," one crazy congresswoman had told the cameras as her bottom-feeder eyes shone with conspiratorial zeal. While the sun and water parboiled her, Connie half agreed that human life had no greater purpose.

The boys refilled her glass as soon as it was empty. Then, when the next glass was half-empty and when Connie asked if there was really a worm at the bottom of a bottle of tequila, one of the boys said, "Let's find out," and refilled her glass again.

The boys talked between themselves about gaming, mountain

bikes, military tests, and ketamine, but really, they were waiting. They didn't wait out of shyness or uncertainty or the residue of a long-dead code that good things are worth waiting for. They waited till she was absolutely drunk enough before taking off their swim shorts and daring her to do the same.

She was too drunk to think why not, though without her bra and panties, she felt somehow less human. She felt like seaweed in a rock pool. Her breasts were bladderwrack. Her pubic hair was thongweed.

When she told the boys these thoughts, one of them called her perverse. She answered, "You have no imagination," and they told her they didn't need to imagine what was laid out before them.

When the grocery boy climbed on top of her and told her that she wanted it, she pushed him off and told him that she didn't. He climbed back on. She pushed him off. He climbed back on, and her head sank beneath the water. She pushed him off and came up sputtering. He climbed back on. Her ass on the shallow underwater seat, her back against the poured plastic edge, he forced her wrists behind her, so her bones dug into the lip. She turned into a gray waxy metamorphic rock, with two eyes looking skyward, and braced herself as he screwed her in stark sunlight.

She stared past his dark hair toward the sky. Steppes. Mountains. From here she couldn't see the ranch, though from the dormer window in the master bedroom, she had a clear sight of the housing estate, whose luxury cannibalized the ground. She opened her eyes wider. Quick fibers of clouds were crossing the mountain peaks, as if that threshold were nothing. She imagined that it hurt the clouds. Or did it hurt the peaks? Maybe it hurt both.

When the boy lifted himself to secure a more gravity-enhanced angle and pushed harder, he blocked her view. Nothing now to see but his chest. A tiny node of dark hair might have been a hole between his nipples. Boys had stupid nipples. Flat, almost inverted. A Jesus Fish tattoo was on his shoulder. It leaped out of the water and flickered in the fading sun. He moved as if he were trying to scrub a stain from an empty bottle in chlorinated water at 104 Fahrenheit. She heard the squeak inside the bottle, but she could no longer tell the difference between hearing and feeling. She'd inched outside her body. She was drifting with the clouds.

When the first boy pulled out, the second boy said, "My turn."

The first one said politely, "Be my guest."

The new boy stood her up and turned her over, and she held tight to the tub to stop her pelvis banging into the plastic shell. He went on for ages behind her. Fucking out her shocked brains and turning them into jelly. He went on and on. Maybe he was in one of those dreams where you're climbing the stairs and your legs are made of oxidizing lead, so you will never reach the top.

But then he peaked. He collapsed against her, his head upon her shoulder, the scent of shampoo rising from his hair. He hadn't rinsed it properly, and the tangy lemon chemicals engulfed her. He held there, motionless, as if he had been shot.

When she turned her head to check, she saw no sign of injury, just the crimson coinage of a dollop of her own blood, spinning slowly in a whirlpool. She looked again toward the mountains; the Saints had not protected her. She felt orphaned. But shock had shut her senses down, and her mind lifted away again, and again she didn't feel much of anything, and suddenly, as if out of nowhere, the sky began to rain.

Shriveled and dizzy and miles from her body, she crouched down on the underwater seat and rested her cheek against the side of the tub. Little blasts from the jets jabbed her thighs. As she ran her fingernail down her arm, a small tag of clay came away from her skin. She rolled it between her fingers into a human shape and let it float off in the water.

She slept, or technically she didn't sleep, but dumbfounded, she dreamed, and she dreamed she was playing a game of Snakes and Ladders with her cousins, and the ladders were entangled snakes.

There was a hand on her shoulder. On her face, the tough drilling rain. The grocery boy was shaking her awake, and the rain had become a storm.

He shouted, "There's lightning. Get out."

Confused by her dream, she asked, "Where are my cousins?"

But he'd already retreated into the house to stay dry, and the other one, his blond accomplice, had disappeared entirely.

Connie couldn't find her panties, which had blown away in the dark wind. The dark wind is only one of thousands of winds, but together with yellow wind, they may stand for them all. But such insights, though they lay embedded in the land beneath the subdivision, belonged to another world, not to Connie.

She did not know if she'd slept a very long time or if the storm had ended the daylight. Darkness, and there was no hour to be known, except that when she rose and walked inside, the grocery boy told her his parents would be returning from work and she had to get going.

"Drive me?" she pleaded, as she found her school uniform on the floor where she'd dumped it.

As she fastened the kilt's mini-belt, the boy leaned against the glass doors watching the battering weather. The Jacuzzi was overflowing in the downpour. The hanging-banana patio umbrella had fallen over and sailed into the railings. Like a maniac parrot thrashing against its confinement, the parasol flapped against the posts. There was a crash, but what made the sound was unseen.

She pleaded again, "Can't you?"

He lent her a garbage bag as a raincoat, using a kitchen

knife to poke two armholes and a head hole. He did that much. And maybe it was true that the three-car garage reserved an empty space, like a vacant seat set for an ancestor at a table. But probably it wasn't.

"I don't have my own car," he said, "and my parents took both of theirs. Don't walk back the way you came. There's a shortcut."

He rattled off directions as he shoved her toward the door, which was decorated with an Easter wreath with plastic hatching eggs. Did boys have inverted nipples so you couldn't bite them off?

Now Connie was outside. In the storm's darkness, the solar-powered numbers glowed. The rain drilled down through the holes in her bag. She was soaked in seconds.

She slipped on a mess of leaves and overturned garbage. She bumped into a stranded bicycle and bruised her shins but didn't feel it. The plastic strap on one of her flip-flops popped out of its rubber hole. She forced it back in twisted, and it ground against her metatarsals. A tree across the luggage rack of a hatchback blocked her way. Climbing over, she couldn't feel the stick that sliced the naked insides of her thighs. Her senses were dulled by booze, but she was sober enough to be frightened, furious, and ashamed. The blood on her thighs washed away in the rain.

When the houses receded behind her, she looked back: their insoluble mass, their girth, a solid darkness in the basin, and their windows slightly blacker than the sky. She walked on. She turned up the shortcut toward the gorge. Her flip-flops slipped in a mudslide, and she fell and she stood and she fell again, and she lost her floppy hat, and she was nothing but mud and blood and more mud, and the shortcut was a stupid and dangerous and crazy idea that she should have known better than to take. If she had walked another way, she might have become someone else.

Somewhere, a cockroach flew across the sky, and across the lower realms, tarantulas were on the crawl. They'd been on the move all day, but only her grandfather had appreciated these portents of a storm. Toads, caught off guard, hopped for cover, while leopard frogs emerged to take the water. Salamanders held tight, their rubbery toes grasping mesquite shrubs that were flicking in the wind. Small birds dissolved in the bushes. Most frightened creatures hid: no free-tailed bats, no barred owls, though the sympathetic darkness of the blotted day might have drawn them out. Snakes arose to feed on the pocket mice running for their pockets. No one could say which was better: being swallowed whole by a snake or drowning in a pocket in the earth. The squirrels in the tree trunks were safer, though the wind sheared the rain at a hard angle so even the hollows filled up. Higher in the trees, hatchlings took cover beneath their mothers' wings, and some of them were lucky, but most were not. The tantrum wind like a tidal surge lifted up their nests and sailed them to the ground. Only insects, being boneless, could survive such falls. Red fire ants came up in the millions, pouring jelly-like out of the earth, evacuating their subways in the high limestone walls of a newly formed river. Huddled together, they melded their bodies into an organic raft, rising with the waters in the gorge. The ants at the bottom died, but even dead, they didn't let go, and the colony above was prepared to drift for weeks.

Over the pounding rain, Connie heard rushing water, where there'd been a dry gulch when her cousins went down to play. She heard a familiar voice shouting for them, and saw the beam of a flashlight but not the hand that held it. Like the sun, which was gone but not descended, her grandmother was hidden by the rain. The old woman's thin voice cut through the dark, over the roiling torrents of the flood.

"Gran!" Connie shouted back, but the switchback wind returned the word to her mouth.

Connie stumbled toward the torchlight, and, unless there was nothing to see because the world had ended, in which case her sight was perfect, the crossways rain blinded her. She didn't have the third eyelid of a bird that blinks sideways in the horizontal rain. After wiping her eyes, they promptly filled again. She couldn't see the nearby cliff, but she heard the white waters below. They pounded under her feet, hurling themselves at the gorge's pliant banks.

"Gran!" Connie howled at the storm.

"Connie, that you?" cried her grandmother.

"Me, Gran," Connie called.

And following each other's voices, the two moved closer.

"Oh, thank God. You got the children?"

"I –" Connie said, but she never finished the sentence.

Waves slammed beneath the levee where she and her grandmother were standing. The gorge walls gave way, the ground split, the levee slipped into the torrent. And because *I* and *aye* sound the same, if that's what the old woman heard, I call it a mercy.

As Connie's feet shot out from under her, a hidden tree root heaved from the earth and smacked her head and snagged her hair and held her by the plastic bag for a moment, before the bag ripped through. Holding fast to the tree root, she pulled herself back to the ledge.

She shouted for her grandmother but got no answer, nothing. Or at least nothing human: rain and black wind and whitecaps, and hundreds of shredded and mobilized things. She called out for Carol but heard nothing. Billy, nothing. Jacob and Arnold, nothing. Tatsie and Quentin, nothing. She spat mud from her lips and howled for everyone again.

The spasmodic rain departed. The wind gusted as if cleaning up. As the clouds moved away, the sun could be seen still setting, a pink glow above the peaks. In the domical sky, the first stars appeared, and though they might have shuddered, nothing up there had altered. But closer down, the whole world had changed. The range was split wide open. Along the ragged banks of a churning river, an enormous bloated bull hung upside-down in a tree. A glass peanut-butter jar sailed by, miraculously intact, the scorpion inside alive.

The rain had gone, and her gran had gone. The ground where she'd stood was no longer ground. And the cousins, though Connie hadn't seen them to say they were ever there, had gone.

As she walked the rim and surveyed the changes, Connie found only two bodies. Quentin and Tatsie were wrapped in each other. His Spider-Man T-shirt coiled around his neck. The Walmart bangles Tatsie wore on her wrists sutured to her tiny biceps. The river had chewed on the children and spat them out.

Connie staggered, dropped her head back, grasped her hair and pulled as hard as she could, but the pain did not make the horror disappear. She knelt beside the luckless children. Her grandmother had told her that the eldest was born to protect the youngest, and her grandfather had warned her that a storm was coming. But thinking only of herself, Connie had not brought the little ones home. She wanted never to think about herself again. Never.

She picked up the dead boy and hooked him on her hip. She leaned down again and picked up the dead girl. It was a slow hard slog through the mud to the ranch. She tripped and dropped them. She turned aside. In her anguish, she vomited tequila into the mire. Then she braced herself and lifted them up again.

If he'd had sight, her grandfather might still not have known what thing it was lumbering toward him. She was brown and red. She was black plastic. She wore panniers of two small corpses. He stood on the porch, not with the intention to greet her but to come as close to the evil of the day as an almost-blind man could. He could see her coming, but he could not know who or what she was.

"Who are you?" he called.

"Connie," she called back.

Then she said it again, as if trying to make it true.

When she reached the porch, she couldn't let go of the two dead children on her hips. Her arms had stiffened around them like dead things themselves. Her grandfather had to peel them off her.

"The others?" he asked as he laid them down and leaned close to the two small faces to decipher whom to mourn. And because death is indecent, he covered his youngest grandchildren with a black industrial tarp.

"None of them," she answered.

Her grandfather would not believe it.

"You saw their bodies? You *saw* them?"

"No," she said, "I saw no one."

There was uncertainty enough to give false comfort.

"And your gran?" he said.

"She was there – I heard her – then she wasn't."

"You didn't *see* her?"

"No."

"Your gran don't die that easy."

He would not believe the worst, not until the waters gave up their bodies, or the cowboys returned empty-handed. The boys were already scouting the range.

Tortured by the clock's tick, they waited in the living room near the empty hearth. The rain had come and gone and taken away everything except the heat. Connie longed to call her parents, but the rotary phone was dead.

Her grandfather sat stiffly, chewing on his lips. It seemed if the cowboys didn't get back soon, he'd eat himself alive.

She paced from the living room to the hall to the kitchen, where the collie in the corner raised its head and watched her. She dried herself with a dishcloth, and it turned black. She threw it in the laundry pile, then retrieved it because, absurdly, she didn't want to part with it.

She found fresh cookies in the oven. They hadn't burned. She fed the collie one and took one for herself and stared at it. When she finally put it in her mouth, she couldn't swallow.

We all know the heart breaks, but the reality is the stomach is the first to go. She spat the cookie in the sink. The bolus sat there, a small butte in a stainless steel desert.

She stared out the window above the sink, gazing through the dark. Visible beyond the kitchen garden, beneath a heavy plywood cover, was a large hidden hole in the earth. The beef continued to slow-cook in the firepit, which glowed like an excavated city whose lamps were still ablaze. The rain had not damped it out.

Returning to the living room, Connie found, just where she'd left it in a different world, her granddad's little pink book. It was a Victorian travelogue, written by a Scotsman as he crossed the American continent. Connie turned it over and over, as if trying to decipher a secret meaning. She pulled the string on the standing lamp to see better, but the power was down to the solar panels.

The clock ticked and ticked and ticked, and the silence between the ticks was hell. In an attempt to shut out the clock and fill the gaps, straining to see in the gloom, Connie began to read aloud. And the collie came in from the kitchen, and because dogs know much without words, laid its head in the old man's lap.

"Monsters," she read, "as conjured by the dreams of children, are said to inhabit these godless lands, savaged by heat. The gila lizard, unlucky fellow, a warty prehistoric specimen, lives alone beneath these ancient rocks. It is given to us to wonder if even Noah's faith faltered briefly before he allowed it aboard his ark. Worse yet are the stories the red men tell, who dwell here like purgatorial ghosts, disappearing as suddenly and silently as they appear. Oh for a patch of grass! Oh for a Highland summer! When one of our party inquired, 'What, Sir, is the name of that flat-topped hill?' the native man informed him, 'Nah-yeh.'

"'And what does Nah-yeh mean, Sir?' he asked.

"'Monster,' said the man, lacking all irony or guile. 'But it's a dead monster. That there,' said the native man, pointing to the baked earth from which he had seemed to take the color and texture of his skin, 'is the blood of monsters. The heroes killed them long ago, but the land kept their corpses.'

"'Surely the corpses would have decomposed!' my compatriot objected. To this the man merely shook his head."

When she paused to turn the page, it was her grandad who shook his head. "Connie," he said, "stop." He did not need to yell it. His quietness was a kind of scream. Accustomed to hollering from his horse across the desert's illimitable distances, his voice had never been so quiet.

As if it were written for children, the book was small enough to hold in one palm, and though Connie flipped it shut, it did not remain so. The velvet and cardboard ends being warped, it reopened of its own accord, and the pages parted one from another.

When the cowboys at last returned, they were empty-handed except for their hats. They did what was prescribed in times like this, as if there had always been times like this: they held their Stetsons and stared at the ground, and no one chewed gum, smoked, shuffled his feet, or coughed.

Connie looked at Henry. There was something in the way he eyed the floor, as if in the scrubbed floorboards he could see her reflection and was sorry for what he saw.

There was no more to be done till dawn. There was no point in searching further. The black moon was a plug in the sky, and surely by now the bodies would have traveled as far as the next county, where the newborn river would deposit them with its bed load along the shores.

The old man looked down at his dog, its black head like a box of ashes in his hands. He did not look at the cowboys, for if he raised his eyes, the world would crack.

"You informed the county sheriff?" he asked.

"Sheriff can't do nothing."

The old man looked up. "It's his bleeding job to do something!"

"Sheriff's got bigger problems."

Just saying there were such things as bigger problems seemed an act of cruelty. But they were trying to tell the truth, though they only knew a slice of it, and the full reach of the day would take months, years, even centuries to discover. Sandbags blocked Interstate 10 and the feeder roads had been closed, and neither FEMA nor the National Guard were on their way.

"Radio says they're heading for the coasts," said Henry.

The radio told them much more.

It revealed a scale so vast it mocked the grief of a grandfather, setting it side by side with an entire world's despair. That a hurricane had rerouted and swept away the old man's loved ones was as small, in the tragic scheme of things, as his youngest grandchildren.

In a span of twelve hours, Greenland's Jakobshavn Glacier had calved over a quarter of its ice mass into the ocean, causing tsunami after tsunami to hit international seaside cities. LA had lost Huntington Beach and Long Beach, which was nothing compared to Manhattan, Boston, and Barcelona, and a surge up the Thames to London. Everywhere, everything was reduced to nothing, nothing on a scale that no one had before imagined.

"Oh my God, Scotland!" Connie cried.

The Seven Hills of Edinburgh were islands. She would never go home again. She would never give her mother that kiss.

She steadied herself on the back of her grandfather's chair and turned the words she'd offered Quentin on herself. *Be tough.*

They listened until the radio could only repeat itself. Then Henry and another cowboy stepped onto the porch to fetch the corpses, and a mean wind blew through the hallway. The bones of history, turned to dust, seethed along the floor, and the drip pan on the hall tree filled with dirt. As the door hung open, decimated bougainvillea petals danced across the floor and a spider whirled on an invisible line and dropped into the flowery purple sea.

Henry returned carrying Tatsie. The other cowboy, carrying Quentin, closed the door with his bootheel. They carried their small, light burdens up the stairs to lay them on a bed.

Connie turned to follow.

"Constance," her granddad said.

He reached out his rough hands to comfort her, but rape and loss had enclosed her in their cell, and she couldn't bear to be touched.

"I'm here," she called from the stairs.

She'd strip, wash, and dress the dead kids while the cowboys built two coffins to be lowered out the window.

"I'll be down when I'm done," she said.

So much she didn't know or feel. She didn't feel the two fertile eggs inside her, or the Y sperm burrowing into the right and the X sperm into the left, about to commence innumerable divisions into the spawn of two nameless fathers, though their own names, Tom and Tam, would become the *rat-a-tat* of machine guns and the sound of bursting seedpods. She did not know what was taking place within her was even a possibility: superfecundation, common enough in cats and dogs but exceptionally rare in humans, the fertilization of two ova in a single estrus by sperm from sequential males, producing twins who are genetically half-twins. She didn't know that she was rare.

Her belly grew as she got thinner. Her feet swelled, and her grandmother's riding boots pinched her toes, and in the mornings she vomited on horseback. She rode to check the fences and brought salt blocks to the summer fields and brought hay to the high elevations and yodeled to call the herd. She learned to rope.

The sun beat down hard, and it was a new dark world for those who'd survived the old one. She roped with four cowboys, until she roped with three. When the world economy collapsed, and Wall Street was physically underwater and, down in the valley, the building society closed, she couldn't even pay for two. She held onto the last one by grit, but eventually it had to be faced: she couldn't pay Henry either.

Having packed his duffel, tomorrow at dawn, he'd be hiking to I-10 and hitchhiking out. Where he was going he didn't say, and probably didn't know. But he had never worked harder than on his final day, hoping if he worked without tiring, the day would never end. He sucked the dregs from the hours, like a bat sucks on the night blooms of organ pipe cactus, having traveled six thousand miles to do just that.

When he couldn't see to work anymore, he stood on the porch and said to Connie, "Say goodbye in the morning?"

"Yeah," she said, having learned an economy of words.

Henry had a surprising surplus of them, and again delaying the end of the day, he picked up a new conversation like an old tin of nails. "If your pony slips on a high trail, you make sure to jump off uphill. Promise you won't jump downhill, or the horse is gonna crush you, okay?"

"Okay."

He was telling her how things worked again, and he looked her straight in her blue eyes, though in the darkness the blue was black.

"It seems obvious," he said, "but obvious don't mean nothing when you're scared."

"Scared of what?" she asked.

"Falling," he fudged, though he typically said what he meant.

"You mean scared of dying," she said.

"Yeah, that too."

"I'm not scared of dying," she said, and didn't offer a description of the hot pregnant nights in her coffin room when death sounded a lot like freedom.

"You still not afraid of the dark?" he asked.

"Just some of the people in it," she said, and glanced down at her belly and beyond it to her varicose veins.

She was resting her bootheel on a wooden Coca-Cola box that had been kicking about the yard for generations, and her grandmother's prairie skirt had slipped above her knee, revealing the blue veins whose valves had given way with pregnancy: a couple of indigo snakes had coiled themselves into the shadow of her knee.

"They're ugly," she said.

"Nah, just life," said Henry.

"You think they look like snakes?" she asked.

"Looks more like a map to me."

"A relief map," she said, pushing at the bulge. "A map of a faraway country," she mused, "where no one's ever been."

"Yeah," said Henry, "'cept somebody's been everywhere."

He was talking about the wind again. He talked about the wind a lot. But she could see that he was tired, and they couldn't go on talking all night.

"Say goodbye in the morning," she said to end it.

"Yeah."

He tipped his hat, and she set her jaw as he walked away, in preparation for the same in the morning. She watched him as he staggered back to his cabin to collapse on his cot exhausted and to sleep quick and deep, still in his jeans and boots.

She didn't plan to join him, but later, after the moon moved upward and Orion set, when her legs walked in the direction of the hands' cabin, there wasn't a watchful creature in the world who was surprised.

Henry didn't awaken when Connie knocked and opened the door and whispered his name and sat beside him. By the crescent moonlight, she watched him sleep on his side, the dry heels of his hands in his closed eyes and his hair, heavy with sweat, cloying at his neck. Even her gaze didn't wake him. But when she lay down beside him and curled her back into his chest, though he didn't speak, he slid his hand around her belly.

A roped calf will lie inert, but Connie was the opposite. In Henry's rough-cut hands, she came untethered. Her mouth closed tight, she shook all over, and when she couldn't help but open it, though she stopped shaking, she sobbed. Henry didn't say, "Don't cry." He didn't try to stop her. He just moved his hand softly back and forth. She was snotty and puffy and reeked of loss, and her ugliness was her beauty. She sobbed until she slept, and he slept too.

It was still dark when both of them opened their eyes, as if awoken by a sound that no technology could record. Connie pulled closer to Henry, and Henry took down his jeans, and neither said a word, but she gave him permission, and he slid inside her.

Henry gently woke her further from the inside. Inside, where she was all-enveloping, Connie held him tight. The momentum of the world paused, and in their embrace was infinite space. Sometimes there was one person, then again there were two people, and once again there was one person, then two; some instants there was no one. It felt more like unmaking than making, but love was made regardless. They tensed. They gasped. They softened. And when, at last, they slept again, Henry abided in her, until he slipped away as all men must.

Because they were ordinary people, the extraordinary happened: there, on a cot in a cabin, where scorpions dodged in and out of holes in the mortar, the two of them fell in love.

In the morning, no goodbyes. Henry unpacked his duffle and returned his Johnny Ringos to underneath his cot. An aficionado of the two-step, he only ever wore his good boots for dancing but would never dance again, because a day has only so many hours, and survival would take every second.

As he unpacked his duffle, Henry stared into the distance, which is also the future. He had a wind inside him that said go, move, walk, ride, roam, wander, and drift, but except for riding the fences, he would never heed it again. He stayed still for Connie because he loved her, and because she loved him.

He would watch her belly grow, then he would watch her children grow, and he would remember a worrisome story told to him by his Navajo grandmother.

Back in one of the early worlds, First Man and First Woman had forgotten how to love each other, and they so reduced marriage to possession, and flora and fauna to objects, that a woman stroking a fuzzy elkhorn gave birth to Horned Monster, and a woman tickling herself with a feather quill gave birth to Monster Eagle, and a crazy woman using a cactus quill gave birth to Monster That Kills with Its Eyes. The monsters rolled across the land for an entire era, killing whatever they found.

The word *monster* may seem fantastical, but another word will suffice. Psychopathy is thought to be a variation of the human genetic code passed between the generations to produce a human being who is arguably inhuman, whose ventromedial prefrontal cortex, controlling empathy and guilt, and whose amygdala, controlling fear, cannot register the emotional reality of others. In other words, a psychopath is born with a monstrous heart, a deficit – or benefit, from the point of view of ruthless dominance – which, in the random division of DNA, may or may not pass on to offspring.

Henry worried that Connie's children, fathered by monsters and conceived in the opposite of love, might be born as monsters themselves. But there is never just one story, and his grandmother had told him a second, which did not contradict the first but completed it, like a snake biting its tail.

It was the time of the monsters, but was also the time of Changing Woman, she-who-becomes-again-and-again. She was lonely in a big empty desert, and she looked up and there was the sun, and looked down and there was the water, coiling through the canyon, where she stopped to rest and bathe. When the sun and water fell in love with her, the sun shone down into her and the river rushed up into her, and the two of them made her pregnant with two babies: Monster Slayer and Child of the Water. The twins had been born to rid the world of monsters, but first they needed time to grow up. When a monster knocked on her juniper hut and shouted, "I want to eat your kids," Changing Woman hid her kids and lied, "I don't got no kids." And when he swore he'd seen their footprints in the dirt, she lied again: "I make those myself when I get lonely." With white lies and fortitude, she gave her children time to grow up.

The morning after lovemaking, Henry kissed Connie one more time, and the man and the woman rode out together to bring salt blocks to the cows and check the fences for breaches, through which a monster might one day enter or a headstrong bull break free.

III

TOM AND TAM

Armed with a rifle, Connie stood guard in the dormer window of the master bedroom. In her holster sat her granddad's antique pistol, which he didn't need anymore, because he was asleep on a cot in the basement, where he'd moved to escape the heat and light. Light and darkness were the only options left to him, and his blind eyes preferred the latter. The rest of the family had worked all night to mend the busted Ford.

Down below in the yard, Henry was visibly submerged beneath the open hood, his mustang tethered to the pickup's side mirror. By moonlight, he'd replaced the brake fluid hose and jerry-rigged a dozen other fixes. Now, racing against the dawn, he was adding a final bungee cord while Tom perused his route to the war front.

A dog-eared map lay on the ground, and Tom's draft card smoldered amid the trash in the oilcan incinerator in the parched and wind-struck yard. Though the draft card called him "Thomas MacAllister", Tom wasn't "Thomas" anymore than Tam was "Tamara". Their names weren't short for anything, nor were they named for anyone, unless Tam was named for Tom when, instead of an afterbirth, a second child had emerged as a surprise from Connie's womb.

Studying his map, Tom squatted on his undercut bootheels. He was dark and handsome, but his good looks were cold and not a single drop of sweat showed on his skin in ninety degrees at dawn. Behind him, Tam was crouching, her thick pale arms coiled around her brother's neck. A rifle strapped to her back nosed up behind her head.

"Happy seventeenth," said Tam, whose birthday it was too.

"Back at you," said Tom and smiled or snarled at his sister; no one could presume to say which.

He'd mastered bait-and-switch: kill-you-as-soon-as-look-at-you one moment, chill-as-death the next, and charming-as-hell if it helped him get what he wanted. *I want* were his favorite words, whether the object of his wanting was benign or blasted evil.

Tom had not as yet shot a creature bigger than a dog. And his sister was the one with a rifle hitched over her shoulder. But if you'd seen him squatting on his haunches in a landscape of bones, he'd have chilled you to yours.

"Wish you were a girl?" asked Tam.

Taller and beefier than her brother, Tam defied the Christian Brigade phenotype charts in which females were portrayed as shorter, weaker, genetically insubstantial, and unfit for war. No draft card had arrived as a birthday present for her, because Unemployed Conscription was limited to out-of-work male Outsiders, aged seventeen and up, resident in the renegade West or the New East's extra-domal wastes.

The CBA and Govcorps, who did not share a bottom line, one glorifying an end time and an afterlife escape for the chosen and the other legislating the Earth's annihilation in service to their shareholders' ongoing pleasure, had, behind closed doors, battled over gender, and the CBA had won. Girls had been made exempt from the draft. Concerning dodgers, however, the alliance spoke as one: punishment was to be determined by the technologies at hand, be it hanging, beheading, drowning, firing squad, or burial alive.

Tom dropped his chin to his sister's fists, and they fused into a two-headed creature. The two were so inseparable that their great-granddad had quit calling them "Tom n' Tam" and had nicknamed them "TNT". They formed a single explosive entity, but they looked alike only to the legally blind.

Tom was dark like his dark-haired father. A high-and-tight recon cut with a short Mohawk landing strip hid beneath his cowboy hat. He was dressed in a dirt-gray tee, black jeans, black Stetson, black pinched Johnny Ringos – Henry's old good ones, which, being too small for Tom, hurt just enough to satisfy his need for pain to feel alive.

Similar to her own father, Tam was pale where she wasn't tan. Her long blond hair reached to the middle of her back. She was big-boned, long armed, and long-legged. Her soiled frock, with wide pockets, had sleeves too short for her strong wrists. The hemline rode above her knees, and over her ample breasts, the fabric fell like a waterfall in a flash flood, though born into perpetual drought she'd never seen a body of water bigger than a kitchen sink, except on TV, while it lasted.

They didn't look like twins, and yet despite their dissimilarity, they resembled each other, because the degradation of place is conjugate to the ruin of persons, and Tom and Tam were the hour they were from.

Out of nowhere, sonic booms. Into a semi-peaceful morning, there was the intrusion of jets. As a formation of F-15XX Silent Eagles broke through the sky, Tam released her grip on her brother in order to shield her ears. Displaying some difference from his sister, Tom did not cover his ears – if anything, they perked up.

"You like the roar?" Tam yelled to Tom.

"Fucking love it," he yelled back.

The shadows of steel birds leaned on the foothills, but when the Eagles roared overhead, the cattle barely heard them. The booms had deafened the five surviving bulls and twenty cows, only three robust enough to carry a calf to birth.

The shadows crossed Tom's face, as his engine-oily fingers traced a lubricous route from his mother's home to the front. Once upon a time in America, a teenage cowboy had wanted nothing better than to rush off to fight for his country, but when Govcorps blew the peaks off the mountains and redirected the rain, most had learned to tell the difference between their country and their country. God-fearing ranchers, whose churches had denied The Change and who'd applauded corporate profits as their historical entitlement, now pointed their guns in the direction to which previously they'd bowed. And hardscrabble kids risked draft dodging in order to join the Outlaws.

Tom's rendezvous with the Outlaws was set for south of Phoenix at a defunct municipal dump. Squatting over his map, he was contemplating the route. Interstate 10-E via 33.4484° N, 112.0740° W (Phoenix) and south, four hours and forty-three minutes at seventy miles a clock hour if you were a slogger or a corp or a shareholder with an insulated SUV. But eight hours minimum if you were Tom. Or no time at all, because a boy in a pickup would be lucky to make it past 33.8303° N, 116.5453° W (Palm Springs) alive.

"Taking Highway Ten?" asked Tam.

"Gotta," said Tom.

"Ten's dangerous," said Tam.

"Yeah, so what?" said Tom as the sun began to lip the mountains. "Everywhere is fucking dangerous."

He traced the route for his sister: he'd turn off the 10 toward the Salton Sea and zigzag down old state roads, crossing the Gila River and its Indian Reservation, which was printed a tawny yellow as if to designate a wasteland even before The Change. But the map wasn't reliable, a mere approximation, because no map could keep up with the times. Blue lines designated rivers where rivers couldn't be found. Like Outlaws hiding in their caves, many rivers had disappeared underground.

"Going to Gila," Tam singsonged as she pinched and killed a spider crawling up her brother's neck.

Tom wiped his dry mouth. Engine oil painted his lips. In the nearby oilcan, his draft card crackled in the fire. Against the low rising sun, he tipped his hat, and his upper face disappeared and the bottom drew back in shadow.

Wind smudged the map with sand. Scrapings swirled in the yard. A tumbleweed snagged against the open hood of the old Ford pickup and shattered like an ice sculpture. As the wind blew, the hours scrambled, and seven generations from the past infiltrated seven generations in the future. Time, trash, and the corpse-dust of a hundred creatures mingled in the wind, which carried the scent of Drifters, those millions without homes who walked the highways till they dropped, so desperate they'd slit your throat for a tin of lard.

Tam stood up when the wind howled. A hunter herself, she knew that hunters were mimics, and there was no saying for sure if the wind was really the wind. With so many boys dodging, Henry buying a brake fluid hose at the Higgly Piggly was enough to rouse suspicion and draw a corp squad up to the ranch.

Fingering her Remington, Tam scanned the brightening wastes. Somewhere over the horizon, like somewhere over the rainbow, the future's horrors were out there, but for the moment, nothing. No special-op corp squads storming up over the gorge. No eyes on the MacAllister ranch, unless the crows were spies. No manhunters in pursuit, but the sun was still rising. Tam disappeared around the side of the house to confirm that the howling wind, now rustling the corn, was nothing but wind in corn. She'd been back and forth all night.

"Almost done?" Tom called to Henry.

"I could use three hands," Henry called back.

Tom left his map to join him, and crossing the yard, he crushed a mound of beetles. Always some plague or other. The lane was tarred with insects.

Tom squinted into the sun, which was cresting the blown-off peaks. The effect in his retinas thrilled him: the sun appeared to burst and explode into a thousand tiny stars. Glad to take credit for everything, whether real or imagined, and responsibility for nothing, Tom enjoyed his illusory power. Fake it till you make it, right?

Henry lowered the Ford's hood slowly, so as not to shy the mustang tied to the side mirror. He said, "Pray that bungee holds."

"It'll hold," said Tom, whose recklessness masqueraded as bravery, which technically it was not, because bravery is contingent on the ability to actually feel fear before you overcome it.

"You so sure?" said Henry.

"It'll hold cause it's gotta," Tom said, kicking at the shiftless dirt.

As he wrestled with doubt, Henry appraised the Ford, whose chassis hung low with munitions. Much of the MacAllister gun collection was being donated to the Outlaw cause. A utility chest mounted to the bed held a wealth of ammunition and four Colt man-stoppers, three semiautomatics – one Simonov, one Chinese lookalike and one 3D-printed – two antique muzzleloaders and a Winchester Model 1892 with a mother-of-pearl sight blade. The semiautomatics had never seen action beyond shooting tin cans off the porch, but one of the man-stoppers had killed its owner, and the shameful Winchester had slaughtered a family of Comanche in their tepee.

"When you get to the dump," Henry said, "don't wander away from the guns. Wait as long it takes. The Outlaws will show when they show. And no one is gonna go look for you if you wander away from the guns."

"I know what to do," said Tom, who, right or wrong, always knew what to do and, whatever he did, was so unapologetic he could convince you it was right.

"You remember what to say if you're pulled over?"

"I'm driving to Phoenix –" said Tom.

"Don't say Phoenix," said Henry. "Corps hate it if you use the name. Just say the trucking town. They'll know where you mean."

"Sure," said Tom, but then said it again. "I'm driving to Phoenix, where my friend, who works as a slogger, has got me a slogging job too."

Now Tam rounded the side of the house, having completed a check of the chicken coop and the hands' cabin and the corn rows in the kitchen garden, delineated by a line of children's gravestones. She moved through the ruined orchard, weaving between avocado pits, which were as hard as she and Tom were and, like the two of them, waiting for the rain to root.

Tom called to her, "Get my smokes."

"Where are they?" Tam asked.

"In the bedroom."

The bedroom was Tam's bedroom, which had previously belonged to Connie, who had never given her children permission to share the tiny bed, though that is what they'd done. Tom was bad with boundaries. What was his was his, and what was Tam's was his too, including the coffin room.

Tam disappeared into the house. She did as she was told. That she obeyed her brother did not mean she was a good girl; it just meant she was good at obeying.

"She's gonna miss you," said Henry. He rubbed his eyes with his greasy hands and the bags underneath blackened.

"You think so?" asked Tom. And then he asked without sympathy, "You tired?"

"Wish I could be," said Henry, for whom sleep would have to wait, because a morning couldn't pass without securing the property's borders, what he still called riding the fences. "But I got too much to do."

Henry glanced up at Connie, stationed in the dormer window. She was peering down the sight of her rifle, aimed at the dry gorge, in case anything moved that shouldn't. Having taken up the weapon later in life, she wasn't the expert shot that her children were, but marksmanship ran in her blood and she could knock a can off a wall okay.

"See anything?" Henry called up to her.

"Nothing but nothing," Connie called down, lowering the gun.

They smiled sadly at each other. They both of them smiled slow as the slow rising of a kestrel in open country: it flies into the headwinds, it hovers there, it inspects the lizard-looking thing unmoving on the ground; the thing turns out to be a brake fluid hose; the kestrel tilts its wings and lifts slowly on the wind. There weren't kestrels anymore, but in a world gone to hell, a person smiled when they could, though usually they smiled sadly.

Connie returned to scanning the horizon, from which no good news comes – according to official news outlets, Govcorps were invariably victorious, and even back channels admitted that Outlaw victory was rare. They were outnumbered and out-armed and lacked central command, unified action, and a leader.

Wiping his palms on his jeans, Henry said to Tom, "It should be me going."

"Going to war?" Tom laughed. When Henry didn't laugh with him, Tom told him why it was funny: "You're old, old man."

Tom was flint striking itself, and life would be more peaceful without him, but he was still the closest thing to a son that Henry (who was thirty-something) had. So Henry grabbed his hand with both his own, held it awkwardly a moment and then reluctantly let Tom go.

Henry unfastened the reins from the pickup's side mirror and swung himself up on his ramshackle steed, which looked as held together by its high-cantle saddle as the Ford was by the bungee cord. From the mustang's offside, he pulled his rifle from its scabbard and propped it on his shoulder. He touched his hat in the manner that he always did on parting.

Riding away on his piebald horse, who'd gone bald around the muzzle, Henry began to whistle. The uneven tune wasn't happy, but it gave forewarning to potential predators, who are particularly dangerous when surprised. Wolves and wildcats were gone, but dogs and humans remained, and the rule pertained to them as well.

The lone horseman rode beyond a meager cow shading itself beneath a basalt rock, like an eroded rock itself, and dissolved into the withholding distance. Then the sun breached the shorn-off mountains, beyond which was the war. It was suddenly time for Tom to go.

"Con! Con!" Tom shouted at the master bedroom window, and he took his impatience out on the pickup's hood.

From the date they learned to talk, he and Tam had called their mother by her abbreviated first name, as if she had no greater distinction than being the tallest amongst them.

"What you waiting for, Con?" he shouted as he pounded on the hood. "I gotta fucking go!"

The wind rattled the dormer hard, and something resembling window putty dropped onto the sill. It was a solid wad of Nicorette, which Connie, who was trying to give up smoking, had stuck to the glass to chew again later. Popping it in her mouth, it sat there without moistening.

"Hold your horses," she called down, stepping away from the window, deep into the master bedroom, a term that mocked her – for if there was a master on Earth, it definitely wasn't her.

As her son banged his presence into the unfortunate Ford, she returned her rifle to the rack, took the bone-handle pistol from the holster on her waist, and deposited the antique gun inside an alligator clutch purse of similar vintage, fashioned in the days when no one thought twice about accessorizing the body parts of creatures.

The pistol was to provide Tom some protection in an emergency, and it was traveling in a handbag because Christian Brigade reductionism cast females as seductresses but otherwise as harmless. If the Ford was stopped and searched, corps would check in the glove compartment, under the seats, and in the utility chest before they deigned to open a symbol of feminine weakness that a scatterbrained woman had left on the passenger seat. The purse would give Tom time to do his worst.

But it was too small to contain both a pistol and a piggybank's worth of cash, and her son needed money too. So, removing a sunhat from where it hung limply on a hook beside the gun rack, Connie dropped the bank into the crown. Then she smashed it with a lump of petrified wood, whose metamorphosis into rock over millions of years in oxygen-minimal zones of mineral-laden water made her own transition from sweet-sixteen to over-the-hill look easy. Now the heads of Truman, Washington, and Jefferson streamed across the remnants of a pig.

Lastly, into the purse, she squeezed the petrified wood, which her granddad years ago had stolen from far-off lands. It was time that it went home. Tom could take it as far as the dump, where drones would reduce it to sand, and the remaining two hundred miles to its Petrified Forest homeland would be up to wind and birds.

"Con! Con!"

Outside, the sun was ever rising. It sat low on the horizon, as innocuous as a neon bulb, but it would be hellfire by high noon.

Connie rushed to the open window and warned, "You'll break the bungee if you bang like that, Tom!"

And she pulled from her pocket a rabbit-foot keychain that was supposed to bring good luck and was as close to a desert hare as anyone had seen since small mammals hightailed it north. From the rabbit foot hung the entirety of circumscribed life: keys to front and back doors, barn door, shed door, cabin door, chicken coop hatch, trapdoor to the root cellar, living room display cabinet, and the Ford ignition key. She removed the car key from the ring and flung it out the window, and it landed at Tom's feet like buckshot in the dirt. "Warm her up," she instructed.

Soon it wasn't warm but hot, and Tam was the one guilty of delaying Tom's departure. Having returned to the house for yet more provisions, she was taking forever.

Tom sat behind the wheel, studying his map, which had split down its seam, and he was turning it this way and that. Restless, he perched his foot on the window ledge, then stuck it in his crotch, then kicked it back into the footwell. In the passenger seat, the sunhat of coins sat by the purse with the rock and gun. In the Ford's bleak interior, the dash ashtray slumped on its springs, inviting another cigarette.

Standing outside the Ford, a Nicorette pebble in her mouth, Connie felt her resolve to quit smoking start to slip away. Gray-red with sunburn and dirt, her white shirt yellow in the pits, and blackness under her nails, she stood stiffly on the same tired feet that had stood her upright all night.

"Is Tam coming?" she asked.

"She's coming," answered Tom, which would prove surprisingly honest.

Tam at last emerged from the house with her rifle slung

over her shoulder, a picnic basket in the crook of her muscular arm and a bottle of whiskey in her hand. In her armpit, she held a paperback book. Previously barefoot, now she was wearing sneakers. As if they were going-away presents, she opened the passenger door and placed the book, bottle, and picnic basket on the passenger seat beside the purse and hat. Then she climbed onto the truck bed and, opening the utility chest, stowed her rifle with the rest of the gun collection.

"What are you doing?" Connie said. "You need your rifle."

Tam's next step was her answer: returning to the open passenger door, she squeezed into the small flip-down seat in the half-back behind her brother.

"Tam!" cried Connie. "Where do you think you're going?"

As if it wasn't obvious.

Tam reached forward and closed and locked the door.

Tom said, "I want her."

"I forbid it!" Connie cried.

But if Tam's free will amounted to choosing whom to obey, the choice had already been made. She was a big girl in a tiny flip-down seat, the ghost of her rifle slung over her shoulder as immobilizing as a splint.

Racing around to the open driver's window, Connie grabbed hold of Tom's arm and implored her son. "Tell her, Tom. Tell her not to. If you love your sister –"

"I want her," he said again.

Connie tightened her grip on his arm, believing he'd never shift her, for though the boy was strong, her will was stronger.

"Getting everything you want will ruin you," she said, sure her words had weight.

"How would you know, Con?" he said, as he pried her fingers off him. "When was the last time you got anything you wanted?"

And, without a goodbye, the Ford pickup tore off downhill.

As it careened down the rutted track, neither twin so much as glanced in the rearview mirror. It disappeared into the valley, and just like that, both of her children were gone.

Connie would write in her diary, "I never dreamt that Tom and Tam …" But Tom and Tam were exactly what she dreamed. What everybody dreamed.

An era seemed to pass as she stood in the lane, stunned and blindly witnessing the emptiness all around her. She refused to waste water by crying, but as the sun moved on and Connie stood still, it stung her eyes and they teared up.

At last; she entered the house and descended the basement stairs to find her granddad seated upright in his cot. Across a wooden packing crate lay his rifle, which he couldn't aim but which he could shoot. On the floor sat a bottle of tequila and a box of salt with a picture of a girl in a raincoat carrying an umbrella.

"That you, Connie?" he asked. When she sat down on the cot beside him, he bent close and smelled her. She reeked of sad insomnia. "What you been doing all night?" he asked and leaned away to light a cigarette off the flame of the lamp, a necessity he'd mastered even blind.

She took a swig from the tequila bottle, and the basement pipes, though empty of water, made a moaning sound. The liquor went to work, numbing her heart while breaking it, like baby Tom biting her nipple with the emergence of his first tooth and her rubbing liquor on his gums to numb his pain. Or maybe it was Tam. Sometimes she forgot.

"Where's TNT?" the old man asked.

In the rush, no one had told him. And what was the honest answer anyway? Ridding the world of monsters or becoming monsters? Her diaries hereafter would report only hearsay and myth.

Faced with a hidden future, Connie didn't have the heart

to pursue the truth. Whether it was a lie or a white lie or true enough, she answered, "It's still early, Granddad. Everyone's asleep."

Elsewhere, the Ford plunged into the valley.

The dirt turned into potted asphalt with mangled street signs. Fanciful names like Wonderland Road and prophetic ones like Red Sky Boulevard were bent double on themselves. The cul-de-sacs were empty. Smashed windows aired lifeless living rooms, graffiti adorned the walls, and Jacuzzis brimmed over with locust shells. A rockslide had buried a port-a-crapper where a kitchen extension had been started and renounced. And, like hard-cast tumbleweed, a recycling box blew along the sidewalk.

In the Higgly Piggly's parking lot, feral dogs slept beneath abandoned cars. A flat-footed woman, freeing a shopping cart from its chains, prepared to roll it down an empty alley. Propped against the automatic doors, which jittered open and shut indecisively, a Drifter with a pack threw a hunchback shadow on the concrete. No clue revealed his homeland: no filthy football jersey or *I Heart Somewhere* button from a bulldozed town in Sacrifice or from Chicago's South Side, discluded when the freshwater city was sealed.

The Higgly Piggly trudged on, but the grocery boy had left and was elsewhere living comfortably under the cover of a New Eastern dome. Eyeballing his victim's growing belly, as if it were some toxic merchandise she'd force him to price and stack, he'd been happy to skip town after the first mountain peak detonations, his family joining the Early Exodus, siphoning out a pass in the San Bernardinos.

Exiting the valley had become more challenging. The interstate arrow pointed at the ground, and at the intersection traffic lights the green and yellow bulbs were smashed and sunshine illuminated the perpetual red lamp. A law-abiding citizen might never find his way out of the valley.

But the Twins weren't law-abiders, and the town soon disappeared behind the Ford. Like a grave dug for a giant rattler, a bone-dry irrigation ditch edged the country road. On the far side of a split-wood fence, what was left of a longhorn herd was decimating what was left of the grasses. On the range rode a cowboy, who, like any remaining cowboy, still wore his Stetson and jeans, cutting a skinny, bent figure, with scars crisscrossing his arms in the shape of barbed-wire fences. He lifted his hand as the Ford sped by.

On the interstate on-ramp, Tom revved the engine, and Tam, in the seat behind him, laughed with pleasure, though, to their disappointment, the pickup spluttered and lurched as they attempted to accelerate along the heavily guarded highway. There was no pretending that their vehicle was supercharged or turbocharged or a hundred-thousand-horsepower. Empty transporters thundered past the Ford.

Though Hollywood had relocated and Disneyland was dead, the LA Port Authority remained busy 24/7. There, the leftovers of dome building and internal dwelling-systems – including uranium, coal, copper, potash, potassium chloride, and sodium sulphate – were packed onto freighters destined for Greater China. Paid by the load, sloggers had dumped their contents at the port and were racing up I-10 to Sacrifice for more. All up and down the east – west corridor, charged with protecting resource, Corporate Regional Police manned the exits and meridians. The cars were black-and-white PPVs, but municipal and state law enforcement had long been stripped of their coppers. No more good cop and bad cop. No one could trust a corp.

One thing hadn't changed: the biblical horsemen still rode. Billboards showed a red equestrian, traversing civil war and flames beneath a nuclear cooling tower, and a black rider, who was backdropped by the gifts of famine, plague, and injustice and a crumbling Mount Rushmore Lincoln. The meaning of the hooded wraith with scythe who accompanied the pale rider was sledgehammer-obvious, but as for the white rider – in one century thought to be Christ and in another considered to be the Antichrist – who could say what he was bringing? One clue was the picture of the snow globe, inside of which stood the White House – where the final president of the United States signed 666 executive orders and the Documents of Incorporation.

Tom grabbed for the gearshift to move into fifth but instead caught the neck of the whiskey bottle. He cussed and corrected his mistake. He was capable of irritation, impatience, desire, and anger, but the rest of the rainbow was missing, and he appreciated the fact. He believed that he – being better than other humans, almost a species apart, and able to function without the handicap of beclouding feelings – shouldn't ever make mistakes. And making them pissed him off.

As the rising sun struck Tom's eyes, the speedometer hit seventy, and the cab rattled as if the Big One had begun. The doors threatened to fall away, and rolling up the window didn't stop the shaking. A bar of sunlight slashed Tom's face, and the hollow in Tam's neck began to drip.

"God, it's hot," said Tam.

"You don't believe in God," said Tom.

"I do when I need Him," she said.

"Tom don't," said Tom.

"Tam does," said Tam.

They both had the disquieting habit of talking about themselves in the third person. Internal differences between them were significant but small, almost non-demonstrable, except in the amount they swore. Tom was the more foul-mouthed.

"But," Tam had defended him, back when they were children and their mother still had the power to send them to their rooms, "*fuck* ain't a cuss."

"It fucking is," Tom had said with pride.

"You know what you sound like?" Connie had said, as she marched him up to his bedroom.

"A Outlaw," Tom had answered, proud as hell.

"A corp," Connie had said.

It hadn't fazed him one bit.

If one child was an Outlaw, the other was an outcast, for Tam had no friend in the world except her brother, a fact that the absence of suitable buddies in the valley could not explain away.

Jamming the dash lighter into its socket and pulling it out and finding it dead, Tom said, "Nothing fucking works in this truck."

He lifted his rump off the seat. He fingered a matchstick from his tight front pocket, while two cigarettes, like buckteeth, protruded from his lips. Leaning over the seat back, as if he were entertaining a baby, he wobbled the glowing cigarettes up and down and prompted Tam to take one from his lips. Doing this while driving was one of his many talents. Another one was making smoke rings. He blew a perfect circle, then drilled a second ring into the first to forge a chain, while Tam made a noise of admiration and clapped. The smoke ring chain was reminiscent of their birth: his umbilical cord wrapped around her wrists like slimy handcuffs, Tom had dragged his sister into the world.

But it was hard to imagine Tam as a baby. Seated in the tiny half-back, she resembled a character from the *Mahabharata*, which Connie had read to them as children: Tam was the mythical giantess who tried to poison the infant Krishna with her breast milk.

Now, suddenly, the fun was over. Just ahead, on the shoulder, sat a string of PPVs and a corp holding a driver in a headlock on his steaming car hood.

Tom slumped deep into his seat and buried his face behind

his arm, ringed with dark tattoos. "I'm getting off the fucking highway," he said.

As if he commanded the universe and bent time and space to his will, he immediately flipped on his blinkers, which didn't blink, and instantly turned onto an off-ramp. There was no way out of the valley without a short stint on the highway, and that stint was over.

The Ford turned south toward the Salton Sea and the struggling town of Mecca, which maintained a strip mall with a dollar shop, a liquor store, a pawnbroker, and several storefront churches. Its tourist days were done. The country club had closed its doors after painting its putting greens emerald, and boarded-up seaside motels advertised slash-and-burn discounts. Because there were more huffers and junkies per capita in Mecca than even in LA, the mining complex on the Salton's southern shore drug-tested its workforce weekly.

Descending Route 86, spray-painted ("pray-painted") Jesus Fish abounded, and not one but a series of highway signs directed the scanty traffic to stop and admire the miracle: a four-story garbage Christ, constructed from a garish colormap of crimson plastic gas jugs, Bud cans and Classic Cokes, silver tinfoil bake trays, strident yellow sippy cups, and Styrofoam disposables. But if the upcycled God-man planned to walk on water, he'd have to do it fast: the Salton Sea was vanishing.

Viewed from a distance, the so-called sea looked beautiful. In its pink and reflective waters, it looked as if Heaven and Earth had merged like two great corporations. But, drawing closer, reality made itself visible. The Salton was a sewage dump that halobacteria had pinked, and it was growing increasingly saline without the monsoon rains. Along the receded shoreline were hillocks of tires and flip-flops. And as the Salton's waters receded, its violent history surfaced. Up from the depths came arrowheads and skulls, a long-ago flooded frontier town, and the restless monster, the San

Andreas Fault. One day, the Salton's waters would entirely cease to be liquid and become a meal of salt flats and dead tilapia.

The Ford chugged past a Brigader subsidiary church that was releasing its congregation. The faithful of all ages, wearing their Sunday best, stained with dust and dirt and splotched with baked beans and soup, were filing past a swimming pool, previously used for baptisms, now an enormous ashtray. Men in sweaty long-sleeved polos and women with covered heads, having received absolution and hope, were making their way on foot to the his-and-her segregated social club, where they would sip thrice-brewed coffee and discuss subjects befitting their gender about their exclusive personal salvation in the nearing apocalypse. Certain they knew the happy ending, they were eager to get to the end of the world's sorry story.

The Ford passed a huddle of under-draft-age teenagers in a vacant lot. The teens would have been huffing, but today they'd found some purpose: they were smashing up a microwave with rocks and baseball bats. A self-appointed demolition crew, home-educated experts on Stingray, Triggerfish, Gossamer, Finfisher, and other surveillance systems, the teenagers understood that any piece of junk could be a spy. They believed that someone somewhere cared enough to surveil them – though in fact no one did, because Meccans were deemed too lost, too faithful, or too stoned to warrant the cost.

Junkies lolled in the shade of their motor homes, and one euphoric tripper walked the interstitial wastelands between the lines of trailers. Splaying out her bloodied hands, she walked through fields of razor-ribbon cholla as if they were feathered grasses, and she felt no pain.

A skin-and-bones cow trotted down the road, while a corvid, riding on its back, pecked at its hide in search of ticks. The bird would hit an artery one day and kill its host and, much like a human being, travel on to find another meal until all hosts were dead and gone, and subsequently the corvid too.

Tom slowed the truck, feeling hungry.

"We're not supposed to stop," said Tam.

"Says who?" said Tom.

"Con and Henry."

"They ain't watching," he said.

He pulled the Ford into a parking lot that was empty of cars except for a dark-windowed SUV. Above a tin-roofed shack, a diner flag accordioned in the wind, one moment reading *din*, another reading *die*, then syncing up into a shapeless hieroglyph.

Over the splintered asphalt, two young malnourished girls were crawling on their chafed and bony knees. They were attempting to catch a horned toad, which despite its name was not a toad but a lizard, like the Salton Sea was not a sea but a watery dump. It had emerged, as if from its grave, through a crack in the crumbling pavement.

Tom called from his open window, "What you gonna do with it if you catch it?"

But the girls, who were so scrawny that their torsos could be birdcages, knew better than to talk to strangers.

So, as the Twins parked the Ford and checked that the guns in the bed were securely locked, they debated the question themselves.

"Play with it?" said Tam.

"Nah," said Tom, taking the sunhat of coins and passing his sister the alligator purse.

"Swallow it whole," said Tam.

It was the more likely outcome.

Two ravens circled in the sky and flew in perfect unison. One cawed and the other chortled, and they tipped their sable wings and purposefully collided. Recovering formation, they repeated this maneuver and its accompanying call and response.

Taught to pay attention to signs, the Twins paused to watch. Two ravens meant something, but what? There were conflicting interpretations. In Scotland, ravens were demons or the souls of murder victims. But up and down the indigenous Pacific coast, a raven's black feathers were a smokescreen to cover his body of light, and though Raven could not be trusted, He had created the Earth. They watched as the ravens' flight-loop widened, and the augury diminished until only one bird was audible, the higher pitch carrying farthest, the other voice inferred.

"You coming?" asked Tom.

"Yep, but first I gotta pee," said Tam, making a beeline for the outhouse.

It stank but was clean enough. No visible rats, and no black widow nesting across the hole. No dedicated toilet paper roll either, with its unblemished end folded into a V, an unimaginable luxury that Tam thought was fake news. A page from an antique *Farmers' Almanac* had been generously left on the floor.

When she joined her brother at the diner counter, Tam wanted to play the kind of game deserving of a road trip. "V for what?" she asked, plunging into the middle of the alphabet game, which she and Tom had played since learning their ABCs.

"V for violence," he answered, always eager to play a game, believing life and death were also a game, like *Mortal Kombat 64* and *Grand Theft Auto: Domes.* "S for what?" he asked, because alphabetic order had no place in a chaotic world.

"Sundown," Tam said.

"Don't be stupid," he said. "The right answer is snake."

Feeling his sister was stupid, he returned to his previous amusement of flirting with the waitress. He was excellent at the seduction game, so good, in fact, that when Tam ordered eggs over easy, the waitress was too hot, flustered, and confused to get it right. Instead of over-easy, a couple of pale-yoked eggs arrived sunny-side-down on the griddle.

Tom kicked his boots under the counter, making his stool spin around. Having procured the waitress's name, he asked, "Paula, you think owls get dizzy turning their heads three-sixty?"

(An owl's head rotates only half that.)

"There aren't no owls no more," said Paula, which was not absolutely true; for though most nocturnal eaters of desert hares had followed their prey northward, the tiny elf owl had stuck around, adapting to a mono-diet of beetles.

The diner door opened, and the two young girls from the parking lot ran in. One was carrying the lizard, which, scared to death, had inflated in size in her tiny skeletal hand. She held it up to the waitress, and though her body was diminutive, her enthusiasm was enormous.

"Look Paula, a horn toad!"

"That's something, all right," said the waitress.

"It's a tough something," said the other girl, reaching over her sister, and, with fingers as fragile as bat bones, giving the horned toad a pat.

"It lived underground with no water," said the girl with the prize in her hand.

"It came out a crack," said the other.

"Is it a miracle, Paula?"

"Is it Lazarus, Paula?"

"What should we feed it?" said the more pragmatic one, though the lizard appeared better fed than she was.

"Gosh, I don't really know," said the waitress.

So Tom and Tam stepped in.

"Spiders or scorpions," Tom said, as if he we were an expert.

"Scorpions," said Tam, "are gonna be easier to trap."

A scorpion was easy to trap because, despite a set of eyes

on the top of its head and another five sets in the corners, a scorpion's vision was poor.

Suddenly returning to the alphabet game, Tom said to Tam, "S isn't for sundown, it's for spiders, scorpions, snakes, or Satan. The s's have got to be poisonous. You know that."

"Sundown is poisonous too," said Tam.

"Sometimes," Tom agreed.

As the Twins talked between themselves, the worried little girls looked shyly from one twin to the other. Neither girl was as tough as a horned toad, and neither could survive a scorpion's sting, let alone a meeting with Satan. Having learned the hard way to avoid strangers, without another word, they took their lizard and retreated out the door.

A sign above the door asked them to COME AGAIN, and with a little luck they would, but their time on Earth was limited. There were other dangers than strangers: viruses followed the Drifter trails, and when the wind blew hard from Sacrifice, tailings entered the lungs. Death would come to the girls as surely as the screen door slamming closed behind them. But though the diner had lodged a security camera behind the COME AGAIN sign, it would not capture their deaths. When the hour came, the girls would pass into another world unnoticed.

The video camera in the COME AGAIN sign was not the deterrent that it intended to be. It didn't have a live feed to a corp station, it was just a rickety security cam producing grainy, choppy, and badly focused footage. But, after the fact, it would prove useful in deciphering exactly what happened in the diner.

Paula and Tom resumed flirting. Smiling, Paula's stained teeth, like a gray dusk, receded into her mouth.

Tom said, "You ever wear lipstick, Paula? You'd look good with lipstick."

"For special guys," she said.

"You think I'm special, Paula?"

"I got a feeling you might be."

"How about I prove it?" asked Tom.

"I got lippy at home," said Paula, and a flick of her hips made it overt that *home* was an invitation.

Watching Tom play with the waitress, Tam ate without expression. She had a talent for public solitude, which made her a good hunter. And with an excellent sense of timing, she knew her brother had no time to go "home." So she snapped open the alligator purse and dug past the bone-handle pistol and beyond the petrified wood to find an old tube of lipstick, dwelling beneath a wadded soiled tissue. She read the faded words at the bottom – *Red Pucker* – and passed the cosmetic to Tom, who passed it onto Paula.

"Put it on for me, Paula," said Tom. "Customer's always right."

As Paula twisted off the bullet-like lid, all revolutions conjoined, from the twirling of Tom's stool, to the head of an owl somewhere, to the sun's apparent circumambulation over the hot tin roof. Paula was happy to oblige, but as another customer flagged her down, she was forced to hurry off with the Red Pucker in her hand.

The only other guests in the diner were a well-heeled family of six, owners of the dark-windowed SUV. They were eating in defensive silence and attempting to take some semblance of refuge in the wall-mounted TV, where a newsman's obsidian desk gleamed like the *mizbeach* in the Bible. The newsman was announcing the latest extension of the war front: 106.3736° W to 111.4517° W by 32.9004° N to 38.4419° N. In a red hematite canyon, jets could be seen strafing the sandstone fangs of Spider Rock, where Spider Woman (who is nothing like the comic book character) had taught Navajo women to weave. The beating heart of resistance, the Four Corners was seen under siege, but the footage was, in fact, a rerun, while a patriotic soundtrack had replaced the blare of antiaircraft guns.

The family was clearly not from Mecca: the fish pendant around the mother's neck had a freshwater pearl for an eyeball, and the father and his scrub-faced kids wore breathable khaki baggies and platform sandals that enabled them to stand above the filth. The father's industry lapel pin, in low-conducting copper alloy, signified a New Eastern-import manager from the Salton mines, a first-year who'd ventured off the compound with his family to visit the garbage Christ. The ill-conceived outing had featured sewage stewing on the beach and breakfast in a grimy diner where food varnished the table. The whole family was in a lousy mood, though it was going to seem a pleasant one compared to what was coming.

When the father thrust a credit card into Paula's hand, she stared at it as if at a flattened reptile and passed the plastic back to him.

"Playing cards only," she joked.

Without humor, he observed, "You don't take American Unity."

"People pay coin or trade," explained Paula. "Eggs, berries, prairie dogs –"

"When was the last time this dump was inspected?" he interrupted.

"Inspected?" she said, looking around the room, hoping his meaning would become self-evident. "You mean cleaned?"

"I mean is there no one left in this godforsaken land who's not a terrorist or a cretin?"

It was a mistake to raise his voice. His spatula lifted like a panhandler's cup, the short-order cook looked up to see *qué pasa*. And, more importantly, Tom and Tam swiveled around to see.

Through a hose hidden by his high starched collar, the head of the well-to-do family was intracellular-hydrating.

He perspired and visibly swelled as he threatened Paula with Health and Safety and waved his hands at the cook in the kitchen and threatened to call Deportation. He oozed the sort of hubris that was typical of the domed. But it was not a Zen-like hubris; it was loud and insecure.

As he returned his credit card to his wallet, his voice shook as he said, "Do I look like the kind of trash that carries coin?" And when Paula failed to answer, he shouted at her, "What the hell do I look like?"

Closing her mouth so tight that her lips went missing, Paula ceased to appear even remotely attractive. "You don't look like nothing," she whimpered, and unsure if she'd given the right answer, glanced behind at Tom, who'd known what to feed a lizard.

Enjoying playing the good guy, Tom stood up from his stool and swaggered toward the table. His heart was beating precisely no faster than usual. His hands rested on his lower back, where the cigarette pack under his tee pretended to be a handgun. His calm was superb. As he answered the guy's question, his voice was like central air set to freezing.

"I know what you look like," said Tom. "You look like a motherfucker."

As if his hose had been cut, the man visibly shrunk, and Tom grew to fill the vacancy left behind.

"You too classy-ass to carry coin?" Tom asked, and called back to Tam, "What do you think he carries, Tam? A squirt gun?"

Expressionless, Tam sat her stool, the clutch purse in her steady hand. "I think he don't carry at all," she answered.

"Don't carry at all," repeated Tom, shaking his head, as if to call it a shame. "How's that TV commercial go, Tam?"

"'Don't leave home without it.'"

"Fucking good advice. But I got a hunch he carries all kinds of crap in his baggy pants, especially when he's shat himself. Think I should find out, Tam?"

"I think you should do what you want, Tom."

So Tom slammed his free hand on the table and, sucking in his breath, barked out, "Empty your pockets, classy-ass motherfucker! Show the waitress what you got to fucking trade!"

The man's frightened wife closed her eyes to pray. And the children, who were orange-skinned from sunscreen and sunburn, plastered themselves like geckos to their sticky seat backs.

"Kids," the man stammered. "I got kids," he said, though he didn't mean to offer them to swap.

Tom laughed in such a way that no one found it funny, except Tam, who halfway smiled.

The man divested. First, a silver lighter. It was impressive. But then, wow, a smartphone. Placed on the table, its small black rectangle sat like a window on the void.

"Take off your sandals," Tom ordered.

When the man bent down, unbuckled, and gave them up, Tom wiped the soles on the guy's starched shirt, then made a present of the shoes to the waitress, whose name he'd already forgotten. But she hadn't forgotten him, and her smile grew wide and dusky.

"Baggy pants too," Tom said. "Take 'em off."

The man blanched. Maybe he was pissing himself, but if he was, it was undetectable, because his baggies, designed to wick sweat away and stow it for future replenishment, worked just as well on urine.

Tom banged his fist on the table again.

He shouted, "Fucking strip!"

"Kids," the man stammered again as one of his children began to cry. "Let my kids wait in the car?"

Tom shot a look at Tam, who sat alert on her stool. Tam raised her blond eyebrows and shrugged.

"What the fuck," said Tom, just glad to get rid of the blubbering.

"Go wait in the car," the man whispered to his kids, and when the youngest took his hand instead, he said it again more loudly.

The children and the mother stood up. She felt included in her offspring's taxonomy by virtue of the fish around her neck, but one noise from Tom and she sat back down again. The crying child ran straight out the door, over which hung the Come Again sign in its thick black frame. After a moment's dithering, the rest of the children followed.

The man split the Velcro at his fly. But the sound of the fly ripping was covered by the diner door swinging open, as if the sign had worked its magic and the traumatized kids had returned. They had not.

A corp strode in, a private hire, his gun up. Heat extractor on, the air rippled around his ballistic face mask and around the suck-tube coiling from his mouth-sieve to the water tank on his back. Tom and Tam should have guessed that a managerial family didn't day-trip west of -101.35 without a corp chauffeur. Waiting in the air-conditioned and limo-tinted SUV, playing games on his iPhone, if he'd been a rattler he'd have bit them the instant they stepped out of the Ford.

Tom and Tam lifted their hands, but no higher than their shoulders. The cook's hands sprung up, and his spatula fell to the ground. As the waitress flapped her arms toward the ceiling, the platform shoes, lipstick and the rest rattled to the floor. And, in an instant, the head-of-the-household had gathered up his things, and he and his wife and his other belongings were out the door.

The small room seemed to tighten. On Paula's forehead, a string of pimples like a pale tiara made themselves visible. The short-order cook appeared molded out of cast plastic. As an egg scorched on the griddle, smoke wafted through the sunlight from the windows, and the room turned dim. Tom and Tam wore the torqued look of two wild creatures determining whether they were the hunters or the hunted, for the venatic order is so intimate, it's reversible.

Like a serial killer or a cat, the corp played with his prey. He frisked Tom for what proved to be a pack of smokes in his back pocket, then shoved him across the room so that he landed in Tam's lap. Next, he let it be known that he wanted a cup of coffee.

"Whatever you want," whimpered the waitress.

"Whatever I want?" the corp repeated.

From inside his hermetic helmet, he eyeballed her. He was standing so close, she could have knelt and shined his steel-tipped boots. Though she was as unappealing as roadkill, working amphetamine hours, he'd screwed worse in the brothels.

"Sure, whatever you want," she whimpered.

But he wasn't going to screw her. He had other games in mind. He told her to pick up the lipstick tube, which was rolling back and forth beneath him in a groove in the floorboard. And because female attachment to small meaningless objects was said to offset greater losses and keep the gender under control, for a moment it seemed he was nothing more than a Brigader who wished to calm down a hysterical woman. But when Paula bent to fetch the lipstick, he grabbed her by the hair.

He spoke without raising his voice. "I want that fucking wetback cook to put his hands on the motherfucking griddle and for you to suck him off while he burns, and I want to watch you while I drink your shitty coffee." Then, waving his air-cooled M4 carbine at the Twins, he said, "After that, I'll fucking decide what I want from the two of them."

His eyes fell on Tam, who gazed straight back at him as if she were daring him to screw her. She was actually appraising the seam in his helmet as a potential entry point for a bullet. Though it was a near impossible target, Tam had a perfect eye.

But though Tam was the better shot, it was Tom who did

the deed, because Tom always had to be first. When the corp lifted his visor to drink the diner's crappy coffee, Tom drew the pistol from the purse and shot him in the face.

The gratuitous details were captured on the security video, but not what was happening outside, where, leaving the eatery's airspace, two ravens, cawing and chortling and corralling the discomposed winds, circled above the Salton trough and spiraled along the drainage canals leading toward the two-thousand-mile Mexican wall. From their bird's-eye view, they saw what no surveillance agency would ever bother to watch.

A female junkie reclined on a tatty lounge chair, barefaced in the searing sun. When her fingernails tapped a glass syringe, it shattered into a thousand rainbow shards. Abandoning a smashed-up microwave, a boy retrieved his cow from the road and returned it to his farmyard, where he and his mother worked the seedy cow manure into the hungry earth. Two scrawny girls sucked on a bottle of sterilized water with an illustration of a mountain stream, and splitting a hunk of bread, each declined the larger portion. Their lizard vanished underground. A man and his weepy family sped off to the safety of a sterile compound on the southern shores, their dark SUV twitching left and right because the driver was unaccustomed to driving his own car. The car sped beyond a hitchhiker outside of a state penitentiary where, in the days when such statistics had been meaningful, seventy-eight percent of inmates were diagnosed psychopaths who manufactured vanity license plates for undiagnosed psychopaths who'd risen to the top of their professions.

Most interesting to the ravens was the lizard. But even a bird's-eye view isn't comprehensive, for there is a hidden world beneath the ground and another beyond the horizon.

The ravens circled back to the diner when they heard the gun go *bang*. They saw the panicked cook sprinting out of the doorway, his hands in the air like liberated birds. The waitress exited next, then leaned on the diner wall and slid downward to assume a ball-like position from which she never wished to emerge. And finally Tom and Tam, clutching a handbag and sunhat, looking like nothing more than a couple of teenage purse thieves.

They watched as Tom put his foot to the accelerator and achieved a whopping seventy-two. Henceforward, the Twins would wish they could fly like ravens, for they'd be on the run. Omnivorous predators, the ravens understood that the chase makes the hunter the hunter and makes the prey the prey, and though running seals its destiny, the prey runs all the same. They watched the Ford diminish. The faster the driver drove, the closer the future came.

The Ford careened out of Mecca, quit the salt lake, and raced east down a side road into the backlands. Where red scree blurred the faded yellow lines, the journey having changed, the Ford cut away from asphalt altogether and climbed a gravel lane. Passing the ruins of a bleached corral, it joined a ghost track hewn by indigenous scouts, wagon trains, and dirt bikes. It lurched through a wash and labored up an eroded slope and crossed a flattened barbed-wire fence, partitioning the blankness. It stopped at a cattle gate, roped closed against the wind, before entering the uncharted white space between the red and blue lines of the map.

The Twins drove toward the sun in the morning and away in the afternoon. When a trail dead-ended at a gulch, they jammed the Ford into reverse and shot backward to the nearest fork. But more often than not, as if imitating life, one path dumped them onto another.

Nothing to see out the window: on a lonesome range, just a cow, just a bird. The cow stood with its head facing north, the magnetite in its brain aligned with the Earth's magnetic field. The bird on its back took off, open-mouthed, magnetite in its thorax and teeth ensuring it would not lose its bearings in the heat-lightning storm to come.

The Twins too had an internal compass, byproduct of the lodestone under the bed in which they slept when Tom, as a child, nightly trolled the hallway to join his sister. Driving unmarked byways, to anyone watching they would have looked lost, but not to themselves. With every backcountry mile, Tom and Tam put the diner behind them, believing the worst was done and over, though what's done is never over.

Through the early afternoon, while Tam napped in the passenger seat, and the broken metal coil in the cushion drilled up between her legs, Tom enjoyed replaying the gratuitous details of the morning, an angry mesquite branch shot through the open window and sliced Tom's neck. He tilted the rearview mirror to inspect the blood-bead choker and, unfazed, rolled up the window. Now a mosquito was imprisoned in the cab, and he was caught between two hells, mesquite and mosquitos being equally brutal things, but so what?

In the late afternoon, Tam drove and Tom curled up in a dark unsleeping mass in the airless sunlight. The mosquito, having gorged itself, rested soporific on the glass. Silence choked up the overheated truck as it drove away from the setting sun.

"You asleep?" asked Tam.

Tom grunted a kind of yes and with excellent aim swatted the mosquito. The mosquito became an abstraction and a smudge of blood on the window.

As the wind gripped the Ford and sandblasted the windshield, Tam poked the wiper button until a spurt of fluid smeared the view. In the cerulean methanol, the late sun flashed and blinded.

The Ford traveled a dismal range incised by a brittle river. Cattle reclined in the shade of skeletal cottonwoods, but a cow lying down was no longer a sign of future rain. The cows were fleshless and picked over. Even what was alive was only half alive and incapable of reproducing. On shriveled and self-amputated cacti, where there should have been blossoms, there were scabs. A prickly-pear cactus, having dropped its kitchen-mitt pads, looked like a bluebottle jellyfish melting on the beach.

But the sun would soon be gone. Night was coming on them quickly. Tam leaned over the wheel to see better. In the evening light, the shadows of rocks were black and cold-blooded creatures. The Ford dipped down and back up the trail, in and out of dry washes, and the last sunbeams chased it, lost it, and pursued it again.

Tam cracked the window, and the wind yowled through the gap. The bipolar wind was up again – up and down, up and down – and over the hood, dust blew back and forth and sideways, uncertain of its preferred direction. According to Henry, whirlwinds spinning clockwise were good and counterclockwise evil, but the wind was far too fickle to test its morality. The wind, the world, the hour, all of it was too fickle, too mobile and unsure. Important questions could not be answered, and Tam wasn't one to ask them. She didn't inquire of her soul, or of her genes, if she and Tom, despite having different fathers, were one and the same, or near-identical, or if near could be far when there is only .1% genetic difference between any two human beings and .2% between a human and a chimp.

Suddenly the pickup's wheel dropped into a rut, and Tom and Tam lurched toward each other, and the ashtray shot out of the dash, and ash blotted the air, and the cash in the sunhat heaved up like silver-stiletto flies off a pile of shit. Quarter bullets flew as Tam drove the gulley hard, leaning heavily on the steering wheel and heaving it around. No power assist. It wasn't easy. And when she finally returned the wheels to even ground, and the gas in the tank resettled, the arrow on the gauge dipped into the red. They were going to run out of gas in the middle of fucking nowhere.

Fuck. Fuck.

Tom couldn't stop cussing.

Tam turned the Ford toward the north. Again, they drove in silence. Windows sealed, with no noise to obstruct their vision, Tom decided the route and Tam obeyed. Both stared at the distance, as if something in the emptiness were staring back and they wouldn't be the first to blink. But they weren't in a showdown with the void, not yet. Accustomed to vast and untenanted lands, while some animals can see in the dark, cowboys can see in the emptiness. "There it is," said Tom, and as if it were a jinx, a millisecond later Tam said, "There it is."

A black vein pulsed in the superheated distance. Once more, it was Interstate 10. Tracking the east-west corridor, they'd been driving parallel to the highway these many hours. Before them, as expected, backlit and luminous, was the tricolor sign of the ExxonMobil, where they definitely wouldn't stop. Just beyond it was an Al's Gas, its incandescents flickering. Once an independent, now a mock-independent, the gas station had been repurposed to catch drivers with good reason to avoid the big guys.

In a hollow beneath the overpass, as industrial-military convoys and Sacrifice sloggers roared over them, the Ford sat alone in a lot. Curved concrete barriers like the rings of Saturn surrounded a plywood convenience store and a couple of rusty gas tanks. The rust was a fact of the past that was hard to accept as reality, but so were the lack of cameras and floodlights and the gas station being open.

Where duct tape covered the credit-card slot on the pump, a handwritten note directed customers to pay inside. There was no doubt that Al's Gas was a flytrap. There'd be a corp alert button under the checkout counter and a Throwaway

Kid at the till: a teenager designed to be killed and replaced. They'd have been better off going elsewhere. *But go fucking where?* asked Tom. They weren't so stupid as to try their luck at an ExxonMobil.

"How much we got?" asked Tom, when Tam finished counting the pennies in the sunhat.

"Enough to run out of gas again."

"Fucking Con," said Tom.

Their mother had given all she had, including the Ford itself, but someone was always to blame, and usually it was her.

As Tom fetched Tam's rifle from the utility chest in the truck bed, Tam surveyed the target. To cut the electricity to kill the corp alert button, she would need to take out the transformer beneath the eaves of the convenience store roof. It was a testament to their innocence, so to speak, that neither twin had heard of magnetic-field technology, and so they presumed that a corp alert would be powered off the mains.

Tom handed Tam her rifle.

"Do it now?" she asked.

"Don't be stupid, Tam. After you fill up the tank."

Carrying the sunhat and purse, Tom strode into Al's Gas.

The teenage clerk at the counter looked only semiconscious. Spider veins mapped her cheeks, a constellation of blackheads on her nose. She needed braces and would never get them, and if she had, she wouldn't have brushed them anyway, so in the end they'd have rotted her teeth. She was chronically depressed, but not so far gone that she'd given up the dream, encouraged on Sundays by her church, that a boy would enter her life one day and save her from her fate. Deep down, she knew the truth that Throwaway Kids – or what Govcorps called Seasonal Labor – weren't awarded happy endings. She knew it, but to rise from bed in the morning she relied on make-believe.

Because the clerk was trained to alert the corps to anything suspicious, until Tam filled the tank and cut the electricity to the alarm, Tom's job was to distract her by flirting.

Entering the store, he paused to admire himself in the security screen mounted to the wall. Despite the piercing heat, no sweat caulked his upper lip, which, in a single day, had bristled out with stubble that looked like spider spit. Tom smirked into the camera, set his coin hat on the counter and ordered a tank of gas, dropping into conversation that the girl at the pump was his sister not his girlfriend. Then, from a selection of snacks, whose chemically long lives had exceeded their use-by dates, he took a jumbo Doritos and a barbecue Jays.

"What do you think, Judy?" he asked, reading the name tag on her red poly vest. "Is it a Dorito day or a Jay day?"

Unaccustomed to chitchat, her answer was stale and bland. "You're the customer," she said.

"So I am," Tom said, pretending to have been enlightened. "I guess I should have it all."

As Judy absorbed what *all* meant, Tom leaned against the counter and played absently with the sunhat, cinching it together and letting it fall apart so the soft lips sloughed open.

Judy's eyes darted from the lurid sunhat to the girl pumping gas out the window, to Tom's strong and stubbly jaw. The pleasure he'd taken that morning in shooting a man in the face (if you can call a corp a man, if his barbarism doesn't preclude it) was still visible in his own, but Judy misinterpreted his pleasure as existing on account of her. Her heart was beating triple-time, but her rosacea made it impossible to tell if she was blushing.

Tom moved swiftly, almost sweetly, like syrup squeezed from a pliable plastic bottle. In no time, he'd maneuvered himself to Judy's side of the counter and had offered her Red Pucker, while the alligator purse stood erect and ready. Touching Judy's hand, Tom told her how her fingers were as long as extinct prairie grasses, and in another life, she must have played piano.

"I don't got a piano," said Judy. Staring at her grubby fingers, she failed to notice the pleasure draining from Tom's face.

Tom was finding there was a problem with pleasure: it didn't last. Killing a man had been such a great relief to his empty discontentment, it would have to be repeated to be sustained. He toyed with Judy's fingers, delighting her while, outside the window, Tam finished at the pump and aimed her rifle at the receiver.

"You played in another life," said Tom. "In another life."

But Judy had never heard of other lives. She looked up and asked, "In Heaven?"

Instantly the power blew. A bang and a flash of light, and Tom's avatar blinked off the security screen, and the fluorescent lamps on the ceiling perished, and the evening sun, stalking the windows, filled the room with glare. But, powered by a magnetic field, the corp alert button under the counter remained aglow.

Tom hated being wrong.

Lacking lightning reflexes, Judy's prairie-grass fingers never reached the button. Instead, she received the full ricocheting force of Tom's self-abnegated shame.

Now, squatting over her body, he felt decidedly better. Pleasure returning, taking the measure of her corpse, Tom had a revelation: life wasn't hard and brittle like he'd previously thought. Life, in fact, was gory, and the gore was hiding just beneath the skin.

He unpinned Judy's name tag. He tucked the memento in his pocket. It would be the first of a collection of such trinkets. He tossed the Doritos and Jay bags into the sunhat and returned the pistol to the purse. Holding the hat and handbag, seen in the blinding glare and the last brutal light, a witness might not have recognized him as a man at all.

When Tam walked into the shop, her eyes glanced over the girl. She hesitated a moment. A bloody tongue of laminate curling away from the edge of the checkout counter curled away a little further. Judy's traumatized brain dampened the cigarette cartons on the shelves. The winds in Judy's body, the ones that stand a person upright, rushed away out a hole on either side of her head and swirled around the aisles of semi-edible foods.

Tam asked, "You killed that kid?"

"Nits make lice," said Tom, usurping a Govcorps saying.

"Huh," answered Tam, and she left it at that.

As the door swung closed behind the two, a cluster of thimble-sized cowbells tinkled dully. And soon the Twins sped on.

The resinous dark was binding, and though distance from Al's Gas increased, Al's gas traveled with them. On a full tank they drove deep into the night, headlights off, directed by the torch of the moon, unable to tell a cactus from a dead man. Only in the picnic basket in the back, in the dog-eared pages of a penny Western, were heroes heroes, villains villains, and only there did fate favor good causes. In the dark world of reality, avenging angels could be demons turned inside out.

They would have sped right through the night if a rattling under the hood hadn't forced them to slow down. As they slowed, the rattling briefly quieted, but shortly it resumed, and they decelerated again, and soon again and again. Then a slap-slap under the hood, and the pickup died on the side of the road.

It was a lonely road but a paved one. It was a haul road from Sacrifice, irregularly patrolled by military. Flares and shellfire in the distance, and the nightglow of industry, where well-paid sloggers trucked out stock and shifted hazmat, and round-the-clock prison labor extracted resource.

"You giving it gas or not?" Tom shouted from the open hood.

Trying to fix the break, under the starry darkness, a wave of his arm conducted Tam's foot on the accelerator. In suspect conjunction, as if he'd hailed the fireball, a star shot across the sky.

"Make a wish," called Tam.

"Just give it fucking gas."

But though Tam gave the pickup gas, whatever magic Tom had intended, the engine did not turn over.

"I can't see a fucking thing," he said and slammed the hood.

"Wait for dawn?" asked Tam.

"Let's get this thing off the road."

Tom shoved and Tam steered, and the pickup rolled in subservience to gravity down an incline toward a cliff, at the edge of which Tam slammed on the foot brake and yanked the hand brake, while Tom wedged rocks under each of the wheels.

Whether or not it was far enough, the pickup sat off the road as far as it could go and still return. Until the sun held a lamp under the hood to reveal what was broken, they could only hope no car would pass and call the nearest corp.

With nothing to do but drink, Tam searched in the footwell for a Styrofoam cup, but if there was one down there, it was hiding, as they were, in the dark. They would have to drink straight from the bottle. Slipping from the dark cab into the blacker darkness, for a moment Tam was gone from sight, though even in broad daylight there was something missing about her. Emerging beside Tom, she passed him the bottle of whiskey.

Tom sucked hard on the neck and wiped his mouth with his tattooed arm, doubly black with engine oil. He sat on the back bumper and gulped down liquor with the confidence of a man who knows he is not a boy anymore and has reason to believe he is not even a human being.

Trying to pass the time, he read aloud from the back of the Doritos bag. "Whole corn, vegetable oil (corn, soybean, and/or sunflower oil), salt, cheddar cheese (milk, cheese cultures, salt, enzymes), maltodextrin, wheat flour, whey, monosodium something. Lactic acid, artificial color (Yellow 6, Yellow 5, Red 40), citric acid, sugar, garlic powder, red and green bell pepper powder, sodium something. This stuff isn't food. It's fucking sick."

Tam nodded in assent. Standing with her foot on the front bumper, she seemed solid yet spectral in the night. The sunhat on her head, she stood with her big pockets overflowing and her hands gleaming with coins. She wasn't prepared when Tom chucked the whiskey bottle over the truck, but nonetheless she plucked it from the air, for even impaired by night, Tam could catch and shoot.

Her reflexes had failed her only one time ever: when, playing in the gorge, Tom had thrown a stone at her head. A scar remained on her forehead, but according to her brother, his culpability had faded away.

"Throw it back," he called.

She did as Tom said, and the bottle orbited back and forth like a quick-fire satellite. When at last the game was over, Tam relinquished the bottle to Tom, and demonstrating how here-one-moment-gone-the-next was the rhythm of the era, she slipped away into the dark.

Now the bottle was severely depleted. Seated sideways in the open driver's door, his feet in the sand, head lolling below his knees, a drunken Tom was watching the insomniac ants descending a cadaverous yucca and disappearing into a hole. He could see time on the move, one creature coming forward, another receding, but no one and nothing truly disappearing. The ants had colonized the desert dance floor, where a hundred million years previously, mating dinosaurs had pounded their footprints into the fast-drying mudflats. The prints were now repositories for double-glazing dust and the small flags of disposable diapers, which would never decompose. Where the ants crawled in and out and maybe even played pinochle in the maze beneath their hole, they navigated a buried skull wearing a Hello Kitty hair clip lying side-by-side underground with prehistoric man, preserved by extreme aridity. The gaseous presence of ghosts rose from the pinprick hole, despite the rituals of ancient peoples designed to stop a haunting. You were as likely as to stop the trash-grass from ravaging the range.

Tom looked up, believing he heard a distant war cry, but it was really a colony of bats, their teeth cracking open the exoskeletons of a swarm of flies. He saw, in a drunken haze, a harras of painted horses trammeling the wild grasses. When he rubbed away the hallucination, the wild grasses were gone, as were the birds who therein nested. Bats alone filled the avifauna void. He lifted the bottle again, and his liver shuddered at the onslaught.

Tom staggered to his feet. Suddenly, he was bored. Always getting bored was inherent to his condition. And bored made him angry.

He removed his shirt, and the moonlight threw its ashen mantle over his naked back, and caged by emptiness, he paced the night's dark cell. His black tattoos shone metallic in the moonlight. He unstrapped the knife he wore at his ankle, and it glinted in his hand as he lifted it to the sky. He set off toward the cliff, under which he'd heard his sister picking about in the scree. He'd heard her peeing some time ago, but nothing for a while. Only the whirr of a locust. Bat prey. But no hunter whizzed by in pursuit.

"Still alive down there?" Tom called.

"Yeah," came her voice from the dark.

"Prove it," Tom directed.

Tam arose from the cliff like a shade from a pit, and the two ascended a hill, Tam following Tom, as she had in birth, and as she would in every conceivable and unspeakable gyration. The Twins fused with the dark, and the walls of the night moved inward. The darkness resembled water. If only you could drink it. But the darkness resembled water in just one way, in the way that sound sweeps across its surface.

Tom said, "Tam?"

"Yeah, Tom?"

"We're gonna be the ones who win this fucking war."

"Tam hopes so."

"Tom knows so."

"You think we're gonna do great things, Tom?"

"We're gonna do whatever we want."

When, at last, the two of them slept, water molecules from their breath joined with other water molecules and rose on the wind, and the thermals tore them apart and blew them away toward Sacrifice, to be converted by the lichen, adapted to toxic slag heaps, into oxygen to be inhaled by future generations. The booze in their blood stank, so the scorpions kept their distance, but a rattlesnake visited them, emboldened by the density of their slumber. And when a bat dipped its wings nearby, the snake slithered off, leaving only its trail, for the rattler is more shy than violent. The bat, however, had never been self-effacing, and it soared back and forth, curious to sense a couple of humans asleep on a rock slab in the middle of nowhere. It seemed to the bat that the Twins had been thrown there by ancient forces long since passed away, the two of them sleeping the clean sleep of children, whatever they were in truth.

When the first sun touched their eyes and the Twins awoke, the sky was adorned by nothing. No clouds or contrails. No birds or surveillance helicopters. It was as if all objects, vaporous and solid, had been sucked out its secret hole. Night's detritus lay in the dirt. An oil patch, a bungee cord, a whiskey bottle, a picnic basket, a water bottle, a book, and a road map pinned under a rock so as not to blow away. Nearby, a tumbleweed and a sorry yucca. Nothing else. The Ford itself, yes, but the tire tracks of its arrival had dispersed in the wind.

The Twins got to work. Two heads under the hood of the pickup, the minutes passed and the sun rose higher. They felt sure to fix the Ford, sure to because they had to, because the dump remained far off, and even if it hadn't, in the heat on the edge of Sacrifice, you did not attempt to walk. Sure to because they had to, because if God in his Heaven was real, there was no counting on His help, because God in His mercy giveth but His habit is to taketh away.

Soon it would be high noon, and the sun would sear through the sunhat, which they traded back and forth. The sun would wither their black and blond hair and deep-fry the lids of their brains, and after it ticked past the zenith, it would not pause to observe the damage done. Like the Twins themselves, the sun would never look over its shoulder at who or what it killed.

Exposed by the sun, they were alert to danger. Anything driving a haul road would not be a four-door with friendly bumper stickers, its GPS politely intoning the route to a better world. They were on their guard, but their heads were under the hood and they were focused on the task at hand when an amber cloud gusted off the earth, something heading west, tearing up the sandy asphalt. When from the earth-cloud there emerged a state-of-the-art ten-wheeler, its semitrailer steel-branded *Yácorp*, line-hauling from Sacrifice, it was too late for them vanish. And unless the earth opened up beneath them, there was nowhere to vanish to.

Asbestos from its howling brakes stank up the stinking

air, and the cab door opened, though Yácorp's number-one slogging rule was to drive on and call it in. Man, woman, child, alive, wounded, or dead, if they weren't wearing a Yácorp jumpsuit, drive on and call it in.

The slogger who stepped out of the cab was a stout man, middle-aged and overweight by about twenty pounds, which made him a sort of miracle. A kind soul, in Tom's judgment he was a fucking idiot, disobeying the slogging rule to follow a gentler one from a better world. The old rule told him to stop, get out of his cab, and offer the kids some help.

"Engine trouble," Tom explained, raising his hand in greeting.

"Let's have a look," said the slogger.

Tom gestured to Tam to step away so that the man could take her place beneath the pickup's hood. And as was expected of girls, Tam flapped her hands and seemed all the more female when she walked around to the passenger door to retrieve her purse and hooked it in the crook of her arm.

"We're heading to Phoenix," said Tom, "where I got a job as a slogger like you. You running hazmat? You driving from the Supermines?"

"Where else?" said the slogger as he poked about in the engine.

"You making the Sacrifice-to-LA run?"

"Yup," said the slogger.

"How many times you made it?"

"God only knows."

"My mom used to fly into LAX."

The slogger looked up from the engine to observe the innocence of youth. "Son," he said, returning to the bowels of the Ford, "you're lucky you're too young to miss the old days."

"Mom calls Los Angeles The City of Angry Angels."

"More like the land of the living dead now. Your mom wouldn't recognize it, son."

"Tom," Tom said.

They almost seemed like friends.

"You drive alone?" asked Tom.

"Solo in and out on the highway."

"Must get lonely."

"Lonely enough to get you killed," said the slogger, obeying yet another defunct rule of the road: that the road was a confessional. "I knew a slogger got killed on a haul road by a dog with a micro-bomb in his collar. Outlaws banked on him stopping. Not just stopping, getting out and following the soft thing. Counted on his being lonely enough to totally lose his mind. He knew the number-two slogging rule, knew it and didn't obey it. It's *never abandon the truck*. The cargo comes first. It's a harsh rule, sure, but it's a safe rule. Safer, anyway. Nothing's really safe. But it's safe enough if you're hauling hazmat, because Outlaws won't spill the hazmat. They've got what they call environmental morals. I'll give them that much anyway, but it's a cheap trick targeting a person's loneliness and planting bombs in dogs."

"Genius," observed Tom.

The slogger paused at the word but, upon a moment's reflection, assumed it to be ironic. "Ugly genius," he agreed. "But, Tom," he said, "it's hard to know who's who or anything anymore."

He glanced above the truck hood toward the watchful sun; then his voice dropped to a whisper, and he said, "Some sloggers swear the dog was a self-bomb. They say Govcorps weed out their weakest sloggers any way they can and call it natural selection."

His grizzled face looked tortured by the thought. But under the shadow of the hood, Tom was the only one to see it, and he didn't care.

"Sorry," said the slogger, "I shouldn't have gone and burdened you. You still want to be a slogger after all of that?"

"Sure," said Tom. "I'm not one of the weak ones."

Removing his head from underneath the hood, the slogger said, "I hate to say it, Tom, but I think the thing's dead."

He looked sadly at the broken-down pickup, which didn't just symbolize American hope and freedom – according to theories of consanguinity, it was those very things. Then, from his Heatwick jumpsuit, he pulled out not a No-Name pack but an actual pack of Marlboros, proving that, though the job was lonely, the pay was excellent. Life in an R-40 vermiculite-insulated truck with full-body wind deflectors and self-cleaning, light-adjusting windows could be good.

When he offered a cigarette to Tom, Tom blew a smoke ring and asked him, "Where you call home?"

"Truck's my home," answered the slogger.

"You weren't born in it," said Tom and slid one ring into another.

"No," said the slogger, "but probably gonna die in it."

Watching the girl walk toward him, the slogger felt uncertain whether to offer her a cigarette, too. He knew girls no longer smoked, but it felt impolite not to even ask. He was trapped between dueling worlds. But when she reached into her purse and something glinted in the sun, his mind caught up with the era: he presumed it was a compact mirror for powdering her nose.

The pistol in Tam's handbag didn't end the slogger's life. The barrel had been emptied in the diner and Al's Gas. But Tam was a strong girl, and the rock did the trick.

Moments later, they were driving toward the dump in a ten-wheeler, extractor fan on, and enjoying smoking Marlboros. The sun grew tall and mean and scowled through the sealed windows. When Tam mopped her neck with a Yácorp hanky, monogrammed with a Y, Tom, sufficiently chilled by his amazing Heatwick jumpsuit, twisted the air jets to cool her down. Seated high in the cab, they watched the land speed by. Out the window, soil on the wind, like souls in transmigration.

Before I get to the dump, I want to pause. I want to attempt to be clear. I wish to be transparent, which is a politically charged word, but the best that I can find. I want to say this: all history, minor and major, intimate and global, is the conjunction of specific, often disparate events, any one of which, not having happened or having happened differently, would irretrievably change the ending. The perfect coming together of parts can and will appear uncanny and yet is mere reality, for the world is a convoluted web given to feedback loops and the interchange between perturbation, resistance, and resilience. No matter how defiant of expectations, synchronicity should not be interpreted as impossible – which is not to dismiss centrally organized conspiracies like self-bombs or own-group assassinations at linchpin moments designed to galvanize a base or justify an agenda. "The Universe is not only queerer than we suppose, but queerer than we *can* suppose," wrote an early-twentieth-century geneticist. Aside from grossly measurable actions, we don't know the subtle journey between cause and effect. We only guess it. We only shorthand it. The pinholes of our senses subtract more than they sense. We speak of the flap of a butterfly wing; we ignore the flap of a bat wing. I am trying to tell the truth here, and it is glib to say truth is relative, for there is a difference between two stories and two sides of a story when one side is a lie. Hyper-relativism played its part in the global catastrophe: leading up to The Change, folks reduced facts to opinions, as if the Earth itself were a partisan issue. Facts are facts are facts, but simultaneously and without contradiction, all history is scribed in lies, which over years of erosion and extrapolation evolve to become what passes as fact. This is my disclaimer: what happened on the Sacrifice front, at the rendezvous at the dump, only approximates truth, which must be sufficient, because approximation is all we have, and all we ever had. Okay, I can continue.

The ten-wheeler sat in the dump, a boneyard of beaten fridges and microwaves, propane and pig-fat furnaces and compacted and derelict cars. In the coolness, the Twins sat inside the cab, listening to the radio. Amid a crackling sea of static, a preacher begged his listeners to repent their sins and enter with the saved into a better world.

"Fuck," grumbled Tom, "wreck the fucking world, then gab on about a better one."

But it was boredom, not indignation, that made him flip off the radio, and, sun be damned, climb onto the semitrailer roof to sit on top of the utility chest, held to its enormous escort by the bungee cord and a frayed rope from the Ford. His sister dutifully followed.

Seated on the guns, the insulated jumpsuit rolled down to his waist so that his chest was bare, Tom scraped the blunt side of his knife across his tattooed arm and watched as a bruise under his skin flared up and faded back again. He sucked his teeth, and his breath released a chemical odor. Her pale skin protected by the sunhat, Tam sat silent by his side, like a hand that has gone to sleep, insensible to its owner but belonging to him nonetheless.

Scanning the horizon, Tom said, "We're gonna find out how rat meat tastes if the Outlaws don't get here soon. A person's only got seventy-two hours before dying of fucking dehydration. It's a mean, slow death compared to most gunshot wounds."

"Quick compared to most cancers," observed Tam.

Because it was something he himself might have said, Tom glanced at Tam admiringly, and something similar to love stirred inside his ribs. Not love, of course, but it felt close enough to the word, the meaning of which he'd never quite deciphered.

He leaned over the edge of the semitrailer and spat. Then, just as quick, dismounted the roof and scraped up the dirty spittle with his knife and wiped it on his jumpsuit. But not because spitting was gross. Organic processes, even those in the end-phase of life, are gross only to people who can't live with the fact that they are themselves organic processes. Conversely, non-decomposable, non-recyclable toxic wastes and plastics – which Govcorps and Brigaders aspired to be like by trying to live forever, whether on Earth or in Heaven – are gross to life itself.

So why did Tom collect his spit? Because it was a basic tenet of witchcraft, as well as genetic engineering, that spit, piss, dandruff, nail parings, or anything carrying a person's code were vulnerable to possession. And though Tom wasn't scared of witchcraft his habits had been forged by Henry's fear of it.

As he hauled himself back up the trailer and resumed his throne on the gun chest, Tom felt increasingly impatient. Henry had told him to wait, but he hadn't said *wait forever*. Having ascended to its apex hours ago and finding nothing at the top worth having, the sun was sliding down. Sunset was on its way.

"They fucking coming?" he complained again to Tam. Then, too impatient to wait for an answer, Tom answered himself: "They'll come if they want the guns."

He squinted into the distance. No windstorm, no artillery fire, no sign of Outlaws, nothing. Stale air. No one could tell dump from not-dump. Just junk and rocks, and rocks that bombs had shattered into more rocks. Such vital markers as Bruised Rock and Gashed Head and The Devil's Iron had been decimated because, after Ground Control collapsed, paralyzing older satellites immediately and Block

II-As soon after, Outlaws had relied on them as landmarks. Without GPS to guide them, Outlaws traveled like birds by ancient navigational systems, by sun, stars, scent, sound, and topographical features. But unlike birds, they named the rocks.

Tom eyeballed the ground below. The Outlaws could come from anywhere. For all he knew, they could pop their heads out of a junkyard mound of snow tires.

Tam's attention was elsewhere. "Look, Tom," she said.

Scuttling across the yard, a lizard had crossed paths with a snake that had been sunning itself on top of a fridge-freezer. The snake was poised to strike, but the lizard was holding motionless, instinctively aware that a snake can't see to strike what doesn't move.

Tam felt the stalemate had lasted long enough. Removing the ribbon on her sunhat, she strung it through the Ford ignition key, which she'd stowed in her frock pocket, and raising her fist, she swung the makeshift weapon like a hunter's bola and let it fly. When the key struck the lizard, it dropped its tail and bolted. Now on the run, the lizard could be seen by the snake. The snake opened its mouth and levitated. Predator and prey conjoining, they vanished into a hole beneath the cars.

"Nice one," said Tom.

Tam smiled and showed her solid teeth.

They were children playing cruel games on a rooftop. But according to the development of vital organs and the regeneration of cells, they were adults, meaning their brain cells were quietly dying, though any absence would not be noticeable until achieving critical mass.

As the day trudged on, the games became more perilous. Pointing to an overturned electricity pylon some hundred and eighty feet long, Tom said, "That." He felt it was an excellent dare. The pylon had fallen uphill and crashed into a car crusher and transformed into a red-hot skyway over a sea of cars.

"Walk it?" asked Tam.

"Do it barefoot," said Tom.

"Tom wants Tam to?"

"Tam's chicken?"

"Chicken enough," said Tam.

The Twins grinned at each other. As well as calling themselves by their own names, they had a special private language, involving inversions of common usages: being *chicken* meant the opposite of what other people meant by being "chicken". But the reversal was realistic, for cocks were bred to fight, and a hungry hen doesn't think twice about eating her own eggs.

Tam kicked off her sneakers. Tying their laces together, she threw them over a girder, where now they hung like rubberized fruit. Her calloused feet could take the burn. Disencumbered except for her rifle, she swung herself up easily and ascended the flaming latticework. She spread her arms like plucked wings.

On top of the pylon, the view expanded. Winds whirled in the plains, and dust-sheets sailed across the flats. Gutter gusts and slurve gusts in the distance sounded suspiciously like tanks or jets. Air currents seesawed up and down and merged and rippled, and everything dissembled. The distance pretended to be water, an inferior mirage, an image located under a reality when hot air rises and cool air drops and many layers commingle, and the image turns unstable and distorted. Nearer the yard, black ash lifted off volcanic buttes that impersonated monuments to Pharaoh.

Everywhere, the wind blew, but not in the dump itself. Here, there were localized doldrums. The wind was as local as incest, and the junkyard abutted a mesa, which blocked the prevailing gusts. There was only a passing downdraft. A black plastic bag sailed by the girder and descended, silent as a vulture, into a wrecked convertible on whose crackled seat lay the fragile bones of a rat or maybe a songbird. Whatever it was, even the bones looked thirsty. The region measured less than a shot glass of rain per year. Even the bones were dreaming that the heavens would one day open and rain would fall like governments.

Walking the scorching girder, Tam performed her task so effortlessly Tom felt there was no fun in it. So he threw a stone at his sister. Immediately, she twisted around and raised her rifle. When she pretended to shoot, the game was on. Tom laughed and dropped to the ground and amassed an arsenal of stones, and as he swerved between junked cars, he hurled them one by one. Except for the occasional pebble that disintegrated in midair because it was actually a clod of dirt, Tam dodged every stone. They rained down on the cars. Tam shot imaginary bullets, and Tom aimed to miss, and the cars took the brunt. In the future, with better weaponry, Tom would achieve reloading times of under three seconds while Tam, employing a side stock, would fire a staggering three hundred rounds per minute with little loss of accuracy. This game, like many games, was really a rehearsal.

But when a car alarm went off, the game was over. The junkyard had been thoroughly scavenged, and as any garbage picker knows, no one leaves behind a functioning car battery. The alarm was clearly purposeful. The alarm was calling someone.

Tam's rifle sight turned toward the horizon. Nothing in the distant plains. Tumbleweed. Nothing. The desert, like a desert person, gave little away to strangers. In the foreground, one butte shielded another, and the mesa was a fortress behind which anything might hide. The sun was well past half-mast, and the lodestar had presented in the sky. Sound travels far in aridity and faster in the heat and even farther at night, and if nothing was out there now, it would be soon. The alarm would call it forth.

Tom had laid his stones on the ground and was walking carefully between the wrecks toward the offending car. The steering column had been busted open, making entry easy, but his acquaintance with the workings of his mother's Ford had never included an alarm. Unsure which wire to cut, he picked through the colored options, his knife held in his teeth. He was about to take the obvious route and cut through the entire tangled knot, but something whispered in his ear and stopped his hand. A fly walked down the windshield: it is not impossible that the fly tipped him off.

He couldn't say why: it just wasn't a good idea. So he yanked the pull in the footwell, and the hood kicked up an inch into a preparatory position, and he stepped around the front of the car to unplug the battery instead. In a second, he'd slide his hand underneath the hood to find the latch.

But his sister hooted loudly. She hooted not exactly like an owl hoots but like wind hoots over empty bottles and through sewer pipes and breath holes between rocks. She pointed with her rifle.

A dog was skulking toward the junkyard. It was mangy and black and appeared to have been shaved by a blunt knife. Why its tail was missing was another story. The more pressing question was whether it was in fact a dog or someone more nefarious who had shape-shifted into a dog. The instant it saw the Twins, it froze and bowed its head and rounded its rump and tried to tuck its tail nub. Then, as it had come, it went, relinquishing sovereignty of the dump, unaware it had briefly played the role of a witch in a fractured landscape.

Tom turned back to the car, but the descending sun had moved along, and a sunbeam had slipped into the gap where his hand was meant to go. It illuminated a copper tripwire the width of a human hair, threaded through the latch under the hood.

Retreating from the booby-trapped car, Tom signaled to his sister, who, descending the girder, retraced her steps exactly.

Now, once again, the Twins sat on the top of the semitrailer. They were staring at the monolithic sky. The setting sun was hard-edged, and the car alarm carved up the emptiness. Leaning back on their hands, Tom's fingers over Tam's, they resembled a couple of sweethearts awaiting the privacy of night, but in fact they were marking a path up the mesa where they could take aim in all directions.

Tom bit his lip to think, and the pain cleared his furious mind. "How we off for water?" he asked.

As if to cover her doubts, Tam covered her mouth with her hand. "We got enough for now," she said.

"Better get going," Tom said, not asking Tam how long was now or how much was enough.

Preferring agility to comfort, he removed the cumbersome jumpsuit from atop his jeans. With the utility chest resting on a couple of scavenged iron bedrails, which distributed the weight across their shoulders, the Twins bore the gun dais up the mesa. They followed an antique trail, passing some simple petroglyphs, two waves and a series of gashes that had once tallied the number of hours by foot to water. Arriving at the flattened summit, the Twins unloaded their burden and surveyed the view.

Nothing. Not yet. Wind moving sand. Dump sand, foreign sand, it had blown in from all over. An orange orb on the horizon. Shadows jittering at the base of a butte. Maybe bats. Probably nothing, but you couldn't be sure.

"Where are they?" said one twin.

"Coming," said the other.

"Motherfuckers," said one twin.

"Takes one to kill one," said the other.

The two chose their weapons.

Sliding his leather belt from its loops, Tom gave it to Tam so she could bind her nondominant arm and restrain sympathetic movement. The tin bronco buckle would slice into her skin, but the bondage would enhance her aim.

Tam descended to an overhang that offered cover and an unobstructed view of the junkyard. Adjusting the cheek piece on her sniper rifle until the stock tapped her jaw, she locked into an anti-materiel, bolt-action Dragunov. Tom remained on top of the mesa, where he could see in three hundred and sixty degrees. He loaded a Simonov with 14.5mm cartridges with armor-piercing cores. He lay down on his belly and lowered his eye to the scope.

The shadows of the buttes ceased to fidget. The air began to agitate. The car alarm kept blaring. The wind rose. The temperature dropped some degrees. Tam's gray frock darkened. And the sun continued turning down the covers of the day as if no more was going to happen.

But everything was going to happen, and happen simultaneously, confirming what most historians believe: that destiny boils down to timing. Even rhythm perhaps, for what happened next in the junkyard was inscribed in the original source material as a song.

As the buttes and flat-topped mesa bounced the car alarm between them and the four directions caterwauled, a tank rolled into the junkyard, like junk blown into a wasteland. It rolled in by the red-hot pylon where a couple of sneakers hung like rubber fruit or strange fruit or antipersonnel mines. And meanwhile up in the sky, a black whirlwind cloud came rolling off the plains.

hey hey hey

With reactive and slat armor, and a top-mounted remote

weapon station armed with a .50-caliber machine gun, the tank rolled into the dump. It rolled up beside the semitrailer loaded up with hazmat. The sun struck the cab's side mirror, the rearview mirror, the vanity mirror, and the *Yá* emblazoned on the flank. It unrolled a luminous red carpet up the mesa trail, toward the hidden Twins. The sun slanted down, dragging down the heat, and meanwhile a black whirlwind cloud came rolling off the plains.

hey hey hey

It was only a single cloud. It had no reinforcements, but no more were needed. It burst upon the junkyard and rained hard on the busted fridges, the microwaves and derelict cars, and the songbird rat bones blanching in a car seat. It pounded down on the semitrailer and the tank beside it, and the many mirrors, making rainbows in the sunlight. It rained cats and dogs, but really it rained spiders.

Nonny nonny nonny!
Hey hey hey!
It was really raining spiders!
Do you believe your eyes?

The song does not explain why it was really raining spiders, but in twenty-first-century Beebe, Arkansas, a cloud rained a thousand blackbirds, and in nineteenth-century Singapore, the clouds flung down carp. These are historically documented occurrences, and neither one was a miracle. Nor was the black whirlwind cloud. It was a tornadic waterspout, which originates over bodies of water and occasionally over salt lakes. Subject to the velocity of the spin, such waterspouts are capable of sucking up creatures from under the water's surface and transporting them hundreds of miles before air currents dump them as rain. The lone black cloud in the junkyard, somewhere in the plains, had sucked up a waterhole of newly hatched spiders. Though nothing explains sufficiently why the icy upper altitudes did not stop their tiny hearts, due to their boneless suppleness the spiders survived their forced migration and their fall from a precipitous height.

Spiders, like black snow, drifted across the junkyard. Spiders, like black ice, paved the route up the mesa. Like deluge off hardpan, they ran off the four armored corps who climbed from the tank to see the miracle of living spiders falling from the sky. Two corps walked between the junkyard cars and marveled at the infestation. They did not believe their eyes. Two astonished corps stayed with the tank, one dodging back to the gun mount, the other leaning out of the hatch. Hidden up on the mesa, the Twins turned black with spiders, and like night inside night became invisible.

hey hey hey

Tam shot a sniper bullet, and it pierced the seam of one corp's armpit, and he lurched and hugged his devils. Tam shot again, and she pierced the seam of another corp's helmet, and blood filled it like a punchbowl. As the nose of the tank swung round, Tom shot a bullet with armor-piercing core, and it pierced the semitrailer's multi-fuel hold, and the hazmat leaped up and fell like a one-horse flaming chariot on the tank. A corp ran round in circles on fire. Inside, unseen, another corp burned up. All over the tank's armor and .50 caliber machine gun, the spiders incinerated much faster.

hey hey hey

Tom stood on the flat-topped mesa, his arms raised to the sky. Tam stood like a giantess on the ledge beneath him. In weather, rage, and dump, Sacrifice had found its heroes. Their fame would speed faster than gunshot. Their fame would speed faster than cancer.

Nonny nonny nonny!
Hey hey hey!
It was really raining spiders!
Do you believe your eyes?

What eyes? Weren't all the witnesses dead? No, because

the corps were not the only ones who had rushed to the dump that evening. Having proceeded there on foot, in the shadows of a butte stood an Outlaw posse, instructed to meet the Ford with the new recruits and guns. They too could not believe their eyes. And one of them, being a songwriter in her previous incarnation, over her chronic tinnitus and in competition with the car alarm, heard lyrics. Soon she would write them down and the wind would pick them up, reshuffling the verses like DNA fragments in directed evolution and calling forth an elite army from the mountains to the coasts.

Black Mouths belonged to Da-Tom, and Ghost Fighters to Tam-Ma, and those who belonged to the Twins renamed themselves such sobriquets as Youngblood, Riptide and Doom, or words untranslatable if they were the sole survivors of their language, or no name at all. Americans, all of them, they came from feuding and polarized peoples, defined by doing unto others what someone or other had done or apparently done unto them. Unified in their devotion to the Twins, whatever historical hostilities existed between them were supplanted by a single enemy, and Jesse James was heralded as each and everyone's paterfamilias – a claim that was verifiably false, though there had been rapes enough on the stagecoach trail to have spawned an army of Jameses.

They fought and won the Seam Slaughter of the Kansas City Dome, the Battle of the Ashes of Phoenix, and the Goldwater Air Force Range Infiltration. They freed thousands from forced labor in the Sacrifice Camps, and they cut off the New Eastern supply chain. They assassinated the first, second and third Govcorps presidents, though such accomplishments were never definitive because Govcorps could not die.

They themselves were mortal and proud of it. They lay down their lives willingly and did not fear to do it, as they rode through the low ways of Sacrifice and were gunned down in the snow-bunny sprawl. In ghost towns and garbage dumps and picked-over slums, they did not fear to die. They rode deep-seat, staggered formation on sure-footed mustangs, their saddle pouches heavy with hardtack, hallucinatory agarikon, edible ants, and locusts. They rode for uncounted days down streets that writhed in the heat-ripple, and the road before them never stopped its writhing. When their bellies sang with hunger, they shouted, "From hunger cometh victory."

They were terrible to behold. Black Mouths were bald with greased scalps, and they were genderless, the females thin and breastless, their genitals hidden in breechclouts, their black-rimmed mouths and eyes like black holes, from which they were said to have emerged. Ghost Fighters wore boneware kilts and ammunition belts but were otherwise naked, and white chalk smeared through their dreadlocks refracted back the sun. Their thunderous horses, nostrils mortared in dust, threw dirt at the sky. Where the clouds had abandoned the sky to the sun, in the blue and nothing but blue, they met their glorious end, desiccated and scorched. They seldom survived a season, but their ranks were always full. They were like lizards who regrow their tails, because no caustic exists to apply to the stump to stop them toadstooling back.

The Candy Wrapper Kids were the real martyrs. Children who had never sat a pony, they did not fight, and yet no life was shorter. Their preteen faces painted silver and charcoal, like moonlight through charred trees, they swept the mines at night so that mounted Black Mouths and Ghost Fighters could outrun the rising sun. Sweat melted the pitch off their temples as they searched for telltale copper wires and found them under candy wrappers or discarded hubcaps. Like beefeaters of old, they died without complaint.

These were the elite, but they were ordinary people. In their previous lives, they'd been cashiers, dishwashers, janitors, teachers, domestic cleaners, backhoe operators, migrant workers, mechanics, lab assistants, and bookies. One Ghost Fighter had turned tricks in a honky-tonk, and a Black Mouth had done the same on the highway. But their past lives were over and done, and when, among the elite divisions, a corp joined forces with a drug lord, no one scoffed or balked. If in their ranks were mayors and senators and even former presidents, when they swore allegiance to the Twins, their mustangs trampled their former identities under their furious hooves. All of them were different now. All of them were the same.

The monikers Da-Tom and Tam-Ma were repeated as mantras over rosaries strung from bullets. They weren't names but *bījas*, mystical seed-syllables that stand for cosmic principles, which, on the level of the word, cannot be defined. When the desert flora threw its dying energy into the production of actual seeds – which can lie dormant for centuries and outlast a drought – the Twins received the praise. And if the American Monsoons reverted westward, they were happy to take the credit.

Spray-painted across the wreckage of shell-shocked towns was their sign: the bloodred hourglass of the Western Black Widow. Spider banners, sewn from bedsheets, hung from busted streetlamps. And at the news that the Twins and their legions would be riding past, the grateful crawled out of bomb shelters and peeked from behind blackout curtains and waited behind blackened screen doors. These were ordinary Outsiders, not Drifters yet, and like so many across Sacrifice, more than one was missing an arm or an eye, but none were without toxic gases in his lungs and plastics in his bloodstream. Spanning the breadth of America, there were women adorned in bright *dupattas*, men with never-cut hair twisted into turbans, pasty John Lennon lookalikes, men and women with afros or cornrows, skinheads, rednecks, nerds, brains, jocks, throwbacks like aging cowgirls and barrel-chested frontiersmen, one freckled man in a bowler hat and one brown lady in a *chuba*, and the lower echelons of the long-sleeved Brigaders, who unlike their wealthier brethren had not made the cut for the domes. There were fewer children than expected – forty-eight percent fewer to be exact, given the smallpox fatality rate amongst an unvaccinated population.

In carnivorous sunlight, they waited to lift up their infants to be kissed and, from their meager holdings, offer presents to the Twins. An elderly man with a wasting disease came prepared with an antique nautical sundial compass with an attached mini-hourglass prized in his family for generations and destined to belong to Da-Tom. A white-haired woman had only a hardboiled egg, transmogrified by a hen out of garbage, to offer up to Tam-Ma. For the unborn child in Tam-Ma's belly, who was prophesied to be female, a small girl had procured a Barbie, unearthed from a pile of rubble. It was not a full-grown Barbie, who had so defined desire that, in a previous, unimaginable world, self-mutilating women had paid surgeons to remove their lower ribs and remake their flesh-and-blood bodies in her plastic image. This Barbie was a preteen Skipper, as yet unmarred by womanhood like the bearer of the gift whose growth had been stunted and whose menses would never come.

They waited all day in their doorways. Their aching feet were a point of pride. For who would dream of missing the Twins? Thousands could live for months upon the hope and fear brought by a moment's sighting.

Da-Tom's cheeks were striped with pitch skimmed from the seeps, copper from the pits oxidizing in his sweat, his jaw marked yellow with uranium, as if anticipating death before cancer, rooster-tail feathers hanging from his earlobes. His uncut hair wicked oil to his shoulders. On his head, a black Stetson. On his neck, a trophy necklace of human teeth. Black jeans. No boots. He was like his mustang, who was unshod and unflappable and so accustomed to the scent of death that even the horsemeat jerky in the saddlebag didn't spook it. He was naked from the waist, except for the body art that blackened and shielded his skin. His lips were marked with fangs containing venom glands, and his cheeks were inked with webs, and the black widow on his Adam's apple came to life whenever he spoke. Over his shoulders hung an albino dog hide, like a fantasy of snow in an inferno.

Riding abreast was Tam-Ma, the chalk line down the bridge of her nose marking her as the leader of the Ghost Fighters. She carried a walnut-and-horn-inlaid Enfield, African style, muzzle forward, her hand on the decorated fore-end, and a Zastava M76 fitted with a ZRAK M76 4× optic and fixed bayonet across her lap. She wore a dogskin tunic, the right sleeve cut off to free her shooting arm, which had grown disproportionately huge. Scar tissue, smooth as a city dome, mottled her big arms. The scars didn't tan, but the sun had bronzed the rest of her, and sandstone dust rouged her lips. In an effort to age her, the sun had bleached her long blond hair, but sweat had darkened it again. She wore it coiled like a snake on her head, highlighting the widow and its eggs tattooed on her forehead. The same arachnoid crest, beaded from PVC wire sleeves, adorned her dress. Not on display was the child in her belly, just hours away from emergence, carried deep between her hip bones.

Beyond the fanfare and cheers, into a moonless night the legion rode in staggered formation toward a safe house of gypsum and limestone caves, reaching one hundred and forty feet toward the core of the Earth. Following a fracking trail, veins marred the emptiness and cul-de-sacs led to disused drill pads, condensate tanks, and emerald wastewater where the drillers had moved on. Passing the distant lights of active mining, they rode mutely toward home until the stench of burning methane suddenly shied their horses. At the smell, they changed course.

Always opportunists, they galloped uplifted and pitched forward, and the dirty wind slapped their faces as they rode toward a burning oil field. They stopped their horses on a dark escarpment and pulled out their scopes and watched. A blowout had ignited a slurry blender and a wireline rig and the wellhead below. A derrick tower blazed at three thousand degrees at eye level, and the release wells burned like candle nubs. Beyond the fires, unmanned and unguarded in the emergency, sat water tanks and pump trucks: freshwater gold, primed for the taking.

They waited as a crane maneuvered a drum of dynamite into the burning wellhead to snuff the fire. When the explosion shook the uplands and powdered their black ponies with a fine toxic snow, which in quantity could lift the paint off cars, it was their time. As the air below blackened and the roughnecks moved through the darkness to cap the well before oxygen reignited the fire, they galloped into the widening penna of smoke and struck fast and hard.

What they did in the oil yard no one lived to say, and no surveillance device survived. But after it was over and done, a dozen eighteen-wheeler tanker trucks, each one holding eleven thousand gallons of fresh potable water, paraded down the beaten roads, driving forth a string of painted ponies. Then, under cover of crude blackness, and under the lampless night, the tankers were stripped and ditched, the hoses left suckling at the valves. Before Govcorps could rally their jets, the clean, fresh water was siphoned down an invisible hole into the cavernous world beneath.

At twice the speed of sound, jets charged across the desert. The horsemen swirled across the sealike plain and scattered like sparks off a Catherine wheel, their white-eyed ponies carrying them in whatever direction they'd spun. Rotary cannons strafed the riders from their saddles, dragged them by the stirrups and harrowed them through the wastes, or charger and rider collapsed as one.

Aerial footage reveals the Twins racing up and down a mesa, Tam-Ma rattling her machine gun at the monsters in the sky and Da-Tom waving his gory keepsakes. Suddenly, Tam-Ma doubles over on her steed. But the Twins are never seen to die, and, in fact, she has gone into labor.

In the forty-eight hours it took to push me out, strange sights were witnessed and reported. A falcon, towering in her pride of place, was by a mousing owl hawked at and killed. Horses broke their stalls, flung out, and ate each other. Across the sky shot stars with trains of fire and dews of blood. A mountain lion passed and did no harm. A hundred ghastly women, transformed with fear, saw men on fire walk up and down the roads. The bird of night did sit, even at noonday, and its hooting and shrieking broke the eardrums of a shareholder and the lid of a city dome. All words or details, having been stolen from Shakespeare plays, these reports are questionable at best. But to the following I will testify:

Four years later, in a cavern underground, a child lay in her reed bed. Her nightie twisted into a tourniquet around her crotch; a black widow tattoo, inscribed on her thigh, crept forth to announce her family of origin. The child hugged her Barbie tight, unable to fall asleep.

In a far-off cavern, Outlaws were celebrating victory in the Second Battle of Glorieta Pass. Shrunken by the heat, a drum burst like a seedling, and the sharp acoustic of the Song Chamber cut across the Mortuary Tunnel, where corpses lay head-to-feet, sage sprigs on their eyelids and a tool, a pot, a book, or a doll under their folded hands, their prized possessions slated to be burned along with their bodies to avoid their rising as ghosts. The casualties at Glorieta were numerous, but death had dulled to a nightly reality, and no one had much to say about it beyond uttering a person's name, sometimes over and over, or someone asking, "You okay?" and someone else answering in the affirmative or not answering at all as they walked among the slain to the tune of raucous parties.

The drums snapped in the child's ears, and, disturbed by the vibrations, bats flew jagged all around her. By sonar, they navigated around her head of blue-black hair, and around the repurposed heating ducts that channeled stolen water through drains in the desert floor to underground plantations where high-density mushrooms incubated in guano. Clean water swished through the aqueducts, while urine trickled along the gullies, eventually to join an urban sewer system where excrement mingled with sweet shampoos, fabric softeners, and the stink of rotting tresses.

Raised in semidarkness, in visual deprivation, the child knew her world by scent. The subtle smell of rocks, laid down through plodding time, recorded the clockless hours. Hermit Shale smelled lonely, while Wescogame smelled sad. Manakacha and Watahomigi smelled nothing like each other, nor like Redwall Limestone, which hailed from the humid Paleozoic, or Bright Angel Shale that interfingered Muav Limestone. Only Vishnu Basement Rocks, dating to the Earth's commencement – and which, the grownups said, would take a megaton explosion to fracture – had no discernible scent.

Clean water pouring through the aqueduct into the adjacent Aquarium Cave was the ultimate prized smell. The lakes were quarantined from the corpses, and the health of their underwater inhabitants was vetted daily. There were blind albino salamanders and blind albino crabs, and the hideous blind anglerfish and briefly-sighted pupfish, whose eyeballs, being a genetic residue of a brighter world, sealed over with a layer of skin as the pup matured. Watching the blind anglerfish enact their monstrous mating practice, the child wished that she were eyeless too: she'd seen the male and the giant female cohere so utterly that their bloodstreams fused and the male degenerated till only his testes remained.

In the darkened underworld, where you knew your kin by scent, even before the Twins emerged, the child smelled a whiff of bitterness. She pretended to be asleep but cracked her eyes.

As Da-Tom strode into the cavern, his ceremonial sword, used for rituals and executions, grazed the walls, and a prehistoric handprint flaked ocher onto the floor. Tam-Ma, following, stood by the hissing glow of a paraffin lamp. Separated from the other Outlaws, they became just Tom and Tam.

When Tom placed his finger on Tam's forehead, where tattooed spiders incubated, Tam's expression was blank.

"When are these eggs gonna hatch?" Tom asked.

Whether or not it was a joke, Tam laughed but didn't smile.

Tom's finger dropped to her chin, and he raised her face to the paraffin glare to read its blankness.

Turning her head as if he were opening a jar, he said, "I can't tell what you're thinking." And when Tam said nothing, Tom said it again: "I can't tell what you're thinking, Tam."

"Because I'm not," she finally answered.

"There's no such thing as not thinking."

"Maybe not for you."

Disliking her answer, Tom showed his teeth. When Tam showed hers, the two repelled like a couple of magnets to either side of the cavern. They were wolves preparing to fight after neither displays subservience, or, equally plausible, they were smiling at each other.

When, standing over the reed bed, Tam stared down at the child pretending to sleep, Tom knew what she was thinking:

"Tam don't want her to go," said Tom.

"The kid don't want to go," Tam corrected her brother.

"Tom wants her to go," said Tom, who always got what he wanted, and though fierceness ran through her blood, Tam didn't try to stop it.

The child couldn't stop it, any more than she could stop the jets or the bombs or the blazing sun above, which, living underground, she'd rarely seen, but she was going to try to stop it anyhow, because futility doesn't equal surrender. Opening her eyes wide, she lurched up in bed and threw her Barbie across the cave, and screamed inchoately, being young enough to understand that sound is stronger than words.

"Shut up! Shut up!" shouted Tom.

Tam, trying a subtler tack, told her the Barbie was crying because the girl was screaming, and it was the doll who wanted her to shut up.

Tom grabbed the Barbie from where it landed, and thrust it back at the child, ordering her to take it and obey.

So the child took it. Sort of. Even at four years old, she'd be damned if she'd obey. Though it was dirty and dented and melted from a life in the sun in a garbage heap, and had weedy tufts for hair because a previous girl had cut it short, the child yanked off the head, leaving behind, in Tom's hand, the hard plastic body with its little penile neck. She shoved the head into her mouth and swallowed. And for a moment, she felt she had won the battle, because Tom shut up. In her momentary victory, everyone was silent. It probably lasted five seconds.

Then Tom shrugged, and turning to Tam, he said, "Your kid, not mine. Get her ready to go." Carrying the severed body, he departed the cavern without saying goodbye.

That night, the child was delivered by several brutal midwives down a narrow black tunnel into another world, where there followed a slow, hard journey, accompanied by a single Ghost Fighter.

In his ghastly arms, on his tireless steed, she slept and woke and slept and woke. She saw the night sky darken to the hue of blue that corpses turn or a person fighting for his breath. She saw the yellow sun rise up and a field of blue corn ripen, and many long and weary hours later, saw the night darken again. Spotlighted by moonlight, she saw an army of Moqui marbles kamikaze across the desert. Sandstone concretions in iron oxide shells, they resembled severed skulls. She saw a colony of sharp-winged bats like a low-flying black cloud, their wings carving the air. Their teeth bit through the armored skins of an insect swarm, like another low-flying cloud.

Though she had imagined nothing was out here, there were bats and there were insects, and neither one was nothing. There was even a raven. There was the concrete footprint of an enormous extinct creature. Signs of men were distant, but their fires outlasted the night. Faraway fires from slash-and-burns, or from blowouts or funeral pyres or wildfires or campfires of Drifters, remained visible at dawn. She had never seen the distance before. The distance was a fearful thing, but also it was a miracle. The distance was the future, and she was riding toward it.

When they stopped again for a third night, the Ghost Fighter kindled their own fire and stood like a ghost outside its protective hoop.

She asked him, "Where we going?"

"Somewhere safe," he said.

"Far away?" she asked.

"Far enough," he said.

"Is it dangerous?"

"Don't ask stupid questions."

But it wasn't a stupid question, and if she'd been older, she'd have asked many more. In the labyrinth of caves and sewer systems, had conjoining twins devoured each other?

Was she Tam-Ma's alone, or was she Da-Tom's too? Did the answer even matter? Or did the effect matter, not the cause, did the flower matter, not the seed? Does survival alone matter, and later you can sort out the details? And haven't we always fought monsters with monsters, though history tells us happier lies? And haven't we always revered the fiercest leaders who display a trait called *fearless dominance*, and if either twin had such a mark, was it not what Cain had aspired to?

"But where we going?" she asked again.

No answer.

"But where?" she asked.

He held his ground. No answer.

"Where?"

No answer. Until he left her at the door of her grandma's house, he wouldn't name her destination.

The campfire swelled and spat at the stars. Stars were something new, yet somehow the child knew to make a wish when a meteoroid entered the atmosphere and snuffed. She wished she was going home.

Curled up in a ball near the fire, she watched the red planet cross the seam of the sky, and the nodes of the moon, severed ends of a serpent, gaze from their disrespectful poles. Beneath the nodes was the Ghost Fighter, who wasn't the least bit nice to her, but under awful circumstances nice isn't all-important.

He would be captured on his return, and blood would paint his skin. His dreadlocks would be blunt-shaved and, like the earth after industrial groundwater pumping, his skull fissured with cracks. A manacle would grip his naked waist, attached to an iron umbilicus from which his captors in the shadows jerked him to his knees and whiplashed him back and forth. And finally when they were finished with him, his head would roll like a Moqui marble across the ravaged desert.

The child could not appreciate her mother's choice of chaperone. But nice wasn't important: he would never reveal the location of the safe house to which he escorted the MacAllister heir.

IV

DOROTHY

I was deposited on the ranch house porch along with an alligator purse containing a bone-handle pistol, a curious kind of dowry. For weeks I wouldn't talk, and needing to call me something, my grandmother called me Dorothy, and as the years progressed, I never offered an alternative.

I grew into the name. Age six, I was seated on a wire-spring cot with a black stain on its mattress, which to my grandmother was her granddad's residuum, while to me, who'd never known him, it was the man himself, and he squeaked when you sat in his lap. I was down in the basement, seated on my great-grandfather, and my grandmother was even farther down, in the root cellar.

"You going to use this paint?" I called, referring to a red paint tin that, having lost its lid, had scabbed itself into another kind of lid. "'Cause if you ain't going to use it –"

"If you *aren't*," she called, doing what she could to undo previous influences, including those on my grammar.

She was simultaneously struggling to reconcile the memory of her grandfather's wisdom with his painting the house red. A sun-absorbent color, it had sucked up the rays until the heat burst out and the house's wooden clapboards heaved away from the studs. It was as foolhardy as a Drifter stripping off his rags to cool down in the desert sun.

"If you aren't, can I?"

"Aye," she said, "just don't paint the house."

"Why?" I asked, which was my favorite question.

"It'll fade in the sun," she said, which was not the entire answer but true enough: the red had faded to pink.

"I don't fade in the sun," I said, rising from the cot and walking to the edge of the root cellar to show off my sunburned arms, which were milk-chocolate brown burned to ripe-cherry red, both foods I'd never heard of.

My knees too were dirty red, because my threadbare dress was short, and the tight puffball sleeves had cut an elastic imprint into my sunburned biceps. The dress was a hand-me-down from Tatsie, who, being a pampered girl, had had no need for muscles, whereas I was sinew and grit.

"Are houses the opposite of humans?" I asked.

Conscious of the smallness of my world, which ended at the dead lilac tree in the front yard, my grandmother respected the queer question. I was always kicking at my suffocating boundaries, and she tried to broaden my territory in every way she could.

"Most things in the world aren't human," she called up from the root cellar, "but there's no such thing as the opposite of human. Even corps aren't the opposite of human."

I watched her blow the dust off a can of beef without success. The dust was so old it had felted. She palmed the can for a bulge and, finding none, took a fountain pen from behind her ear to put a cross through a tick on the wall. She kept careful track of the finite rations.

"What are we up to?" I asked.

"Another five down," she said.

I thought five down was a good thing, because the threat of starvation was one of many dangers that my grandmother kept to herself. The last beef had been canned, and no fifteen-hundred-pound creatures grazed between the fences anymore. But seen from the dead lilac tree, a basalt boulder in the thermal haze resembled a Black Angus, and she let me believe it was one. When I thought the rocks were cows, my grandmother did not disillusion me. Truth was shifty anyway: given enough time or sunshine, red became pink, and in the root cellar her hair looked dark, though in other locations it was gray.

"A snake!" I shouted, rushing away to investigate what proved to be a loop of disused electrical wire in the exposed joists of the ceiling.

No cows, no snakes, no friends, no one but my grandmother and Henry. Through no fault of my own, I lacked companions, because when snakes came, they didn't stay but moved on somewhere better. I loved the mangy collie who sometimes nosed around, but he wasn't allowed in the house, and what rats arrived were trapped and cooked to save on beef. As to the thousands of Drifters who passed through the valley each day, they no longer dared to cross our barbed-wire fence. Henry scared them off, but how he scared them off I didn't know.

"Fake snake," I whispered into a boiler duct that hung off the ceiling. "I hate fake snakes." Though my words carried to the kitchen above, there was no one up there to answer. I stepped back and tapped the duct. No water. "What's this thing for, anyway?" I called down to the root cellar.

"Moving hot air from room to room," called my grandmother.

"Why would someone want to?"

"It was cold in winter once."

"Cold enough to snow?" I asked, obsessed by the idea of atmospheric water frozen into crystals descending from the sky.

"Snow was always a dream," she said, "but sometimes it rained hard."

"Sing the song?" I asked, for the conversation was a repeat I never tired of, and which always ended with "A Hard Rain's a-Gonna Fall."

As my grandmother crooned in the root cellar, I hooted Shakespeare into the boiler duct. Due to a shortage of age-appropriate bedtime books, and because a person can only be read *The Wonderful Wizard of Oz* so many times, I had at age six already heard the Scottish Play and memorized my favorite line. "Tomorrow and tomorrow and tomorrow," I hooted up.

I was counting on tomorrow. Tomorrow, my grandmother had assured me, the monsoons were coming home. It hadn't rained all winter, but the monsoons were inching west, and they were sure to arrive tomorrow. The question was which tomorrow.

Down in the root cellar, my grandmother was excavating three potatoes from a crate of sawdust, as if from a family crypt. She pulled a gin bottle from a shelf, opened it and sniffed. Because nobody threw things out, she'd repurposed her empties to store water from the well, and a gin-gin bottle versus a water-gin bottle were lookalikes that were deciphered by the smell. Officially, she'd given up booze and conscripted Henry to do the same. Unofficially, on the worst nights, she drank to escape the world.

I hadn't yet been read the *Four Quartets*, but if it could have spoken from the bookshelf, it would have explained, "Humankind cannot bear very much reality." Some terrible nights, my grandmother definitely couldn't. But most days, she lived by a different adage: if you want to change reality, or even just survive it, look it in the eye.

Passing up a water-gin bottle, she said, "It's heavy. Don't lose your balance. Careful not to fall in the pit."

"I can do it," I said, knowing I wasn't as strong as a male dung beetle, which can carry one-thousand-one-hundred-and-forty-one times its weight, but I was almost as strong as an African bush elephant, if one still existed.

"I don't doubt it," she said as she climbed out of the cellar toting a dusty beef can, a bunch of potatoes, and a stale carton of no-name cigarettes, because life was too short to fuss about cancer. "You can do whatever you have to."

Now, seeping through the detritus in the window well, the low sun struck her hair, which turned a more honest gray.

When my stomach growled, my grandmother asked, "You hungry?" In the past, she might have said "starving," but she no longer used the word lightly.

"Hungry," I agreed, because I also didn't exaggerate.

"Let's get cooking," she said.

Up in the kitchen, I sat on the counter, watching her scoop the beef from the can and whack it with a spatula. Out the sink window, dusk and last light teased each other. The bone-handle pistol sat on the drying rack on one side of the sink. My grandmother's eyes were fixed on the horizon. Henry was out there somewhere scaring away the Drifters, what he still called "riding the fences," his rifle slung over his back. She was hoping to see him riding homeward and was afraid she'd see something else. She knew what I did not: though there were no cattle to break out, anything might break in, and beyond the bleak horizon, the enemy was everywhere.

"Henry coming?" I asked.

"Soon," said my grandmother, who lived in fear he wasn't.

I was feeling bored, but I was used to being bored and amusing myself with simple things, like singing, humming, whistling, pounding, and twirling. Now, in the tedium, as I waited for my dinner, I thumped my feet against a cabinet door so that the faulty latch clicked shut then helpfully released, allowing me to kick it again. My skirt snagged on a loose sheet of laminate, and hiked up to my thigh, and when my spider tattoo crept into sight, my grandmother's face darkened. She knew the mark of her twins like she knew her own varicose veins, but it never ceased to upset her when she saw it on my thigh. It brought forth uncomfortable questions, like whose child was I, exactly? While I beat the cabinet door with my heels, she slapped the meat with the spatula, harder than was necessary.

Just then, the room shook, and on the shelf above the counter, the mugs and glasses rattled and a nineteenth-century bone china teacup, illustrated with a boy and girl skating arm in arm, jostled toward the shelf's precipice and fell. My grandmother caught it just in time.

"Lucky," I said; it was my favorite cup, because ice was as mysterious as snow.

"Stop pounding the cabinets," she commanded, as if I had made the little earthquake, though industrially-induced tremors were commonplace since the Salton Sea mines had become a repository for Sacrifice slurry.

"Did I make the earthquake?" I asked.

"You know full well you didn't."

"Did God make the earthquake?" I asked.

"You believe in God today?"

"Today, a bit," I said.

"Frackers made the earthquake, Dorothy."

"Then I could make an earthquake, too."

"You're too little to make an earthquake."

"Tomorrow will I be big enough?"

"One of these tomorrows."

Then, curtailing the inane conversation and serving up the beef and potatoes, she said, "Eat. You've got to eat to stay alive if you want to make an earthquake and change the world."

"Can I change it?"

"Sure."

"How do you know?"

"Because someone's got to change it."

"Why?"

"Because a lot of folks still love it," she said. "Eat."

My grandmother had used a word that I struggled to

define, because even the books she read me used the word *love* carelessly, as if it meant liking or enjoying or taking pleasure from or stealing pleasure from, or plundering until there was nothing remaining of the one you love. My grandmother didn't use it carelessly, but she sometimes confused it with *guilt*, though her only crime had been to look away from a coming storm, and who could say they hadn't?

Glancing out the kitchen window at the gravestones that demarcated the garden, my grandmother sighed, breathing out a suffering recycled through millennia, which has passed in and out of ragweed, sagebrush, enemy, and friend. She wiped down the wooden counter, where dry-rot spores were sealed beneath a heavy coat of shellac like a specimen in amber. She squeezed the water from the sponge into the empty meat tin to reuse it, because even pongy water could not go to waste. And when Henry at last walked through the kitchen, she almost strangled him with relief.

That, I think, was love. I could not define the word, but even at six years old I understood two things about it: when I care for your well-being, love begins, and when I care for your well-being as much as I care for myself, love begins growing up. That's all I can say about age six.

As for the next two years, little to report. Nothing to make the news. Games were played, like hide-and-seek, where my grandmother hid in the hallway crawl space underneath the eaves. When she did it once too often and I complained that she wanted to get caught, she found other hiding places, which weren't so stifling hot and which spared her lower back.

The alphabet game served as education in disguise, as well as domestic resistance to the Coordinate Shift. The strategy was threefold. I studied a coffee-stained *Rand McNally USA Road Atlas*, which gave the false impression that all locations were papery and flat and their size and importance defined by a red splotch. Then my grandmother named a kind of wind, the possibilities being endless, from solar wind to hurricanes to the winds that stand you upright, and I provided its geographical counterpart, beginning with a corresponding sound.

"Cyclones," she prompted.

"Salina, Kansas," I answered.

"That's an S not a C, but I'll give it to you. Tornados?"

"Topeka, Kansas."

"El Niño?"

"El Paso."

"La Niña?"

"Las Vegas."

"Diablo?"

"Denver."

"Dancing devils?"

"Detroit."

"Dust whirls?"

"Daytona Beach."

According to the rules of the game, the place had to still exist, and Daytona Beach was only allowed because the news of its submergence beneath the sea had never reached us.

Charades were played, but I usually lost. When she stuck out her thumb, I guessed she was lighting a match.

"I'm thumbing it," she explained.

"Doing what?" I asked.

"Hitchhiking."

"Doing what?" I had never seen a car.

"It's how you catch a lift on a horse," she said.

Then, to change the subject – because hitchhiking had been a failure, serving only to remind me that, under or over the earth, I was still a child who was raised in a holding cell – she pretended to read my palm.

"You have a stubborn thumb, like me," she said, which was all she recalled learning from a party-trick palm reader who'd declared her teenage thumb to be "stubborn" and her future to be very "bright," neglecting to say what *bright* meant.

Books, of course, were read, and sometimes looked at for hours. I'd devoured the illustrations in the *Encyclopedia of Nature*, where I marveled repeatedly at the mysterious rat kangaroo, and page after page of wildflowers so realistically rendered that I'd left my bedroom window open so that bees could make honey in the book. And when I'd learned that bees had gone extinct, I'd thanked God for wasps and other pollinators. Anything involving flora and fauna was invariably a success with me. Creeping insects, sucking insects, flying insects: I thanked God for them all.

The hardest game to teach me was what my grandmother called the long game. "Govcorps play the short game," she said, "but the Earth plays the long game, and you've got to play the long game, too."

"I don't know how," I said.

"You're already playing it," she said.

"But what am I supposed to do?"

"Just keep walking in the same direction."

"But I'm just sitting here," I said.

"That's part of the long game," she explained.

The long game, like much of my life – the thousands of other hours in which we were neither talking nor reading nor playing games – sounded excruciatingly boring. Even though I loved my grandmother, I hated my forced confinement. I wanted to ride around like Henry. Before the hens boiled to death, I was allowed to walk as far as the chicken coop to check the rat trap, but without flesh or blood to lure them, the rats had moved on elsewhere, and I had no excuse to walk beyond the cousins' gravestones. One tomorrow was much like another. The dirty line where the earth fell off was all I could see of the gorge. And in the distance, the white cul-de-sac houses with blackened windows looked like dominoes turned inside out.

Though I disproportionately remember games, in reality, games were rare. Usually there were daily worries, which often reached the status of fears. Some nights after Henry rode home, he left again so quickly, I wasn't sure why he'd come at all. Just time enough to drop his Stetson on the table, like nightfall on the steppe, and make the day begin a second time by lifting it again. "Maybe they'll know more at The Pig by now," he'd say as he strode out the kitchen door.

On such nights, until Henry returned, my grandmother stood at the sink, holding the china teacup so hard it threatened to break. Puffing on a cigarette as if she were eating it, she stared out the kitchen window at the dusking nothingness into which Henry had ridden. Joining her at the window, I too gazed out at the darkening, beyond the corn and the empty chicken coop to the bleary horizon, where the black-market Pig trudged on.

It was no longer the Higgly Piggly. Having survived by cutthroat adaptation, the grocery store had become another species altogether. The lone outlet for miles, The Pig provided an assortment of services from parking-lot campsites for Drifters, to news from the front, to the sale of valuable information to the highest bidder, whether Govcorps or Outlaw.

The Pig was the primary reason I wasn't allowed beyond the dead tree at the front of the house and the gravestones in the back. Anything could be sold to anyone, and my presence at the ranch was gold. Though Henry and my grandmother regularly visited The Pig, I never went anywhere near it, and when a couple of Drifters breached our fence, I was not allowed to meet them. I was hidden away in the hallway crawl space, where it was cruelly hot.

Over a matter of weeks, each had arrived separately, begging a glass of water. The first Drifter proved to be a good man and the second a bad man, after whose visit no Drifters broke through again. In the darkness of my hiding place, I imagined them as identical men: their lips burned, their eyelids too, dirt, mucus and calcareous sandstone crusting their lashes. Heard from the hallway crawl space, their voices were the voices of premature age, and before their words came out, a noise arose from their throats like wind raking through trash.

Standing at the bottom of the stairs, the good Drifter said to my grandmother, "Ford died."

"Where'd it die?" she asked, as she served him a glass of water and a plate of saltines.

"Could be anywhere," he answered, because it had died long ago.

My grandmother glanced up the stairs toward the crawl space, as if it could be there.

"I'm not a Drifter though," the good Drifter said. "Just trying to get back home."

"Better to drift than die."

"Sometimes hard to see the difference."

"I had a Ford pickup," my grandmother said, making conversation, because if you want to feel safe with a stranger, as fast as you can, don't be one yourself. "There are days that I miss it, but other than The Pig, there's nowhere to drive to anyway."

After finishing his water, the Drifter said, "Thank you, Ma'am. You're a good lady." And returning his cup and plate, he said, "I'm glad to know there's still such a thing, and good don't just disappear."

Opening the door to see him out and gesturing toward the enveloping land, inside which the gesture and all good and bad things intermingled, my grandmother observed, "Nothing disappears in the desert. It lasts for generations." Then she shut the door and called me out of hiding.

That the good Drifter left the house without incident didn't in itself make him a good man, and he didn't claim to be one, but he became one when the memory of his visit was laid side by side with the arrival of the next Drifter.

When the bad Drifter knocked on the door, the interview began in a similar fashion.

"Pickup died."

"Where'd it die?"

"Somewhere."

"So you're a Drifter now?"

"I'm just a good man who's done some bad things."

Though my grandmother disapproved of the answer, she allowed him a cup of water and crackers all the same. Watching him eat and drink, she said, "My granddad used to say a guy is the things he does, and he's no one else underneath."

"I guess your granddad didn't believe in a soul," the bad Drifter said.

"He just didn't believe in excuses."

"Thank you, Ma'am," he said and, in a show of deference, returned the empty cup with both his hands. Then he pretended to leave, but in fact he snuck around the back and killed and ate the stray dog who was my only friend.

I cried for a week. The canyons had been firebombed, the mountain peaks blown away, and deep as the Vishnu Basement Rocks, the Earth's foundations were shaking, but I cried for a dog.

My grandmother blamed herself for not taking the bad Drifter's measure in the same manner as she marked my height on the kitchen wall. But she was no longer a teenager who thought she knew it all, and though politics and religion reduced the world to black and white, mixing every color of light made white and mixing every color of pigment made black, and neither light nor pigment were moral values. Also,

Henry had a different take altogether: though translated as *good* and *evil*, the Navajo words *hózhó* and *hochxo* were not opposites or fixed dispositions. They were pairings that turned like the wind, without whom nothing happens. They were coordinates or directions in a journey that is never stationary.

When I almost died, the virus that tried to kill me could be called *hochxo*, but it's absurd to call it *evil.* My grandmother sat at my bedside day and night, waiting for a sign of health, and as the hours lengthened, she didn't feel like she was waiting, more like she was aging.

Rain pummeled the roof above my coffin bedroom. The monsoons hadn't come, but the Los Angeles inferno was burning so hot it had conjured a thunderhead and created its own weather.

When Henry returned from riding the fences, water off the brim of his Stetson puddled on the floor. Having grown out his hair, the braid down his back was a gray spine that carried a drop of water and placed it on my pillow.

"You been here all day?" he asked my grandma.

"Where else should I be?" she said.

"Let me sit a stretch," he said and took her place by my bed.

He held my inert hand, even though his own grandmother had warned him that, though dark winds can enter through the mouth, nose, and eyes, more often they burrow deep through the whorls of the fingertips.

When his wife lingered in the doorway, he said, "Con, get some sleep. Dor is just like you: if she gets it into her head to do something, she's gonna do it. And she's got it in her head to survive."

The sickness came and went, and when my grandmother caught it, it was my turn to sit by the bedside. I sat and I said nothing, afraid of words making thoughts come true. And so it was in a whisper that I eventually asked Henry, "Is she gonna die?"

It took him a long time to answer, and I feared that he didn't know, or if he did, he didn't want to say. But my fears were nothing but fears: it was just that before he could answer, he had to tell me a story.

Once upon a time, there was an old cowboy whose face resembled popcorn from having smallpox in his youth. The rest of him was a solid mass of sun damage and scar tissue, because he'd been hoofed by a horse, gored by a bull, and gone tumbling down a canyon entangled in his stirrups, his pony rolling with him, and more than once. At the age of one hundred and twelve, the cowboy worried he'd become too tough to die. He worried that, without his even knowing it, he'd turned into a witch, who aims never to die and steals the space allotted to the future's children. The cowboy didn't believe in witches, but he worried about it all the same. So he went to see the world. It was only the second time he'd left his home state. The first time he'd joined the US Marines and flown to another country where he'd shot at strangers, and they had shot at him. But this time he did not bring a gun or leave the country. He just boarded a Greyhound bus to visit a faraway city. He wasn't going any farther than the Greyhound central depot. He stood on the tarmac with his duffle slung over his old broad shoulders and stared at the rainbows that were dancing off the skyscrapers. He stood there a long time. He stood there until another bus, having completed a cross-country trip and returning to where it began, backed up and ran him down.

"That's your grandma," said Henry. "It'd take a bus to kill her."

As if wanting to prove him right, the virus came and went in my grandmother, leapfrogging over Henry to enter another ranch house beyond the boundaries of my existence.

But there were nights when my grandmother seemed nothing like the undying cowboy. Nights when bad news entered, and she sat and drank until she couldn't stand, and when she yanked on a cabinet door handle for assistance, rather than propelling her to her feet, it opened and slammed against her shins, and failing to overcome her stupor, she felt obligated to try and fail again. Each bruising, for a moment, offset her deeper pains and fears. Would her children be gunned down from the sky, or buried alive in the caves, or lowered by ropes and gears onto a Judas cradle? Or would they embark upon a self-inflicted transformation that was so monstrous it made her feel guilty just to imagine it might be so? Was T for Terror or for Twins? Were they monsters or heroes? Her mind flip-flopped as if she were slapping flatbread until, wadding the world up in a ball, there were no sides, just an orb as hot as the sun and the numbing relief of a gin-gin bottle from the root cellar.

One dark-wind night, I entered the kitchen to find a meat tin dumped on the counter, half-opened and baring its teeth. My grandmother was unscrewing the cap on a bottle that pretended to be water but smelled like antiseptic.

"When's Henry getting back?" I asked, trying to sound unworried.

"When he's back," she said and filled her teacup and drank, poured again and drank again.

She picked up the bottle and cigarettes and left the kitchen behind, along with all hope of dinner. She collapsed on the living room couch, the bottle wedged between the cushions, her eyes like piggybank coin slots.

When I sat down beside her, she warned me, "I stink like a pig."

"No you don't," I said.

I hoped the words would make it true. When she held her teacup slantwise and slopped gin on the floor, happy to have a reason to help, I ran to get a mop. At the hallway closet, an earthquake suddenly hit, and various cleaning supplies burst out. Back in the living room, the teacup flew from my grandmother's hand. The cup flew straight and the gin drops scattershot, and the Royal Doulton spalled across the floor. Equipped with dustpan, brush, and mop, I rushed back to the living room to collect, and one day fix, the broken china world.

But moved by the force of erosion, my grandmother stood to depart, and she carried the gin bottle with her.

"Where are you going, Grandma?" I asked.

"Nowhere," she said, as she mounted the stairs.

I knelt in front of the hearth and gathered the parts of the teacup to reassemble the skaters. I stood up and whacked my head on the mantel, which was inscribed with a mysterious language. Then I walked to the stairs and listened. The bed creaked in the master bedroom – she hadn't even taken off her boots. Uncertain what to do, I returned to the fireplace and stood. If I'd had a dog, I'd have pet it, but being all alone I stood by the so-called heart of the house until Henry at last came home.

I told him, "I bumped my head."

"You okay?" he asked.

Did he mean my head or my heart? Whichever one he meant, and regardless of whether it was true, I answered, "Yes."

"She'll be better in the morning," he said, but the way he fingered the brim of his hat and stared at it made me doubt him.

"Really?" I asked.

"Sure."

We stood there without speaking. Henry was a man who was good at silence and didn't speak if he didn't want to, but when he wanted to, he told the truth. Believing him, I started to relax.

"I gotta unsaddle my horse. You wanna come?" he asked.

"I'm not allowed to go to the stable," I said.

"You are tonight," he said. "I got something to show you."

I followed him into the darkness. It was a place he knew well, for though he was out on the range all day, if La Niña brought a heat dome, dropping a lid on the terrestrial cooking pot and turbocharging the heat beneath, Henry worked at night, his white Stetson on his head as if he were wearing the moon. But tonight he was dressed as if for a funeral, and his black hat resembled the hole where the new moon was hiding.

"What's up there?" I asked, when he stopped and stared at the sky.

"It'll come soon," he answered.

Then he wiped down his tired horse and pulled back each hoof to dig out the stones. His mare was so accustomed to the ritual that, even as he prodded and tugged her, she slept, defiant of gravity.

"Do you like the smell of your horse?" I asked.

"I liked it better when she was younger," he said. "She's starting to smell like glue."

"Do you like to ride the fences?"

"I like to keep moving," he said.

For a straight talker, it was a careful evasion. Henry had a flat way of talking, almost never excitable, like the trails he rode daily, so compacted they resisted the wind.

What did I know about him? He could eat prickly pear cactus without getting pricked. He could fix a broken harness, and he whistled in the saddle so as not to agitate predators by riding up on them silent. And he claimed he was from everywhere, though he never talked about anywhere except the ranch where we lived and the land of his Navajo grandmother. Maybe he was like the constellation of the hunter and his dogs, strong and clear in the sky but with a story that is ever changing: sometimes the hunter was a pesky boy chasing seven girls; sometimes he was a blind man who regained his sight after a soothsayer instructed him to walk into the sunrise. Certain peoples knew that the greater dog was actually a wolf. Others saw no wolf, just two bored snakes following around a bat. "There it is. Look up, Dor," said Henry.

I did as I was told. A meteor shower had commenced, and I'd never seen anything like it. As one star after another fell, I felt like hardpan in a monsoon rain: I couldn't absorb a drop of it, but it just kept coming. Needing something in my hand to steady myself, I held onto the horse's hoof pick. Blood rushed to my throat and sat there. The beauty of the flowering sky snuffed out every utterance. No *wow* or *cool* or *holy shit*. I didn't say a word. So much space. So much movement and possibility. So much life that human life cannot account for or possess. Standing as silent as the flight of owls, I couldn't even ask why.

"*Sa'ah naaghái bik'eh hózhó*," said Henry.

It is not an easy phrase to translate and was never meant to be known comparatively, but whole unto itself. I knew the word *hózhó* but nothing more, and I am not, even now, equipped to render the meaning intact. I can only report what it *sort of* means. It sort of means "long life and happiness," or sort of "in old age walking the beauty trail," or sort of "I have become perfect (or real? or complete?) and I have become again, as I have and do and will again and again become."

"What does it mean, Henry?" I asked.

He thought a while and shook his head. "You gonna call me 'Henry' forever?" he asked. "You ain't ever gonna call me 'Granddad'?"

When the heart of the meteor shower had passed and Henry and I returned to the house, the creaking of the upstairs floorboards had ceased: my grandmother was asleep.

"She'll be better in the morning?" I asked, wanting him to say it again.

"She plans on it," he said.

Though a plan is one thing and a journey another, my

grandmother planned to rejoin the living in the morning, and sure enough, that next morning she did. She awoke in her sweaty bed and scratched her burlap skin, mosquitos having bit her all over, the bone-handle pistol on the bedside table providing an invitation to suicide, which she wouldn't accept. She met the wretched day dead on, because, if there is hope, it lies in hard-nosed attention to the suffering world we love.

I told her about the shooting stars, and she was sorry to have missed them. The wind in the night had torn the lid off the sky and set the hot air free, making the wretched day a good one to work outside from dawn to dusk. Together we plucked cutworms and applied snakeweed to the corn to deter the rats. When the tallest ears nodded in the wind, I wanted to pretend they were people, but in the relative coolness, my grandmother preferred to talk.

"When I was your age," she said, "farmers had to fight off the crows and ravens to stop them from stealing the corn. Birds were a big problem, but a good problem to have. Sadly, you aren't likely to stumble onto a raven's funeral anymore."

"Ravens don't have funerals," I told her, certain I knew that much about the world.

"You think they don't, but they do. I went to one when the twins were kids, and I wasn't a welcome guest. Finding a raven lying dead on the ground, I didn't think twice about picking it up to bury it in the orchard to help keep the trees alive. But before I knew it, twenty ravens were screeching at me and dive-bombing me and jeering at me so loud I thought they'd shake the clouds out of the sky. I had interrupted a raven funeral. So I lay the dead bird down, exactly where I found it, and backed away slow. Tom thought I was a fool not to seize the corpse and run."

She taught me a lot about birds that day. First, the astonishing news that ravens ritualized death; then, a tale of cuckoos that I would never forget. A cuckoo had, once upon a time on the ranch, glommed onto a bull's testicles as if they were a feeding trough. The salient feature was not the testicles, but the fact that the bird was a cuckoo. It was not a magpie, which are insect-eaters known for their symbiotic relationship with cattle and which a rancher often found affixed to the more tender parts of bulls.

My grandmother explained, "It must have been a Scottish cuckoo who somehow found itself in America."

"Why a Scottish cuckoo?" I asked.

She told me that, unlike the American variety, Scottish cuckoos were brood parasites, purposely orphaned and planted as moles in other species' nests. They survived through imitation. A Scottish cuckoo could conceivably have been planted in a magpie's nest, and raised by the cattle-loving insect eater, have adapted to behave as one.

"Did it know it was a cuckoo and not a magpie?"

"Probably not," she said.

"Did it live like a magpie all its life?"

"Definitely not,' she said. "Scottish cuckoos behaved like their adopted family for a very long time, and maybe even thought they were some other kind of bird, but there always came a day when they realized they were cuckoos and flew off to join their people and have chicks, and start the cycle all over again."

"But how did they know their way home to their own people?"

"I don't ken," said my Scottish grandmother, "but somehow they always did."

Now she ran a handful of dirt between her fingers, attempting to read its contents, everything that went into it, what she'd done to it over the years, what had stuck, what was wasted, and what it wanted next. And taking up her hoe, she hoed under a patch of oxidizing brush.

I took my smaller hoe and did the same, being careful not

to hit a cluster of boreholes and disturb their architects, who, if they were creeping insects, might have moved on already, but if they were the sucking kind, wouldn't travel more than a few centimeters in their lifetime. While the sun parched the earth to its subsoil, with the help of friendly insects, we would bring up corn and potatoes and squash with delicate white blossoms.

We worked until the evening, until a coven of small flying gnats agitated the light, and the rocks drew the last heat from the late sun, planning to savor it deep into the night. Splashed across the sky was a glory of pink and reds.

"Look at that," said my grandmother, leaning against her hoe.

"Aren't we lucky?" I said, leaning against mine.

My grandmother nodded. "I've gotta think about dinner," she said.

"Meat tonight," I reminded her.

It was the end of the week, and the beef, in short supply, was only served on Sundays.

Working alone till dinner, I contemplated the story of the cuckoo, which perplexed me. Due to the *Encyclopedia of Nature*, I knew that most migrations were seasonal or light-induced or, like a caterpillar born to be a butterfly, involved some kind of morphing. But a cuckoo was something different. A cuckoo began her long migration when she remembered who she was.

And now it was another night. It could have been any night. The moon came, went, the stars fell, then pretended to stand still, and it was another night. I was gazing in the small warped mirror that hung on my bedroom wall. Behind it was hidden a fist hole, testament to Tom's discontentment even as a child. I, too, was looking discontented.

"Is it true people start to look like their dogs?" I asked, swiping the sweat off my upper lip with an equally sweaty arm, unaware that dogs didn't sweat.

"Sometimes," my grandmother answered, pulling open the curtains, which she kept closed against the heat of the day. To save on lantern oil, she read bedtime books by moonlight.

"Why?" I asked.

"Because human beings are plastic."

"Like Barbie?"

"Not that kind of plastic. It just means people change."

"I have a Barbie in the caves."

"You *had* a Barbie," she said. "You don't have a Barbie now."

It was a curious quirk that, regardless of getting older and more worldly-wise, I sometimes confused the present and past tense. It was as if, by scrambling syntax, I was trying to be realistic, for life has a way of circling round, bringing the past to life. The dog was a case in point: the stray collie had been eaten by the bad Drifter, but then, one day, another collie – chocolate and white instead of black and white – came nosing up the hill.

I tilted my head and, in the mirror, attempted to look up my nose. In the stray collie's nostril, a worm could be seen to piston in and out every time it breathed. I'd tried to yank it out once, but the dog had inhaled too furiously to catch hold of the jellied parasite.

"I don't want to look like the collie," I said.

"I don't either," said my grandmother, though it was the least of her worries.

She was standing by the window, looking down to the valley where the highway was a luminous snake of gasoline torches. Drifters were on the move, though there was nowhere to go. The freshwater cities had all closed their domes, and LA was ash and rubble, and the front was drawing closer. There was fighting in the flat-topped mountains, where the morbid fireworks had become so normalized that I neglected to fear them and fretted about looking like a dog.

Though I had been hidden in the crawl space twice and

been ordered more than once to stand between the corn rows when they were high enough to shield me from view, somehow I couldn't imagine that my own life was in danger; but I did worry for the dog's. Drifter packs calling themselves "werewolves" hunted poor stray dogs to supply fresh meat to The Pig.

Not real werewolves. I understood that. Wolves hadn't been seen in decades and their favorite foods, cows and sheep, only existed in farm factories, and black rocks were not Angus. But according to Henry, whom I sometimes called Granddad, the werewolves might, in fact, be skinwalkers, shapeshifters who traditionally turned themselves into coyotes. Witchcraft was adaptive to new realities, and witches can possess you with the smallest of your body parts.

When a Drifter pack howled in the distance, I bit off the tip of a fingernail then looked for somewhere to hide it.

"Give it here," said my grandmother, and tucked the clipping away in her pocket. "They're just a bunch of fakes," she said.

Standing at the bedroom window, she weighed the pros and cons of closing it. On one hand, the breeze was welcome; on the other, the hunters were howling up a storm.

"They don't even know how to howl right," she said. "Real wolves didn't howl to scare a person. Real wolves howled to say, 'I'm here,' or because they missed their mates. My granddad knew wolves so well, he could tell which one was which just by its howling."

"Is that true?" I asked.

"Aye, and if you pay close enough attention, you can learn where a bird is from by the accent in its song."

"Is that true?" I asked.

"Aye, it used to be."

It was true before the grasses ceased to seed and so the songbirds left, and with them the toads and frogs, and various kinds of snakes and finally even cicadas – because you don't have to lose much before you lose a lot. It was true that birds sang in the vernacular. The mundane world was a wonder, but if you pay no attention, it eventually gives up and leaves.

My grandmother again checked the window, which she no longer called a coffin window, for fear of making it so. Not a witch's window either, for if the diagonal kept out necromancers, it also affirmed their existence, and what protection it offered, it replaced with fear.

Beyond the single glazing, the moon shone like a tired sun, and its blues brought forth the shadows. The sun had set hours earlier, but Henry was still out there working. It was the season to burn mesquite, and the scent of creosote perfumed the room.

"You shouldn't believe in witches," she said, fingering her pistol.

"Granddad does," I said. "Why don't you?"

"Because he's got his thoughts and I've got mine."

"Do you believe in ghosts?" I asked.

"Not really," she hedged, though ghosts, who infilled the canyons, were the very ground she stood on.

The first MacAllister was out there in the dust, still crossing the desert by wagon train, deceived by the dunes of machair that it would be no drier than home. Out there too were Kit Carson and the US Army, still rounding up Henry's progenitors like wolves and marching them to internment camps along a soulless corpse-strewn route. Unacknowledged and unforgiven, seething between the grains of sand, the past remained the pattern of the future.

"Don't you believe in anything?" I asked, sure the desert was the Grand Central Station of ghosts (an expression that still existed, though the train station did not.)

"I believe in *you*," she said as she placed her gun on the

bedside table and picked up a book. "And I believe I won't be reading to you unless you get into bed this minute."

As she tucked me under a thin sheet, I rolled into a dip in the mattress, as generations had done before. It was still unclear whether the problem lay with the mattress's inner springs or with the magnetic pull of lodestones underground.

"It's an Indian story," she said, attempting to give some context to the Sanskrit epic whose abridged and translated version she planned to read me. "But not the American kind, not Henry's grandmother's kind. There's another kind of Indian. There used to be a place called India."

This explanation badly failed. Transposing the Great Indian Desert into the Great American Desert, which was the only desert I knew, when the blind king and barren queen gave birth to a ball of iron flesh, I imagined it as a Moqui marble rolling through the night. The sound of its tumbling was its name: *moqui, moqui* it rumbled, which means *dead* in the Uto-Aztecan language of the Hopi.

The *Mahabharata* continued: the ball was weeping though it had no eyes, and gnashing its teeth though it had no mouth. Its objection to life was so loud and consuming, its cries were heard by the gods, who sprinkled the orb with water and smeared it with clarified butter, and carved it into an army, at the head of which emerged a full-grown man: a handsome, dark-haired, dark-brained prince, who, ungrateful for his transformation, sprung into existence shouting, "But I want to be discontented!"

I couldn't bear it. I shot upright in bed, kicked off my sheet, flipped my pillow over and flipped it over again, unable to find the good side. I punched it to make a dent for my head, then flipped it over again. But I couldn't get away from the memory, and my squirming entrapped me further, for between the past and present lies a vacuum, which, like a hunter, is made stronger by that which struggles to escape it. I clutched my stomach, certain I could feel the Skipper head stuck inside me. Mortar fire in the distance became the popping of drums, and somewhere two anglerfish fused in a hideous merger.

My grandmother's worried bottom lip slipped underneath her teeth. "What's the matter, Dor?"

"I don't want you to read anymore."

"Okay."

After she closed the book and tucked me in, in the paralysis of the twin bed, it appeared as if some incubus compelled me deep into the mattress. My round face stared up at her like a anti-personnel land mine. I looked unnervingly like Tom.

She closed the drape to shut out the light. The moon's lamp disappeared and the room turned grainy and uncertain, as if gray were the color of the world that people had crawled up to.

"I'm glad you're here," she said, as she did every night. "I'm always glad you're here. Try to sleep." She took her gun and left the room.

I did as she had told me. I tried. When I failed, I lay in bed with my eyes wide open, listening to the shamming wolves in the valley and mortar fire in the mountains, and remembering other sleepless nights.

It was not the morning after the first reading of *The Mahabharata*, but a similar one sometime later, after we'd resumed the epic and a god had stopped time on a battlefield, and a warrior had learned the lesson that you act because you must, irrespective of success, because the world is not measured by the smallness of your sight. On this morning, my grandparents, both wearing heavy chainsaw gloves, entered my little bedroom.

"You going to be okay?" asked my grandmother, who hated leaving me alone all day but who had no better option. While burning mesquite was a one-man job, harvesting it was not, and it was too dangerous to take me with them into the open range.

"Have you seen the dog?" I answered.

Neither side understood why the other was worried.

"No," said my grandmother.

"Not in a while," said Henry, who did not define *a while*, which made me worry more.

I hadn't seen the collie in forever, which in reality was about a week, but I couldn't say how long a week was. An hour, of course, had sixty minutes, which in my boredom I'd calculated as having three-thousand-six-hundred seconds, but a single second could harbor years of memories that stretch out for generations.

When my grandmother said, "The collie's probably down in the valley looking for something to eat," the situation worsened further.

The werewolves had been howling all night, and though at that point I still believed the ranch to be safe, I understood the valley was dangerous, especially for a dog. My conception of the ranch's farthest fence, which separated life on the hill from what passed as life below, was defined by never having seen it. I imagined some kind of force field, like the urban domes that repelled the weather or the line of magic flint that protected the Outlaws' caves. Ever since the bad Drifter, no one came through the fence without permission, and through it no one went unarmed. Except now it appeared the dog had.

I bit at my lip.

"You okay, Dor?" asked Henry.

I bit and nodded without commitment.

Despite every precaution, my grandmother did not share my full confidence in the fence's defensive magic. Leaving me all alone for the day, she planned to lock the front and kitchen door from the outside and close the curtains in every room. She wasn't taking any chances.

"I'm leaving her the gun," she said to Henry.

Henry sucked in his breath, and not because the small bedroom was a squeeze for two adults with big mitts, a rifle over the man's broad shoulders, a pistol in the holster around the woman's skinny hips.

"She's too young," he said.

"She knows how to use it if she needs it."

"It's a mistake. I don't like it."

"You don't have to like it, because I've made up my mind."

They were neither of them consistent. He thought I could safely wander between the outbuildings and the house, and she thought I couldn't, and she thought I could be left alone with a loaded gun, and he thought I couldn't.

My grandmother removed the book on my bedside table and moved aside her old fountain pen, which had long ago run out of ink and subsequently been lost, and which I had found in the garden. "I'm leaving the gun here," she said, and lay the pistol on the table with its nose pointing at the wall. "You are not to touch it, unless you've got no other choice. And don't open any curtains."

Their undercut bootheels fading away down the hall, Henry said again, "I don't like it."

"I don't like any of it."

"I don't like leaving her armed."

"Well, I don't love leaving her alone."

"I still don't like it."

This did not amount to a fight. As if the world depended on harmony between a man and a woman, conversations between the two always stopped short of a fight.

My day began with a breakfast of long-life crackers and queer-tasting water, its hydrating properties enhanced by a pinch of sugar and salt. But at least it wasn't brown: pumped manually from the well, it had bypassed the rusty pipes. It was unusual to be alone in the house, and I was determined to make the most of it. I did my best to put the collie out of mind.

In the living room, I sort of played piano, poking discordant keys that refused to harmonize, and the discord gave me a headache. So I pulled a book from the bookshelf, but the words proved too grown-up. Sounding out the saying that was engraved on the mantel, I mangled the language that my grandmother's poor pronunciation had forever changed. I attempted to stroke the stuffed javelina above the fireplace, but I found I was still too short. It was not a good beginning, and I still had a full day ahead.

At the display cabinet, I turned the only key in the house not designed to keep me in or out but which stopped the glass door from flying open in an earthquake. I flicked my finger at a doll, but the spring in its head had broken the last time I'd done so, and now it refused to nod. Disappointed, I locked it back in its case, in much the same way as I myself had been locked in the house.

I reclimbed the stairs to my bedroom. I stared awhile at the bone-handle gun before I picked it up and turned it over and put it back upside down to test the limits of my imprisonment. I was forbidden from touching it, but would anyone even notice this small change?

The room uncomfortably dark and stuffy, I pushed back the drapes and opened the skewed window and watched the sand puffs scudding down the roof. I leaned farther out the window.

The wind outside was gentle, but it was not asleep, and might wake up any second, rousing the ghosts in the earth, who would sweep past on horseback, following game and weather. And the shades of wolves would howl with the wind, chasing game and weather too. And a whirlwind would rush through the window and attempt to spin the pistol but find it too heavy to budge. But, as it was, the most restless wind was inside of me. *I go around* in Navajo translates as *I am alive* in English, but if to stay alive I wasn't allowed to go anywhere, was I living or dead?

The soft winds were riling the dust below, revealing what was previously hidden. In the yard and in the garden, there would be arrowheads and potsherds. It was a fine day for a treasure hunt.

I pulled on my sneakers, which, being too small, had become sandals, their canvas toes cut out to make them fit. I hiked myself up by the sill. Aside from rolling off the roof or being guillotined by the window sliding suddenly closed, there was, I thought, no danger as long as I stayed near the house.

I was going out but didn't mean to go far out. I crawled through the window, slid down the roof, walked across the porch roof, and scrambled down a pillar. On the obedient side of the dead lilac, the boundary line, I kicked at the dirt, certain of a find.

I didn't expect another fountain pen or any significant treasure. Small wind brought small prizes, and it would take a tornado to bring what I wanted most, which was a wolf's bone, one that wasn't really a dog's.

I stopped agitating the dirt a moment to consider the missing collie, and then the wind surged and agitated it for me. Lodestones chafing in the yellow lands, their black magnetic sands went airborne. The dark stones saltated. They hopped and banged about and abraded down to cinders. Though I covered my eyes and closed my mouth, particles inched between my lips while tiny magnetite slivers clung to my sneakers' metal eyelets.

I stood unmoving, waiting for the wind to do the same, which eventually it did without warning. Wind was infinitely variable. As it had risen, it fell, and the earth dropped back into place, though not the place of its beginning.

A cast plastic nob stuck out of the earth, and even before I dug it up, I knew it was a Barbie. The headless neck had been chewed on, the hard plastic torso was scratched, and the rubbery legs were studded with pebbles. Though judging by the breasts it was not a preteen, nonetheless it seemed the spiritual return of the Barbie from the caves.

Just then I heard a noise. Looking over my shoulder, I saw the collie loping across the barrens and growing larger as he neared. I couldn't believe my luck. First the Barbie, and now the dog had returned. Who was next?

When I called to the collie and he answered by coming, I could see that he was limping. I hurried to the lilac boundary to call again, but though he came, he stopped short of the bush, and when I called him closer he refused to obey. But he lifted his paw to show me, then winced back his gums and gnawed at the wound.

A dog can pull a stone or a thorn out himself, but if he has been bitten by a snake, he cannot suck out the poison. And if he tried, worse yet, for he wouldn't know to spit. I knew by the way he looked at me that the collie was asking for my help.

Against the locked front door, I propped the headless doll under a horseshoe, so it wouldn't blow away in the next upheaving wind. I then crossed the lilac line to where the dog was waiting.

But as I neared, he backed away. And when I followed, he backed off further. He backed right up and backed right up, until he reached the dry gulch. And I followed. And when he turned to descend, I hesitated only an instant.

The sky grew wide and the house disappeared. The world turned to bone. Only rocks shaded themselves beneath the sapped and uprooted cottonwoods. The land looked dead, which didn't mean it was, or that it would be forever. Signs of desert life are subtle, and no-water followed by too-much-water followed by no-water had always been the rhythm. There was not nothing. A hunkered-down prickly pear cactus subsisted. Devil-awned speargrass grew. And, so much more delicate, in the dark of a rock, a single white Mohave aster curled over a seasonal seep.

Down in the dry gulch, dirt frothed in the wind, an echo of water pouring forward and overflowing. As my grandmother had promised, tomorrow was on its way. As if the patterns of the world were resolute, and the sky had its own ideas, the monsoon thunderstorms were increasingly finding new routes to old destinations.

While the dog paused to worry its paw, I studied the plated limestone. Beneath an old sepia flood line were the names of my grandmother's cousins, and above the line, *Tom* and *Tam*, like crosswords from a single T. No honorary titles. They had not been Da-Tom and Tam-Ma, they had merely been Tom and Tam. And the vanished cousins had not been the first to carve their marks in the stone. A bullseye, a sun-dagger, and two linked solar orbs had been inscribed by an ancient people, before they, too, disappeared. I wanted to join the ledger. I wanted to be part of the hour. I looked about for a sharp rock to employ as a pen, but when the dog barked and limped forward, I had no choice and followed without leaving so much as a scratch.

The day wasn't a scorcher, the kind where you have to remind yourself that the sun's return to the anvil is more welcome than its dousing altogether, but it was hot enough. And the hot scree stung my toes as I scrambled up the far bank and skipped over the blistering fields, arriving at the barbed-wire fence that delineated the end of the ranch.

A tumbleweed struggled in its grasp, and the wind drew spirals of sand up its split-wood posts. Hitched to the wire, a collection of Coke cans tinkled like toneless wind chimes. It didn't look like a force field, but I knew better than to believe my eyes.

"Stop," I said to the collie. "It's dangerous over there."

But the dog spoke a different language, and he did not turn back as I instructed but instead slunk beneath the wires, then glanced over his mangy shoulder and asked if I was chicken. *It happened in a time when dogs talked* was a common beginning to a story, and though this was not that time, the collie's mind was transparent.

"I didn't bring the gun," I warned him.

But the dog didn't care, so I didn't let the oversight stop me. I twisted my long dark hair into a knot, and was squeezing through the gap in the wires when the bun slipped and my hair tangled in a barb. Yanking it free, I stumbled and tore a tag of flesh from my knee.

As the small pain pushed aside bigger fears, I found myself on the other side of the boundary line, with nothing worse than a cut. Crossing the fence, I thought, was the bravest thing I'd ever do, but it wasn't by a long shot. From the vantage point of the ground, I could see the tiny copper trip wires positioned here and there on my family's side of the fence. Not familiar with land mines, I didn't feel fear or vertigo or inordinate good luck when I saw my own footprint a hair's breadth from a wire.

Down empty dead ends the dog smelled his way, slipping from front yard to back, and in and out of black carapaces. Street numbers no longer distinguished the darkened houses. Fire had spared one room and seared another or carbonized a lawn and deformed identical Jacuzzis into a grotesque menagerie. The dog stopped to sniff at urine stains as well as a warped tire swing hanging from a charred tree. Above the swing, on a naked branch, spun the frame of a whirligig, minus its colorful sails. It squeaked and it clicked, being a substitute for songbirds where only lonely ravens cawed and vultures hardly made a sound.

The dog strode down deserted streets as if he owned them. On the commercial strip, at the Burger King, no stinky residue remained of the beef patties. The fast-food joint had become a tattoo parlor before that, too, was abandoned. From behind the signage of a boarded-over pawnbroker's peeked the emerald queen of a Starbucks. The Cinemax was a graveyard, its seats buried in silt, and their valuable brass labels commemorating generous patrons had been stolen long ago. The mouth of an ATM was stuffed with trash. Graffiti branded walls, and the sidewalk slabs were tagged. Everywhere was the black widow spider, like the tattoo on my thigh, which my short skirt barely covered and which advertised my origins to anyone who wanted to look.

Despite his limp, the dog sprinted when he smelled food. High noon and stinking hot I ran down the blazing tarmac, its broken yellow lines the sun itself had broken, while to protect his burning paws the dog dipped into a gully where darkening urine lay stagnant, the sun sucking it away. The ammoniac air stung my eyes as the dog and I turned corner after corner. Suddenly my loneliness fell back behind me, for here were more people than I'd thought the entire world contained.

A thousand Drifter tents sprawled past the boundaries of the Pig's parking lot, and for the hundred tents going up, an equal number were coming down at gunpoint. The Pig, a privatized short-stay shanty city, had a strict three-day buy-or-get-out limit, and the instant a resident had nothing left to trade, they were evicted – or disposed of, if they were dead.

The best of the tents on the lettered tarmac were the dedicated pup tents in section A, situated far from the pits and the urine gullies and protected by the windbreak of The Pig. Semi-shaded in B was a conical frame sheathed by an American flag, monochromatic with filth, and several family-sized yomes with wind-resistant tensile membranes but worthless waterproofing. The patchwork tents in C had been sewn from offcast clothes, mostly T-shirts and jeans, and they resembled messy rooms. One was constructed from a prom dress and a tux, and another from a bathrobe with an embroidered HILTON. In C too was a tepee skinned with Tyvek HomeWrap. Another tepee, made of plastic vapor barriers, sweated in D's direct sun, its listless inhabitants visible like goldfish in a plastic bag. But F was by far the worst. There, muculent garbage-bag lean-tos sagged and puddled in the sun, dissolving into the urine gullies.

Everywhere, Drifters crouched in shadows and scuttled along the ground to avoid the scorching rays that tracked them by the hour. They carried Stone Age weapons: sticks, clubs, bludgeons, slingshots, and flint knives. Relinquishment of more sophisticated arms was mandatory, and if any Drifter still had a gun, it was hiding. They were sluggish; some were dying; some were dead. A naked man lay belly-up to the sky and barely breathing, no family to watch him depart the world. Families were in the minority, though orphans banded together, headed up by a dominant teenage male.

A hymn arose from a church. The most permanent structure in the parking lot, its walls were cobbled together from hollow-core doors and inspiring product billboards – COKE: IT'S THE REAL THING – and road signs that doubled as prayers – WATCH FOR WATER. A torn yellow raincoat overhung its entrance, and above it, an embalmed Salton carp. Inside its walls, a devout chorus evoked the trampling of vineyards.

Because the dog didn't pause to listen, I did not either. He tore on toward the trash buttes, and it seemed nothing could deter him. But as he passed The Pig's entrance, the heavy glass doors slid open as if of their own accord. They were no longer automatic, but whatever hands had moved them were invisible. The opportunistic collie shifted course and entered. He turned down an aisle of freezers stacked with no-name boxes and disappeared into The Pig's dim interior, serenely quiet despite the many shoppers in its aisles. The unconditioned air stank of flesh and meat.

I was inside The Pig. I was standing in front of a cardboard giantess with golden hair in a wind-resistant up-do. A water tube inched from the ruffled collar of her ice-white gown to loop around her ear and pump through a hole in her cheek. Seen through grinning red lips, her brilliant teeth glistened with spit, proving the discreet efficiency of the Heatwick Hydration Units for which she was an advertisement. A pyramid of black-market inventory was piled high behind her. The cardboard queen was dazzling, and if she was meant to paralyze, she did. She was supposed to be Tam-Ma, but I had never seen my mother's teeth so white. I did not hear the doors close behind me.

From the back of a checkout counter, a thin man wearing a baseball cap and seated in an office chair wheeled himself across the floor. He pulled up beside me and applied the brakes. He stuck his long fingers in his dry mouth, and dredging out a gobbet of trash-grass, rested it on the arm of his chair. Lifting a sip-cup from his crotch, he sucked on the plastic nub before reclaiming the gobbet and resuming open-mouth chewing.

He was staring at my sneakers, then my shirt and skirt. "That all you got to trade?"

Down the meat aisle, there was a brief commotion: barking followed by swearing, then a whimper. A bald man emerged, dragging my collie by the scruff. Like his mangy victim, the man's hairless skin was blotchy; unlike my dog, whose eyes were luminous black, his eyes were soapy. The collie had bit his hand, which, holding the dog by the neck, was bleeding all over its fur.

Amused by the bald man's blood, the thin man laughed,

exposing the yellow fibers wedged between his teeth. "Bitch got you," he guffawed, although my dog was a boy.

The bald man said, "The trick is to enjoy the pain."

They spoke as if I were absent, and though shoppers filled the cavernous Pig, I might as well have been negative space. Drifters lumbered down the aisles carrying their meager provisions and did not raise their eyes to observe what was unfolding at the counter. They knew their place: troublemakers had been weeded out, and for those who remained, whatever The Pig intended to do to a girl and her dog was not their business. The only interested party was the worm popping in and out of a dry nostril as the frightened collie panted. The men spoke as if I were absent even when the topic turned to me.

"The girl's got nothing," said the thin man.

The bald man expressed disbelief. "No one comes in here with nothing. Must have thought she could barter the dog."

"Dogs are finders-keepers," said the thin man.

The bald man agreed.

The thin man was struck by the kind of idea that he thought would make his vile day. "But she's gotta have something to trade," he said, eyeballing my naked legs. "Something up her dirty sleeve, or up her short skirt."

When his infinitely long index finger ran back and forth along my hem, I wanted to close my eyes and pretend to be asleep. Instead, I froze with my eyes open, like ice beneath a skater's blade. I didn't try to speak: fear blew away my words.

Thinking a childish vocabulary could sweeten the sick in his mouth, the thin man began to baby-talk. "Pretty girly," he said, his fingers exploring my skirt more freely, "I bet the boys sniff round you like your doggie sniffing round the meat counter. I bet you drive boysies so mad they'd trade anything you want for a eensy-weensy kiss." Then, turning to his bald compatriot, he asked, "What do you think?"

But the bald man was a philosopher and uninterested in sex. The scene, it seemed to him, was congruent with a Civil War diary authored by the fourth president of the Church of Jesus Christ of Latter-day Saints, which he'd read so many times he'd memorized his favorite passages.

He offered up a quote: "The American nation is doomed to destruction, and no power can save it. It is decreed that the measure they meted out to the Saints shall be meted out to them. And they are hastening onto their work of desolation, war, bloodshed and destruction, and woe, woe is their doom. The Spirit of Prophecy would cry, 'Oh, Lord, hasten thy work. Let the wicked slay the wicked, until the whole land is cleansed."

Uncertain what this had to do with his desire for a little girl, the baby-talker was unimpressed. Reaching a stick-finger under the rim of his baseball cap to scratch his head, it appeared that he was thinking. But he wasn't thinking, and he said as much.

"I don't need a prophet," he said. "I know what I want, and I want what I want. I don't even gotta think about it."

He leaned forward, and the bile on his breath came forward with him, and his hand slipped under my skirt. "When I get to the end of the song," he instructed me, "you tell me what you want from The Pig. We've got Campbell's soup. We've even got old Ben and Jerry's pops."

But unlike him, I was in fact thinking, and as the milliseconds passed, as his fingers climbed up my thigh, I had slow, expansive thoughts.

"Itsy-bitsy spider –" he sang.

I knew how to shoot the pistol.

"Crawling up the spout –"

But I didn't bring it with me.

"Down comes the rain –"

I could have shot his brains out.

"Wipes the spider out –"

Fear feels like a fetus rolling over in your belly.

"Up comes the sun –"

Grandma said when she taught me cards, "Hearts trump diamonds, and a brave heart trumps fear."

"Dries up all the rain –"

It would be smart to scream, but no one would care if I did, but it would be smart to scream anyhow.

"And the itsy-bitsy spider crawls up the spout again."

I screamed, and the dog was inspired to bark, but neither sound actually scared the men: the outcry simply coincided with their fear. My skirt up to my hips now, in the gleam from The Pig's skylight, there was my tattoo. Like sprayed wasps, their flaccid hands dropped: the thin man's from my crotch, the bald man's from the neck of the collie.

At the door, I wedged my fingers between the panes and spread them. Into a windstorm, the dog and I ran out.

Outside, the world had changed, for a breakneck foehn had risen. Struggling in the gale, the tent city was mayhem. A sandal, become a bird, slapped my face. A tent ripped up its seam, and its streamers snagged my ankles. Another tent ballooned and overturned and steamrolled down another tent. Everywhere, Drifters turned on Drifters. They scrambled to secure their few possessions or steal someone else's. They clung to their collapsing homes and called for help to God or their gang leaders or the Twins, but the wind, aligned with no higher power, returned their words to their mouths. When the downward gusts about-faced, the reversing wind ascended. The garbage bag tents leavened, and the blue sky blackened with polyethylene souls like a besmirched resurrection.

My dog and I leapt across the patchwork wreckage, and not by accident a man knocked into us as he jumped in the other direction. He lunged at me, and I dodged him, and in an instant he was gone, my collie with him. As machine guns fired, I ran back into the fray, but I was not returning for the dog. Even I declined to risk my life for the doomed collie, but I had spotted, sealed beneath a trash bag, a human baby thrashing like a drowning kitten in protest at its premature death as the black plastic mucosa closed upon his mouth.

I lifted the infant clear of his shroud. I held him in my arms and turned this way and that, hopeful some mother would come. But no one came to claim him. So I shoved back the raincoat at the church entrance, where believers sang through the storm as the mail flaps in the door-walls clacked a frenzied beat. I held out the babe, and some good soul received him.

From behind The Pig's glass entrance, the thin man and the bald man grinned, watching with anticipatory pleasure as the spider tattooed on my thigh took off for the hills. I was the mother of all trades, but my identity and coordinates were not a barter to be rushed. The hunter who'd been dispatched to track me would not make himself known, for it would take a little time to secure the highest bidder for the only MacAllister heir.

Without the dog to lead me out of the valley, I traveled empty roads that led to empty avenues that dropped me in dead-end lanes. I met no one except a raven, shining black and blue in the sunlight, and a red-and-black striped snake. *If red touches black, you're okay, Jack … if red touches yellow, you're a dead fellow.* Thank God for the wisdom of rhymes. I had nothing to fear from the reptile.

I complained to the snake of the heat. "Don't you hate it?" I asked. In answer, it slithered off to find itself some shade.

I was black and red too. I was dirty and flushed, and so dehydrated I'd stopped sweating. I'd been a long time in the sun, and with nothing to cover my head. I'd neglected to bring the gun, but worse, I'd brought no hat, and only tourists, fools, and suicides walk in a desert without a hat. Panting like a dog didn't help to cool me down. One knee clicked and my hip wobbled. I was becoming an old lady. The other knee throbbed, where the wound incurred from crossing the fence was trying to scab over. When a stone entered the pocked rubber of my sneaker tread, every step forward rattled, and the rattling copied my bones shaking. I shivered with mounting heatstroke, and with shock and fear, but not with cold.

By the time I crossed the barbed-wire boundary onto my grandmother's land, the sun had unraveled my mind, and yet somehow I was cognizant of dangers that earlier that day I'd been too young to understand: sensing the buried copper wires were bad, I followed my own footprints, and wherever the wind had stolen them I followed the deeper imprints of Henry's mustang. The safe side of the fence didn't seem so safe anymore, and even nearing home, the fear did not let up, for fear is like heat, which once it has entered the blood remains long after its cause is gone.

A good song could have helped, but it was a bad one that sprang from the recesses of my most meaningless recollections: "The grand old Duke of York," I rasped, "he had ten thousand men; he marched them up to the top of the hill and he marched them down again; and when they were up, they were up; and when they were down, they were down; and when they were only halfway up, they were neither up nor down."

As I paused to wet my lips, a single cloud in the sky above chided me and refused to darken into rain. I would not need shelter from the storm (as in the song), for the afternoon delight (as in the song) was the sun. And now the sun berated me.

He said the Duke of York wasn't *grand*, just a monster with a hump in a Shakespeare play, which always ends one way, with one person killing another, and if my people and I sang a better song, we would have changed ourselves and not the weather.

I agreed to sing a different song: "Up and down, up and down, I will lead you up and down, I am feared in field and town." But I didn't know the tune, because it wasn't even a song.

I was finding it difficult to talk, let alone to sing, and now the sun was swearing: *fucking Shakespeare*. I didn't have the spit for sound-making, and I was increasingly unsure who exactly was dehydrating. "Who am I?" is not an easy question like "What is two times six?" or "What's the capital of former Kansas?" So I closed my frizzled mouth and staggered home in silence.

I entered the reverse way I'd exited: up a pillar, over the roof, and in through my bedroom window. I needed water and wanted darkness. I hobbled down to the kitchen and retrieved the water bottle from the table and a solar flashlight from a drawer. Returning to the upstairs hallway, I shut myself in the crawl space. I would have opted for the root cellar, where the earth held the temperature down, but my grandmother had locked the basement. Though the cubby beneath the eaves was stifling, at least it was dark. There I sat like a red-and-black snake, curled up tight to hide from predators.

Though time passed, I had no idea how much time passed, nor did I know the hour it was when I entered my shelter. And I didn't consider the headless Barbie waiting at the front door as if to be allowed in, a sure sign I'd gone out.

What did I do in the crawl space all that time? At first, absolutely nothing. But when the fear and heat finally left my blood and I felt like myself again, I opened a tennis bag with a lightning decal and found it was stuffed full of diaries: an even better treasure than the fountain pen that had made them possible, writing religiously year after year until the ink ran out.

As I read by the solar flashlight, weakened by its days in the drawer, my grandmother's life grew with me like a skin graft. I imagined the grocery boy and his blond accomplice, all those years ago, growing up to be the men at The Pig. And in the birth of Tom and Tam, I navigated a dark and tangled timeline in which I gave birth to my beginnings. I read, I think, for hours, until my reading was interrupted by shouting: my grandparents had come home and found the Barbie at the door.

"Dorothy!" my grandmother shouted, running up the stairs and straight past my hiding place to fling open my bedroom door and grab the loaded pistol, exactly where she'd left it. While Henry checked the kitchen and basement, she tore up and down the hall several times, passing me repeatedly, Barbie in her fist, where, in the dirty whorls of her fingertips, whirlwinds had entered at birth.

Rushing downstairs to join Henry, my grandmother cried, "Oh God, oh Christ, where is she?" And because she was starting to cry, I emerged onto the landing.

Her terror gave way to fury. "You went out!" she shouted.

"Not far out," I lied.

"Where?" demanded Henry.

"Nowhere."

"Where is 'nowhere'?"

"The lilac."

"Don't lie to us," demanded my grandmother.

"The barbed-wire fence."

"Oh God!"

"Did you cross it?" demanded Henry.

"Not really."

"What do you mean 'not really'?" demanded my grandmother.

"No."

"Did anyone see you?" demanded Henry.

"No."

"Did anyone see you, Dorothy?" demanded my grandmother.

"No."

My grandparents looked at each other, silently asking if they could believe me. In my grandmother's hand, the Barbie resembled a wild tuber for dinner.

Tamping down the fear in her voice, my grandmother said, "Go clean up, Dorothy. You're filthy."

Henry said, "Afterwards, you help your grandma cook."

"And I won't be reading you a bedtime book for a week."

I obeyed and did as they said.

Henry had asked, "Did anyone see you?" Then my grandmother had asked, "Did anyone see you?" But if they'd wanted the truth, someone should have asked a third time.

Three's status as a magic number was not a childhood superstition that would pass as I grew older. A prime and a super-prime and the closest simple number to pi, three manifests as three dimensions, primary colors and divisions of time. DNA is read in triplet codes, and when such exclusive clubs existed, men knocked three times to enter a Freemason's lodge. In Greater China three means *alive*, and in Navajo tradition it is linked to unraveling, exorcism, and a journey through dangerous country. Three is the metaphorical child engendered from two parents. Three is clearly magic.

Asked a third time, I would have felt obliged to confess, and everything might have been different.

As they walked down the hall toward the kitchen, my grandmother said to Henry, "I should never have left her alone."

"Mesquite don't make charcoal itself."

"If The Pig had seen her –"

"It don't bear thinking about."

The moon hunts the sun, however slowly. This is one of many natural facts lost to a domed generation. In exactly six months, the acolyte moon would rise during waking hours to stand in the place that its master, the sun, had occupied six months previously. But in a race between The Pig and the moon, The Pig is the quicker predator. And though flies and other airborne insects may be swift and stealthy spies, they are sometimes double agents: something was going to warn the Twins that the location of the heir apparent had been compromised.

But first, they are riding unaware.

They are riding their painted mustangs, whose manes are coiled with ribbons as frayed as the untraveled roads. Their legions are riding a raiding trail between sandstone hoodoos, down fossilized dinosaur highways where jungle predated ice age and ice age predated prairie, where hundreds of species of songbirds predated clouds of black flies and the soil seethes across the duricrust composed of pulverized bird bones. They are following tangled paths at the mercy of glacial architecture.

The waning sickle moon slices the sky above them, and yellow sand whirls over red in the wash of a lifeless river, first reduced by drought, then emptied in its entirety by hydraulic fracking wells. They sidestep a witch's dunking chair, where the verdict was always guilty. Over hoardings of hard river stones, employed in the name of justice, their nimble ponies high-step. Beyond the decayed sentinels of piñon trees, they ride degraded slopes, passing the leavings of soapberry and netleaf hackberry and the relic of a Gambel oak, marred by a mule deer's antlers in the days of their abundance. They zigzag through sycamore scaffolds, in whose emaciated shade the bones of something have crumbled. A stray dog has joined their legion and, like a tiny colt, runs beneath the legs of their low steeds. They water their horses at a seep, and no No Trespassing sign can stop them. They ride deep into a rock tunnel where carvings of suns, moons, and flute players were forfeited by original peoples to a rancher with a questionable quitclaim deed, though all such legalities are moot. In the sandstone funnel, the retributive winds flick sand at their inked faces, and nuggets of polished chert seethe through the scree in the shape of arrowheads.

Entering an empty country where tough-skinned ranchers held back the end a minute, they ride over hillocks of bones, through dugouts, and over defensive berms and through breaches in high picket fences, the pickets chiseled into spikes. Mesquite, hacked down, has resurrected, meaner and thicker than its first mean iteration. It has devoured greener pastures. Their ponies jump a barbed-wire fence, around which hangs old baling wire. In the distance, an abandoned ranch house.

They ride like mute and implacable neighbors come to see the misfortune of others, or census takers to count heads. The house's siding has cracked like the earth, and a cheap tar paper fix is bleeding in the heat. The front door is missing and the living room windows smashed. A screen door sags aslant on its hinges, the netting slashed, the shellac husked away. The entry hall is varnished with dust. In the kitchen, a lidless crate of empty bottles whistles a tone-deaf song. A wall clock has stopped at 1:12, and a mantel clock at 1:25: the house has been gunned to time-stopping silence in only thirteen minutes.

It has been picked over not just once and not by just one side. The strings have been removed from the piano, and the plaster walls rived open to strip the electrical wires. Someone has stolen the thickest books from the bookcase to sew into the lining of a semi-bulletproof vest. The basement heating ducts are gone. An open attic hatch rains termite dust and fiberglass insulation, and in the yellow miasma of sunlight sits an antique traveling trunk inside of which someone has hidden and bled. Now only a threadbare tartan and the wings of a harvest of moths.

Outside, a dry well has been repurposed into a crematorium, and the portion of a person that is water has seeped into the thirsty silt. The kitchen garden is spent, but, fertilized by death, a green finger of a tender sprout is breaking through the ground. There is nothing here they need.

Leaving the house to its demise, they ride into another day. When at high noon, the sun pauses at its zenith, like high noon themselves, they pause too and sleep. Bivouacked in their saddles, with mounded shoulders, chins on their chests, in the altering shadows of an overhang, they resemble hanged men.

But suddenly they awaken with new purpose. Something has brought recognizance, and no history documents its source. A Swiftfoot or Tattler or some color of the wind? If it was a biting insect, the knowledge entered directly into their bloodstreams. If it was a dream, it reset the magnetite compasses in their brains. The Twins awaken from their sleep and turn in a new direction. Employing bewilderment techniques, they backtrack and hash-tag their hoofprints or void them altogether. Then, with Black Mouths and Ghost Fighters beside them, they grab their reins and spur their horses and ride across the anvil into another night.

Surely they are blessed by tailwinds, for no one can ride so fast and far on such poor and tired ponies. They navigate without the aid of the Comanche Moon, which bears the name of the tribe that raided by its fullness, mutilating their enemies so no witch could resurrect them.

Soon they will ride under cover of the new moon, which is also a moon of no apologies and whose darkness holds their own names. Only Hydra will crowd the sky: a nine-headed water monster that, when the hero lopped off one head, sprouted two for each one lost. The sky, indistinguishable from other skies, will forbid signs of the hour's importance: no meteor shower, not a single cloud, no lunar eclipse, no moon at all, just lightning and thunder in the mountains, the war cresting the flat peaks, as the sun does daily.

Their horses will pick their way through the matted wreckage of a great forgotten flood. Following a winding gulch, at a barbed-wire fence, their legions will dismount and tie their steeds to deadwood and river flotsam. Side by side, the Twins will squat and sit on their haunches to read the lethal pattern of land mines, which their own army had provided for the ranch's security. Then their legion will approach with confidence. And together they will breach the fence and walk forth up the gorge.

Their arrival was imminent. A Swiftfoot had brought us the message that afternoon, and my grandparents and I had taken turns all evening watching from the dormer window. Now tumbleweeds, rolling in the starlight, might have been packs of wild dogs, for the night was a lavish deprivation out of which anything could crawl. Its blackness flattened the mountains and infilled the gorge and erased the very place from which they were coming to take me away.

I didn't want to be taken away. And my grandparents wanted to hoist me onto Henry's horse, slap it off into the mountains, and do what generations before had failed to do – to protect the future in the form of a child in whom the next world incubated. But out there was wasteland and war; there was nowhere to ride or run.

In the dark master bedroom, drapes drawn against the moonless night, the slimmest aperture in the curtains allowed in a seam of starlight. It was late according to the casement clock, but the clock couldn't be trusted. The tiniest earthquakes advanced the hour, and the second hand jittered like a metronome and sometimes even ran backward.

The clock's mechanisms were noisy. The tick asked, "Now?" The tock said, "No." The tick asked again and again. Meanwhile, outside the wind harassed a tarp on the compost pile, and its slack end snapped, monosyllabic and repetitive: *Tom, Tam, Tom, Tam, Tom.*

In the light from the oil lamp, a tumbler of gin twinkled on the bedside table, and the lamplight flashed off the bone-handle pistol in my grandmother's hand. Eyes closed, but upright against her headboard, she was as semitranslucent as a corpse flower that blooms without chlorophyll. But she wasn't dead or dead drunk or even drunk at all. I lay with my head in her lap, trying to stop the time with my eyes closed too, trying and failing, for the clock ticked hard inside my ears. Peeking through my closed eyes I saw how, like a flower straightening in the rain, so gradual it is imperceptible, my grandmother's grip had tightened on the gun.

In his black Stetson and with his rifle slung over his shoulder, Henry stood alert in the dormer window. He'd seen something move in the orchard, between the snags of avocado and persimmon, which in one generation had borne good fruit and in the next bad, and which in mine was dead or awaiting resurrection. But he figured it was only the tarp that covered the compost pile.

"I'm going to pin down that tarp," said Henry, "and stop it banging about in the wind."

"Wait for me," I said.

Slipping out from beneath my grandmother's arm and promising to bring her a cup of stickweed tea, I followed Henry to the kitchen, where, believing there was time for something other than goodbye, he walked silently out the door.

Having poured the tea into my favorite teacup, I carried the painted skaters into the hall. I was about to mount the stairs when the first owl hooted. Owls hadn't been heard in years, and the sound reached my ears like the whirling of wind through tunnels. Memories sometimes return after years of laborious writing, or sometimes with a bang. I remembered my mother's call. I knew there wouldn't be one alone – at least two, often three – and as I awaited another signal, I could feel my heartbeat in my hand, which was sweating with the steaming tea. When at last it came, I left the teacup on the hallway floor and ran to the living-room window to see a dark wave like a second night sweep up and out of the gulch.

The dead orchard turned solid with Black Mouths and Ghost Fighters, who, like snake handlers, carried twitching machine guns. Their naked skins were etched or painted charcoal gray, and a darker streak beneath their cheekbones mirrored the night's horizon, and their carbines were a horizontal band of darkness. The Twins remained, as yet, a black hole in the night, but in a moment they'd step onto the porch and knock on the ranch house door, and for the first time since their ascension, every MacAllister would be gathered together, above ground, under a clear sky and under a single roof.

I raced back to the hallway to call up to my grandmother, or to run out the kitchen door to my grandfather, or to greet them alone at the front door. I will never know which. In the living room where I'd stood a moment before, a mortar bomb ripped through the wall.

A swift black wind ran through the house. The oil lamps snuffed out. In the moonless sky, other lamps flashed on. The clapboard face of the house tore open. The air turned blue. The living-room windows sprayed glass as far as the hallway threshold, and on the other side, the kitchen windows discharged. Winds hit from all directions. The front wall of the house vanished. In its place, a wall of noise. Sharp rain, or something like it, beat down from the sky. Bomb blast gave way to gun volley. Hats ran past the breach. A black hat, a white hat. A bald head. A baseball cap. A corp helmet. Glass shone like northern ice under helicopter floodlights.

The front door had been blown off its hinges, and the hat rack, with its dry drip pans, had gored the hallway's walls. I was on the floor, my face in the welcome mat, the stink of burning flesh in my nostrils. My skirt was doused in blood, only some of it my own. Glass had barbed my arm, and the tea had leapt up and burned my hand, yet the china cup, with its skaters glued together, was a delicate, pristine miracle intact on the floor.

I lifted my face from the mat. Seen through the blown-open doorway, body parts littered the porch. A torso reclined without a head. An arm had pierced a leg. If any of these belonged to either Twin, who was who or which was which? One body was alive but dying, and it had become them both. As if someone had died years before, midnight-dark dried blood had matted into a frazzled blond wig. An uplifted scalp gushed fresh blood into their red eyes. Their dog-dress-dog-cloak was shredded. Spiders and scars darkened and lightened their skin. Shaking out their last breath, a thousand arachnids trembled, and the dying thing was neither man nor woman nor anyone in between, and not one or two but thousands of shuddering creatures. If I yanked their dress over their hips, would it be singular, then?

"Tom, Tam, Tom, Tam, Tom," yelled the machine guns outside, though outside and inside were one. The grafted creature was staring at me. It was attempting to speak. Its tarry lips smacked together. Its last sentence would never be finished, or maybe it was all it had to say: "I want –"

I inched back into the house. My legs and lungs were suddenly useless. I crawled up the stairs, struggling for air, but even upstairs, the air was missing. The thin hallway walls tipped toward me, though the banister helped me to stand. In the dark coffin bedroom, I pushed up the window, but like a trap on a rat, it slammed down on my hand. I knew better than to scream. I spun about in a circle, as if to unwind the pain. My good hand was now the burned one. With it, I pushed up the window again. I leaned out and gasped for air.

Boots pounded up the stairs. I was almost out the window when a corp grabbed my legs. I tore a shingle off the roof as he pulled me down and flipped me over and threw me on the bed. The red high beam on his helmet hit my face, and it made me red with fury, and the fury drove out the fear. Suddenly, I was breathing freely. I grabbed the lantern from the bedside table and smashed it against his helmet. Glass and kerosene poured down on me. The corp slammed my hand against the headboard, and the lantern base flew across the room. I reached for the table again. My hand skimmed across the headless Barbie. It could do nothing to protect me. I found the uncapped fountain pen. I raised it like a knife. I drove the nib into his weak spot, where his helmet joined his collar. His gloved hands snapped to his neck and released me, and I took off down the hall.

But I was trapped at the top of the stairs. Below, in the entry, they were fighting hand to hand. A crowbar swung, and the butt of a semiautomatic. I turned to flee down the hall, but the corp had emerged from my bedroom, the pen still fused to his throat. I looked about for a weapon but nothing offered assistance. A rough plaster wall. A floppy stairway runner. Floorboards, nailed down. Nothing volunteered to fight for me. I pounded my fist on the busted banister, but I couldn't break it off. I turned to face my attacker empty-handed when the door to the master bedroom swung open, and my grandmother stepped out.

Her wizened hair was felted; her ruddy skin was hammered tin; her shirt sweat-yellow and booze-soiled and worn bare at the elbows, and a tail of eyelet fringe peeling from her prairie skirt. But she glistened with the shattered dormer window in her hair, in her skin, and, like sequins, the glass adorned her sleeves. And she knew how to use the bone-handle pistol in her ghostly hands.

The bullet hit his crotch, and his artery burst and he buckled. As he twisted on the ground, she fired again, but this time the bullet missed the seam and ricocheted off his armor. And before she could shoot a third time, lying on his back, blood pumping from his groin, he raised his gun and his aim was practiced. My grandmother's stomach blossomed.

There was no time to feel her death as anything more than a fact. The corp was still alive. I stepped toward him and, in my open-mouthed sneakers, stomped on the pen in his neck. When my grandmother's fountain pen entered deep, I leaned down and yanked it out. I was sprayed by a geyser of blood, and he was dead.

The windows were no longer viable exits. The shattered absent moon was sending forth its avatars, and helicopters were dropping more corps into the yard. The only option was to hide. I closed the crawl space door behind me, and in the creaturely darkness, I touched my way over the tennis bag that contained my grandmother's diaries. Then, in the biggest suitcase, like a portable fetus, I curled up inside. I closed it. I zipped it. I left only the smallest gap by which to reclaim the zipper tag.

They were storming up the stairs, their shouting distorted by respirators. They fired into my grandmother's corpse. They shot her sixteen times, as if she were a thing that could not adequately be killed. When the crawl space door flew open, and a red high beam glowed pink through the zipper on my suitcase, I held my breath. My next exhalation would be noisy. But before carbon dioxide levels forced me to breathe out, the crawl space door shut again, and my hiding place went dark.

My grandmother had died, not me. Beyond all jets and helicopters, the watchful sky had watched out for me. Why?

Why hadn't the corp just shot me while I was climbing out the bedroom window? Was I valuable to them alive or was I lucky, or had I become a witch and could not die? Why would the sky watch out for me when I was guilty?

Time tipped in and out of silence. Inside the polycarbonate shell of the suitcase, I breathed hot plastic in and out. The footsteps in the hallway became lighter and then heavier, then lighter again and less rushed. There were still lighter footsteps: rats were evacuating their nests in the ruined walls. But the corps themselves were more like ants, dragging dead bodies away. I was alerted to the sound of zipping. They had sealed my grandmother's corpse sack. My suitcase became wet and salty, but I was careful not to sob aloud.

After they descended the stairs with her body, for some time I heard nothing. I waited for the silence to prove permanent. But just when I thought the corps had gone, a floorboard creaked, and I had to start waiting again. Again, the silence stockpiled; then suddenly a door shut somewhere. When I fell asleep in silence and woke in silence, I couldn't say whether or not I'd slept in silence. Curled up in the suitcase, my limbs throbbed, and my burn was filling with liquid, and my bruises were turning fabulous colors, though I couldn't see them. If I moved, so did the glass shards in my skin.

The first pang of hunger was pleasant, because something in life was normal. But when the thirst arrived, it scared me. I had seventy-two hours to live without water, and no idea how many hours had already come and gone. I had to get out of there. Unzipping sounded thunderous. Could it be heard for miles? In a suitcase, like a cave, you lose all sense of the world's scope.

In the hallway, the dark runner rug had drunk up the blood and made it vanish, but the afternoon sun, slashing through the open bedroom doors, struck the splattered walls, which would never fade to pink. All over the house, the dead bodies were missing. Loose pages of books flapped in the wind, and the blue sky filled the blasted-out windows, and the rubble glittered like precious gems, but no body parts. In the basement, the heating ducts had jostled to the ground and the paint tin had rolled and opened and inscribed the floor. I pushed away the splintered root cellar door and climbed down into the pit. Glass crunched like ice beneath my feet, but the water-gin bottles were thick and not all of them had broken. I drank until it hurt.

I filled the tennis bag I'd taken from the crawl space, having removed my grandmother's diaries and left them stacked on the floor in the dark. I filled it with a water-gin bottle and a gin-gin bottle and a few tins of meat. Climbing back out of the root cellar, if this had been another world in a better time, I might have been ascending from a kiva into the morning light, except the cellar in the basement was not a ceremonial pit: it was a pit inside a pit.

Returning to the kitchen, I saw what I hadn't before, and if it had been a snake, it's true that it would have bit me. In my single-minded thirst, I'd walked right by the pink plastic udder hanging from the mug hooks beneath the upper cupboards: an electrolyte-infused rehydration canteen.

I stood as still as I could, trying to listen for a telltale noise, but I couldn't hear anything over my own heartbeat pounding in my ears. So I leaned over the counter and peered through the shattered window. No corps, no jeeps, no helicopters, no life to speak of, just a crater where the corn had been. The chicken coop stood, minus the top of its wind tower, and the sun shot down through the shaft. Nothing out there, I thought, except the vast and eerie dryness. The corps had forgotten an udder. More good luck?

I added it to my bag. Then I packed a pot and a pan, and from a utensils drawer, which had ejected itself across the kitchen, a dessert spoon, because I'd need to dig things up. Also a sharp paring knife, small enough to hide in my shirtsleeve. I found a set of oven mitts to protect my hands from the sun, and a tea towel, which was filthy but too dark blue to show it. Because I had no hat, I tied a large dingy dishcloth, splattered brown and yellow, into a kerchief on my head. Then, wiping away the glass shards, I climbed onto the counter and tapped about on the highest shelf, trying to locate the tartan shortbread tin that my grandmother had used as a piggy bank. It had orbited the kitchen, and I found it near the door. Always hard to open, the seal had held, and breaking a nail while prying up the lid, I instinctively pocketed the shard. I added the contents of the bank to my bag, but after I tested the weight, I discarded the pennies and replaced the iron cook pot with an aluminum one.

I couldn't leave by the front door, for the pillars had kicked from under the porch roof and the roof had fallen, leaving a long seismic gash in the clapboards. The kitchen door hung off its hinges, and I paused briefly at the threshold. The final MacAllister was forfeiting her home to a silence such as it had never known. Already, the house had begun its transition into a pixilation on a Govcorps surveillance screen.

Stepping into the garden, I didn't find a garden. Corn kernels studded the dust, and the gravestones had cracked. The firepit's plywood cover had become a gate on a road to nowhere: tattered and jagged, impaled in the ground, it stood upright on one end. The pit itself had been shoveled in, and whirlwinds feathered the boot prints in the dirt. It was a mass grave, but no ghost called to me because no one I loved was down there, their corpses being too valuable to dump.

But something else was calling from the chicken coop. Not calling, exactly: banging. And it wasn't the wind flapping the damper in the silo, which lay busted and splintered on the ground.

I was not the only one to hear it. I'd been wrong about the canteen and the luck. As if inspired by his location in the hands' cabin down the lane, a corp emerged in its doorway, shouting, "I'll cut your fucking hands off this time!"

I slipped around the rear of the coop. Peering through the gaps in the split-wood wall, what I witnessed, the years would never take back.

In one corner was an empty garden chair with a synthetic woven seat, sagging from the many hours the corp had sat there. A shovel was propped against the roosting-shelves. And on the ground, arranged in what appeared to be some deliberate and personal order, were ranch tools, extracted from a wooden box with a faded Coca-Cola logo. An ax-head, skewers, a sander, wire cutters, a fence chain strainer, pliers, a stockpile of nails.

In the other corner, Henry. His shapeless ankle held in a wolf trap, which had also lived in that box, he sat hunched on an upturned bucket. Even naked, bloody, and swollen from having been beaten, his hair chopped off and his back to me, I knew he was my grandfather.

He had caught a rat. He had killed it by banging it against the bucket. The same banging had brought the corp out of the cabin. Now he had it in his mouth and was sucking on its blood, because, before all other causes, Henry was dying of thirst.

When the corp swooped under the henhouse door, grabbed the shovel and smashed it across the side of Henry's head, the rat – like a flying squirrel, if such a creature still existed – flew out of his hand. His head swung round like an owl's, so that he and I were face to face, divided only by the split-wood wall. Though he could not see me, I saw him indelibly, as he would never see himself. His gouged-out eyes were sinkholes.

I ran. Wind shuddered through the rubble and the hollows. My sneakers flapped against the rocks. My getaway bag over my shoulder, I scrambled through the dry gulch, following the footprints of the Twins and the Black Mouths and the Ghost Fighters, only in reverse. I did not hesitate at the fence, even at the sight of their slaughtered ponies. My breathing grew hard and loud, and I sang painfully as I ran.

My song was not a random song this time. This time, my song was not a useless song, without power to change the world. My song was an ancestor's gift to me, whatever my parentage was. It was a song that had survived for generations, though its singers had died, and it had weathered hundreds of years of war and systematic silencing. Sung right, the song, from the start, drove demons from the heart. Everything will change, but the song remains.

Down in the valley, in a gutted house, on a road bearing no name, I stopped, but not to rest. Seated on the floor with my legs in front of me, I unpacked the gin and paring knife. I knocked back the gin and splashed it on the blade. And inch by inch, I cut away the spider on my thigh.

I did not cry out or lose my nerve. I quit only to douse the gash with gin and slap my hands together in an attempt to stop them shaking, then resumed. I moaned but I did not scream as a hallucinatory pain shot up my thigh into my spine, then into the base of my neck, where it displaced deeper horrors. The dark blue tea towel was a night hiding filth, and with it, I bound my wound.

I performed these acts for my own protection. I sawed off my hair and buried the locks. Then, gathering my few belongings, I limped toward the highway.

Like other species, extant or extinct, I would travel far. A night moth's migration is so extensive it spans generations, and no individual night moth knows both beginning and end. No longer with us, the monarch butterfly once crisscrossed the planet, seeking milkweed like a teat, and snow geese and sandhill cranes seared off every ounce of body fat in their annual flight.

Even now, the tiny blackpoll warbler flies what equals ten times to the moon and back in its little life. It was my turn.

I held close to my fellow Drifters, who followed graffiti maps between black-market oases. In this, I was not so birdlike, for some birds will strike out solo, following risky paths in competition to spread their genes. Nor was my walk as long as most avian flights, but being a human it seemed it, because we can retell the past and imagine the future.

When at last it ended, it wasn't ever over.

Every official radio station, website, platform, and billboard had announced the Demon Twins' death, and, as intended, it had sent an earthquake across the Outlaw ranks. Old faultlines had opened up. Black Mouths had fought with Ghost Fighters, red with blue, males with females, husbands with wives, the old with the young, brothers with sisters, priests with preachers, preachers with atheists, hunters with farmers, cowboys with Indians, you name it. Govcorps had exploited the rifts, and the war had dwindled to scattered resistance, called "Terrorism in Peacetime" as if it were a song. Like a song, it would have endless refrains.

The dignitaries gathered for the Reconstitution Signing Ceremony beneath a New Eastern dome, and among them sat the officials of Yácorp and, on a folding chair in the hardscape Rose Garden, a promising intern named Joel Saunders, who would rise with the years through the ranks. McDonald's burgers were served, but otherwise the highly choreographed ceremony was modeled on an historically inaccurate painting from the first Revolutionary War that depicted the Founding Fathers gathered in pleasant accord. The signing established Govcorps' infinitude and the permanency of the First Intercorporate Congress and its regulatory body, the Christian Brigade Association, or CBA.

The National Sacrifice Area now extended to the Pacific Ocean. A twenty-four-hundred-mile fence ran north/south along -101.35, from the southern border of Free Nunavut Canada to the Great Mexican Wall. Beyond it, all property, assets, and lives, including human lives, were forfeit. The White House press secretary explained it as a long-needed downsizing, a small price paid for the New East's American Way of Life. People did their best to nod.

The populations in the domes, the majority of whom were not psychopaths or even malignant narcissists but just ordinary people, soothed their guilty consciences with calming lies and distraction. Retro was back, and it was all the rage. Nintendo. Xbox. There was a boom in babies, both real and AI-generated. And beginning in CB grade school, teachers explained to pupils that the sacrifice of land as resource was the natural basis for the commodification of people as resource. No one saw a Drifter anyhow, and because, as the White House spun it, they wished to live outside, they were increasingly called Outsiders.

"Commodification is charity" was a surprisingly effective slogan, and a nineteenth-century expression, resurrected from the Indian Wars – "nits make lice," – was equally effective; both successfully redefined the innocence of children. Kids proved to be a viable workforce unless they were sickly and weak, in which case, like adult males and senior citizens, their culling was systematic. In the roundup, the older ranks of children, capable of working the mines, were traded in groups of a dozen, while the fates of budding female preteens were determined on a case-by-case basis, informed by secondary sexual features.

Not all dome dwellers, however, were so heartless. Though the Christian Brigade Association never made a formal objection, some renegade Brigaders declared the Drifter policy to be a sin. One particularly strongheaded woman became "a bulldog running along at the feet of Jesus, barking at what He doesn't like," and staging hatchetations and breaking the windows of Walmart. To quiet the bleeding hearts and protect private property, the Adoption Alternative was instituted.

But it wasn't easy to get to the Distribution Wheel. Boys were not invited, only the prettiest girls up to nine years old, displaying no deformities, breaks, fractures, or tooth rot and free from chronic cough. If, in addition, they showed a regular heartbeat and a strong steady pulse, they were spared commodification. They were sent to a cattle auction house situated along the former Kansas border, where, if you played your cards right, you just might get adopted.

Like the other competitors, my head was shaved and I wore a colorless smock, but I'd rolled up the sleeves to expose my muscles. I wasn't leaving my future to luck. I knew how to lie and had already received Christ with enthusiasm. Waiting my turn in the viewing spoke, I darkened my lashes with spit and cleaned one fingernail with another. Then I pinched my cheeks.

I'd carefully prepared my answers.

"Where are you from?"

"My father came from Idaho. My mother came from Utah."

"What's your family name?"

"York."

"How did you get that scar on your thigh?"

"A pack of wild dogs."

When the alarm sounded and the gates opened, I walked into the pen and planted my feet wide and stood on the hot fierce earth. My bare feet could take it. When my would-be mother reached a hand through the bars to touch me, I smiled to show off my good teeth.

V

SACRIFICE

In the substrata of Ulysses's Grand Hotel, entering Departures, the heat slapped my face like a pimp. I waited as a parade of armored cars rolled over a spike strip and ascended an out-ramp. The steel gates opened and closed, and the outdoor air poured in.

A hot gale blew, part atmospheric pressure, part helicopters agitating the upper dark, their searchlights tracking targets in the streets. Wearing insulated body sheathing and cradling assault rifles, ground-corps manned the cleft between inside and out. When, beyond the iron cordons, pedestrian gangs stampeded cars, they fired. The gangs were dominated by children, because Outsiders died young.

The spotlights seared the rain. When had the deluge begun? If I could miss something as fundamental as rain, what else had I overlooked?

Waiting for the Yácorp limo to pull through Vetting, I imagined myself again in the elevator, counting the numbers upwards, preparing to resume my position in bed across from my sleeping husband, having forgotten why I rode down in the first place. But I could not forget. For while much may be forgiven, some things must not be forgotten.

No surprise that the Yácorp limo was ushered through Vetting without being detained. It drew up on the second. 23:59:59. I touched the security chit to the scanner and glanced into the retina reader, and the passenger door swung open of its own accord.

"Hot out there," I said, as the door closed behind me, and I immediately cooled off in the perfect temperature.

Protected daily from the bitter sun by tinted bulletproof glass, the driver's skin looked pasty and smelled flammable with aftershave. His fingernails were imprinted with the Yácorp logo. He was a typical Govcorps chauffeur, accustomed to absorbing blame.

"Sorry," he said.

"The heat isn't your fault," I answered, "any more than anyone else's."

What personal atrocities he'd committed I can't say and for all I knew, he was somehow or other a primary cause of The Change. But though our individual stories are different, our DNA is near identical: the heat is the responsibility of us all.

In the rearview mirror, the chauffeur's eyes were unreadable, as everything would be from here. I had absolved him of the weather, but he merely repeated, "Sorry, Mr. Saunders."

Don't trust your senses, trust your betters was a rule, and following the rules perfectly, he expressed no doubt about my title. If Yácorp had confirmed his passenger as Mr. Joel Saunders, and security chit and biometric identification had reconfirmed it, it was not for a chauffeur to wonder at my dress, heels, and breasts. Though gender reassignment was illegal, a Yácorp bigwig could get away with murder.

At the exit, the guards stepped back from the limo. The steel sheet opened. Ascending into the downpour, the chauffeur put his foot to the floor while cameras flashed and whited out his face. The air thrummed with sirens, and in the echo chamber beneath farmscrapers and high-rises, I could not say if the corp tanks were tailing us or were a city mile away.

"Are those sirens for us?" I asked.

Misunderstanding my concern, he apologized again, this

time on behalf of Yácorp. I had, he explained, contacted Central Hub too late to arrange for a corp escort. Then he assured me that we were sufficiently armed.

The gun strapped to his ankle bulged beneath his trouser cuff. There'd be another under his seat, and a third beneath the lip of the wheel well.

The limo took the corners at fifty, the straight urban runs at seventy. No speed limits in Ulysses. The only speed bumps were the people in the road, whom you couldn't really call pedestrians. The worst of them were on their stumps, the better-off on their peg legs. As sludge drained from the farmscrapers, Outsiders crawled through it.

The car slowed.

"Is your door locked, Mr. Saunders?"

He was reciting a redundant script, for the door had locked automatically upon my entry.

"Why are we stopping?" I asked.

"Restricted road. Awaiting clearance."

I pressed my face to the window. Beyond it, in the downpour were children protected from the rain, if they were protected at all, by shredded garbage bags. In the sky, a rainbow lullaby's multicolored lights, and HIGH AS AN ELEPHANT'S EYE, as if somewhere in the world there were elephants.

Six hundred and fifty thousand sandhill cranes had once sky-surfed ineffable tributaries to join the great Central Flyway, crossing over Kansas. They had heeded no human boundaries, but, adaptive, had fed on waste crop as they slog-flapped up the north/south airscape of invisible rivers and streams, in their multi-thousand-mile migration toward the ice sheets. Did they pause in Oklahoma on a beautiful morning when the corn hit the height of an African species encaged in American zoos? Did they pierce a rainbow in Kansas? Maybe. But without a doubt, they flew, and every year they flew again. I only write *they flew* because English is restricted to a firm past tense. Some languages, like Navajo, have the option of a repetitive tense, where *it happened* means *it happened again*. Or, like most varieties of Chinese, no tense at all. Thus time, and therefore space, are not straight and narrow. No sandhill cranes in the sky tonight, but one night soon, I promise you, the origami versions will rise.

I slid my wedding ring off my finger and dropped the gold band through the charity hole. The children swarmed; a panel in the air flashed YÁCORP. The chauffeur accelerated hard, and the children fell away like snow, leaving smudges on my window.

On the chauffeur's neck, a wormlike mound of smooth skin extended under his collar. I asked, "How did you get that scar?"

It was an intimate and inappropriate question, especially coming from "Mr. Saunders", the repetition of whose name became an act of absolution: if Mr. Saunders had to kill the chauffeur, it would not be I who did the deed. But I didn't assume Mr. Saunders would have to kill the chauffeur at all. My journey from here on wasn't history – not written, not predestined – and in the first frontier, even the dreaded Comanche were as likely to adopt a captive as to torture and slowly kill him.

"Wild dogs," said the chauffeur, and though I felt a solidarity with his answer, I knew that he was lying.

Through the hard rain falling, toward the granular beams of the searchlights, the limo drove a desolate road. It had taken less than a half an hour to exit the city proper and enter the flat yellow expanse of stars and dust and wind. And, as the limo moved west, the rain cleared even quicker than it had arrived.

Not a living soul in sight. Speeding toward the fence, the speedometer hit 120. Soon we would traverse the threshold to the voided and sacrificial miles.

Others had made this trip before me. Snakes had crossed the fence at a weak point accessible to reptiles up to 3.5 inches in width, and having integrated antipersonnel land mines into the matrix of their fears, they had successfully navigated a hundred-mile minefield. In the lab at my university, their skins had been encrypted using a simple substitutionary binary code (A and C: 0; T and G: 1) capable of being decrypted using remedial technology – equally simple biological computers, powered by coenzymes. Urged on by the scent of water and leaving waves in the sand for the winds to subtract, the snakes had carried their missives to the single Outsider Outlaw community, west of -101.35, with whom Insider Outlaws had successfully maintained contact after the erection of the fence.

The first such snake had extended our range: carrying coordinates provided by Joel Saunders, it had transmitted the positions of other holdouts, thus enabling the reunification of an army of mustangs in Carlsbad watched over by a band of kids who were now fully fledged adults, with subterranean gardens and arsenals in Lechuguilla, where vast underground communities waited to be reactivated. The second snake, following some years later, had reported the existence and precise location of the MacAllister homestead, where a collection of diaries could be retrieved, confirming the identity of the agent responsible for such rare intelligence.

There were many snakes thereafter. There were snakes throughout my marriage. Nietzsche wrote that a snake who cannot cast his skin must die, but I write a snake is a snake *because* he casts his skin. You cannot separate being and doing. The ultimate snake – the *go* snake – did not move for years. When it did, it read simply, "Mobilize. Our girl is coming home."

In the double darkness of night and limousine, I might have believed myself young again. I leaned my head against the memory-foam headrest. I stared at the scarlike band on my ring finger. I opened my purse and stared at the protective Faraday bag, inside of which my phone held maps and photos and every accessible document from my husband's palm-reader.

If I could have risked opening it, in the phone's blue light, I'd have typed Joel's name – typed *goodbye* and erased it, typed it again and erased it. Too trite, too clichéd, and even if it was true, too final. In the end, I'd have written:

Joel,

You asked who the hell I think I am.
I am the girl who got away.
I am the woman who keeps going.
That's who the hell I am.

There is much more I wanted to write. For really, who am I? I am the caves. I am the ranch. I am the desert that's never as dead as it looks. I am the tree that loses every limb but survives because its roots dig into deeper sources or are fused with living roots. I am the place I am from. I am the boy and the girl. El Niño, La Niña. I am the fickle monsoons. I am the taste of a woolly mammoth forgotten for ten thousand years.

But I am also the scentless shopping mall. I am the settler's smoking gun. I am the Scotch broom, introduced as an ornamental and killing everything before me. I am an invasive species, though all species are now endangered.

I am the bullet and the wound. I am the whirligig of history. I am the past and the future. I am the heir of heroes and monsters, and I am no one of consequence. I am solitude standing alone, and I am the mosh pit of ghosts. I am the twisted mesquite, and I am the hidden water hole. I am the drought and the sun and the gentle rain and the nightfall. I am the downpour and the flood and shelter from the storm. I am perfectly ordinary. I am power and powerlessness. I am resistance and compliance.

I am the person who turned the heat up and then blamed someone else. I am the one who remade the diverse and multitudinous Earth in my monopolistic image and flattened myself to a screen. I am the one who forced the desert to bloom like a rose, without ever inquiring what in their own right a desert or a rose were, and what on Earth was a gardener. I am the one who, from seabeds to accessible planets, conflated every sign of life with resource and vanquished anything that staked a claim to existence that did not serve my interests. I am the secret diary of our shame. I am the instrument of The Change, which was not reducible to CO_2 but arrived when humans so reduced place to object – we reduced person to the same. I am the Christian who said to the Devil, *I want*, two innocuous words which are his catechism. But I am the one who also said, *get thee behind me*, and *hallelujah*, and *sa'ah naaghai bik'eh hózhó*, even if I only saw dimly into the meaning of my words.

I am the Earth who gave birth to monsters to rid herself of monsters. I am the hope that the place we are from is, in the end, resilient. I am the wind and its whirling. I am imperfection, neither good nor evil, but a good place to begin. I am the one who knows love is the single hole in the sky, the only exit offered from our flat existence. I am the one who has loved, and I am the one who has failed to love. I am the teller of a story that won't begin with *in the beginning*, because we begin and we begin again and we begin and we begin again, and even when it seems too late – the crops have failed and the plague descended – we have only one option before us, which is to begin. I am not the ending.

I am the song that changes. I am the one whose grandparents taught that the world continues if the song goes on. I am the song that goes. The song that goes how? I don't really know, but I am the one to find out, as the music picks up speed and shuffles time and scrambles generations, proving if something can change, it can change again. For I am the witness and I am the agent. And I am none of these. For I am the conscious boundless sky watching the heartbreaking play.

And you, Joel, who are you? Who the hell are you? Are you really so different?

Of course, I wrote no such thing, and my phone remained encased in lead. Looking through the limo window, I gazed past my own reflection toward the stricken land. Like any migratory animal, I did not know where I was going and yet knew how to get there.

There is a black limousine. It has tinted windows. In the backseat minibar are several water bottles illustrated with a picture of a rippling mountain stream. Nothing could seem more normal.

It has traveled west down a central artery that teams with sloggers in their sixteen-wheelers, conveying hazmat and commodities and perched as high as eagles in their cabs. On this industrially trafficked highway, it has passed a silo like a reliquary and a weather-stripped barn with a faded evangelical broadside. It has passed a fleet of abandoned airplanes at a defunct municipal airport. It has traversed rocks and bones, and a predator and its prey, who are both alert and motionless and easily mistaken for stones. Speeding through a windstorm, tailings of history have been spattered on its windshield while the heavier leavings of time seethe along the highway's shoulder. There is a flip-flop and a spearhead. Mano and metate. A Bakelite necklace and a cradleboard. A mug, a jug, a basket, in shards and unravelings, or miraculously intact after thousands of years, or miraculously brand new. This is not an empty continent. It never was.

Night and tinted glass shield the driver in the driver's seat, who has switched roles with the chauffeur, who now occupies the front passenger seat. As is customary with visiting dignitaries, the trucks yield to the limo, let it pass.

In the monochrome twilight before dawn, the car turns onto a numberless road. The driver swerves to avoid the potholes, not just to save the tires. She knows how the enemy thinks. If she were to lay a land mine, she too would use the holes that the weather so generously provided.

The sun rises. The sun rises. That is certain. The heat rises, and the road loses anchorage, and it waves in the steaming mirage. Softening asphalt sticks to the rubber tires. The limo turns up a route unknown into rough and open country, uncharted since the days of gunslingers, hungry settlers, and assaulted Indians, where dry streams continue to dream of water, though more often they gushed with blood.

In the limo's many mirrors, a yellow eye is staring. In the rearview mirror, the side mirrors and the vanity mirror too. As the Earth spins, it will always seem the sun rises, and its yellow eye watches brazenly, while at night it watches with stealth, enlisting the moon as its mirror to see around dark corners. The limo jogs in and out of its glare as the land begins to roll.

The sun tries to melt the driver's chocolate skin. Her undersides are sweaty – under her breasts, behind her earlobes, behind her knees, and beneath her armpits. Wherever the sweat evaporates, as if her skin were a diary, it leaves an inscription of salt.

"We'll die," says the chauffeur beside her, though he does not insist, and it is perhaps a question.

She neither confirms nor denies. The desert is bigger than language, and the driver too is driving through the dark. She does not claim to be a prophet. It is enough that she keeps on driving, aware she is an ordinary person, with doubt and fear and uncertainty, knowing violence and cruelty are also ordinary and wars have no beginnings or ends, just mutations that never develop into full speciation, so that any violence can mate with any violence to viably reproduce. And she knows the hero is often corrupt, and all primogenitors are, by definition, incestuous, and despite the Bible's *son of man*, the human heart is the true sacrifice.

The end out of sight, she does not know if the future will be evil or, if it is, whether the journey might still be good. Unsure who her father is, or if her parents are seeds inside her that are waiting for optimal weather, she has cause to fear her parentage, but dig deep enough and we all do.

She has taken stock of darkness. Her eyes adjust to night. Yet in her dark vision is hope. And this is, she hopes, the beginning. Her heart lifts up to the mountains at the smell of the brooding dirt and the scent of the taunting rain. She knows history is things change, or, that is, things repeat but with essential variations, and exact repetition is impossible in a temporal world. How lucky she is, really, for though she is destined to repeat the past, she might achieve a different end.

What she does not know is as important as the facts. She does not know the location of the emergence of the future. She does not know tomorrow or tomorrow or tomorrow. She does not know the intricacies of deep and unseen cause and effect, about which so many questions are left unanswered by science and religion alike.

What is the outcome of small actions between warm hearts in tiny rooms? What is the upshot of vast and violent dreams? What ripples from a song? Is it possible that, since the invention of the wheel, we have recited the wrong story? If we spoke a different language, what words would become things? Why would we lose our fur, claws, and sharp incisors, and stand upright with our fontanels open to the sky and our organs exposed for anyone to gut, unless the human evolved to love? And if we do not love, will our children die?

There is a bird circling the upwinds, too far off for the woman to say what species. It may be a raven, a turkey buzzard, or an eagle. Nameless as yet, it flies.

Inside her, a sperm has entered an egg.

The wind too is inside her.

It goes about. It goes around.

It sings like this: *I am alive.*

The gas tank arrow hits zero.

The car stops.

The arrow drops into the negatives.

High above, but not far away, a gray cloud is a hole in the blue.

Give it time, it too will descend.

She removes her heels. Finally, she is barefoot.

She opens the door for the chauffeur.

"From here we walk," she says.

ABOUT EXTRAORDINARY BOOKS

Extraordinary Books is a not-for-profit company bringing a new approach to publishing. We were founded with a sense of outrage at the ever-growing monopoly exerted by the big publishers, and a desire to subvert the current state of the industry.

Here's what that looks like:

- We're seeking authors with something unique to contribute – a book only they could have written. Whether an author has thousands of followers on social media, or has never heard those two words joined before, we're committed. No platform? No problem. We're not driven by market trends; we look for books that are one of a kind.
- All our books receive equal, substantial attention and marketing budgets, and we share profits with our authors 50/50. As for us? We only need enough to keep publishing without compromise.
- We're guided by curatorial openness: our experienced team commissions books in-house, and our visionary editorial collective helps uncover singular writing.

Whether speculative fiction, art, memoir or anything in between, our books have this in common: a distinctive pairing of author and subject.

If that means publishing niche books, so be it. If it means going beyond the constraints of genre, we're up for that. If it means taking risks, bring it on.

We're for readers. *Not for profit.*